THE LYNX ASSASSIN

BOOK 2 OF THE SOCIETY SERIES

KAREN GUYLER

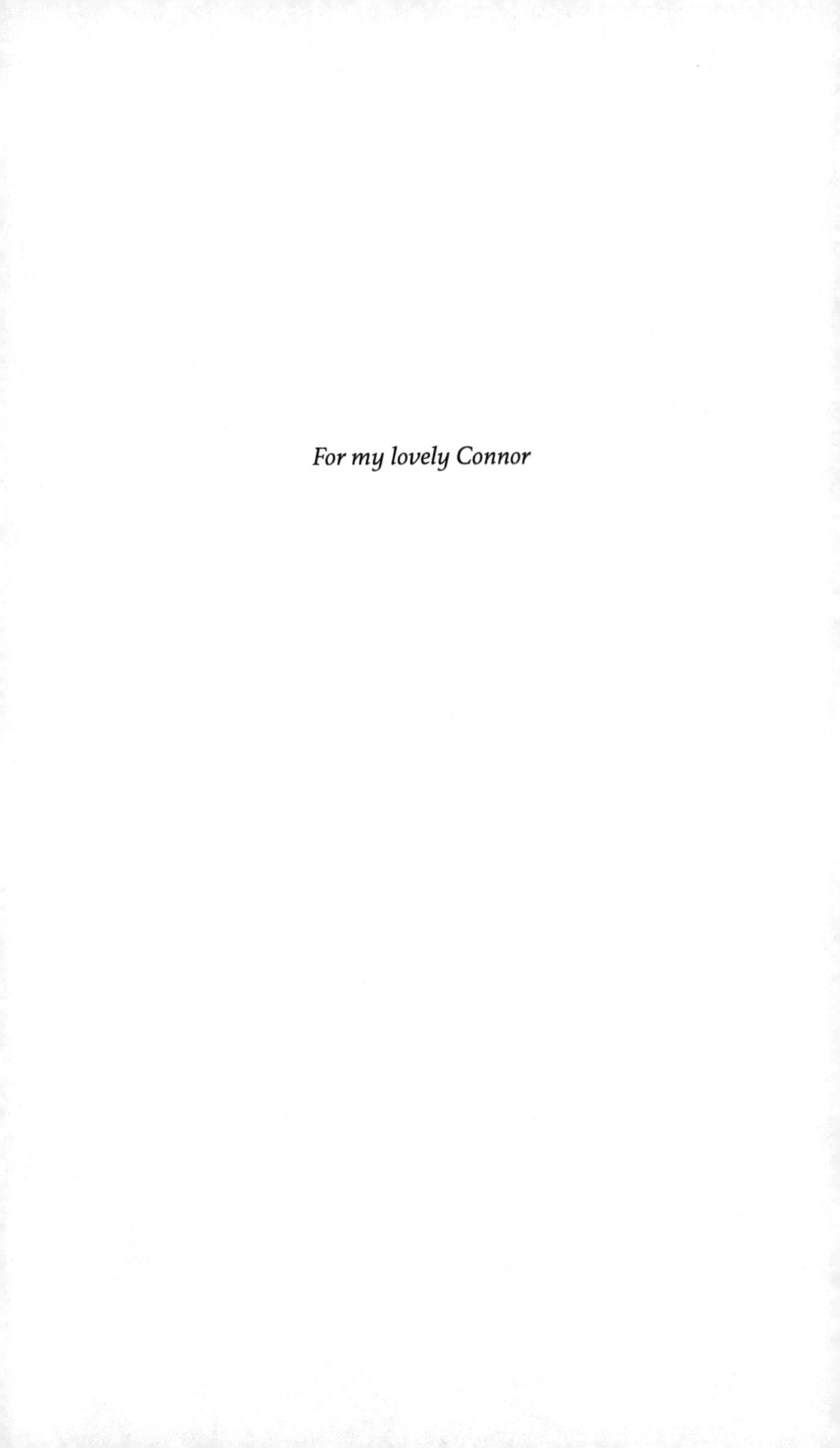

For my lovely Connor

1

A few minutes late would be better for his alibi. Carl Rubin instructed his bodyguard to slow down.

"Your reservation is at seven." Sean Finch reminded him.

Rubin knew his diary better than Finch, but he admired he understood what he liked. Sloppy habits carried risk, that would headline Rubin's obituary, if it were to be written by anyone who knew him.

Finch took his foot off the accelerator, letting the big car slow on its own. Out of his eyeline in the back seat, Rubin nodded his approval. The roads might have been snow-ploughed today, but ice would be a factor as the temperature plummeted.

"Arrive at seven past seven." That had a perfect synchronicity to it.

Rubin turned his attention away from the arresting view of Bergen at night, an arctic wonderland of warm welcoming lights in low-slung buildings. He reread the report from Denmark open on his tablet. The latest modelling test for Yellowstone had assimilated his recommended changes. The results were excellent, better than he'd hoped. It was time to test it in the real world.

"Seven past seven." Finch turned into the road at the end of which was Rubin's favourite fish restaurant.

Another car raced to get into the entrance ahead of them.

"Let them in first." Rubin instructed.

Finch did as he was told, well-trained.

As was Goran Willander, feet stamping in front of the pile of freshly shovelled snow on the right-hand frontage of the restaurant. Rubin remembered when those monuments had been as tall as him by the end of winter. But the evils of climate change reached its talons even there, he could have leapfrogged the one tonight. Willander seemed oblivious, bending down, beckoning Rubin out to join him.

Rubin threw his tablet into his briefcase, snapped it closed, waited for the click of the electronic lock. "You can leave now but no need to go far."

He left his cold weather coat on the back seat, it was only a short walk from the car into the restaurant, where the staff would be watching for his arrival.

Willander shuffled forward to greet his partner as Finch did as he was told. "Carl, I was beginning to think I'd got the time wrong, you're not usually late."

Rubin held out his gloved hand, shook Willander's heartily, his left hand clapped Willander's arm. "Snow on the road, can't be too careful in a big car like that."

"I know you're not a fan but you can't beat a Volvo, built for a climate like ours, solid, dependable."

"Like you, in fact." Rubin said. "But not as environmentally sound as the Tesla."

"I'll get onto the borough, they should be more on top of the weather."

Their hands dropped apart.

"Are those my . . .?" Willander gestured at Rubin's gloves.

"They are. Found them in the office. Very nice." Rubin flexed his hands. "Are they pinseal?" Willander looked away, even though Rubin was careful to keep his tone good-natured.

"They're from a reputable source," he justified them. "The law clearly states products made by indigenous people are a legal use of seal pelts. They're not stripping resources."

Willander's flat nose and weathered face hinted at a smattering of Eskimo in his genes somewhere in his family's lineage, so he could claim it wasn't a big deal for him to have the gloves. But he'd always been fairer than Rubin, and with his sandy blond hair and blue eyes, laughter-lined behind round glasses, more Viking. Beside him, Rubin's ancestry wasn't so clear-cut, brown hair which he was holding onto more successfully than his partner, brown eyes that didn't yet need glasses. Rubin looked the younger of them, though mid-forties wasn't any age at all. Not to have achieved everything he had, not to be poised ready to springboard off those accomplishments to greatness.

"Glad to hear it. They are comfortable, warm, like a second skin." It was as much a concession as Rubin could give as they were better left on the seal. He placed a hand on his partner's winter coat-covered chest. It was a tighter fit than it should be. Excessive living was dangerous for everyone but Rubin held back his instinctive lecture, patting Willander's coat instead. "I wish I'd worn mine. Here."

Carefully, he peeled off the gloves, handing them back to their owner one at a time.

"What's the big emergency you wanted to talk about?"

Rubin thrust his hands in his trouser pockets, grasping the things in them, a fob, a couple of coins, but even a 100% wool suit wasn't so warm in these temperatures. A shiver shuddered through him, but he welcomed it, the weather behaving how it should.

"There's a troubling amount of Futura Energy funds going to a Danish bank." Willander said.

"And you didn't want to discuss this in the office?"

"It has to be someone in accounts instructing the transfers. I thought it prudent to not tip them off."

Rubin gestured between them. "We meet all the time, part of running the company, no one would suspect anything."

Willander shook his head. "Not so much these days, Carl."

"How did you catch it?"

"Quite by accident. We need to set a trap for whoever's doing it to get them when they make the next instruction. In the meantime, I'll do some more digging to find out how much has gone and to where."

Rubin shivered and gestured at the welcome waiting inside. "Shall we?" He set a slow pace along the front of the restaurant. "You're so certain there'll be another transaction?"

Willander nodded. "They won't stop while it's working, the sums are sizeable, but they don't understand banking laws very well."

"What makes you say that?"

"They didn't choose an offshore bank, one based in a country with more impenetrable—"

"Goran, will you look at that," Rubin pointed at the sky. "A shooting star."

Willander frowned. "I don't see it."

"There, to the right."

Rubin's heart rate was far higher than his physician would like. Still in his business shoes, the cold penetrated through to his merino wool socks. He pushed his hands further into his trouser pockets, took a step away from his partner, half a step back.

"Still can't—"

He didn't hear it, fancying afterwards that he only felt the impact on some level. No warning, just two men together looking up at the sky, then the ouff of air escaping Willander's lungs, his collapse onto the ground, the snow changing colour.

The plummeting temperature forgotten, Rubin looked at the sky, down to the crime scene tableau at his feet.

A flutter of feathers spiralled around the hole in Willander's chest. He looked puzzled, at his untimely end, or was he still searching for the shooting star? Rubin scooped up the sealskin gloves, shadows on the snow, and barged, slipping, sliding into the restaurant.

"Call an ambulance, there's been a—" What was it? "An accident. He's been shot, my colleague's been shot." Rubin stumbled in the thick warmth. The maître d' was there, soothing, smoothing, issuing orders, sitting Rubin down, proffering a generous tumbler of brandy for his most respected customer.

"Are you hurt, Mr Rubin?" He gestured at the tiny spray of crimson that had rainbowed part of Rubin's crisp white shirt.

"No, I, not me, but. . ."

The maître d's expression of growing horror summed up what Rubin hinted at.

"You're quite safe in here." He sounded certain but offered the manager's office at the rear of the restaurant, away from other diners' gazes, suppositions, away from the windows, as a safer place to wait for the police. Rubin agreed. Closer to the kitchen too, from where the smell of the house special teased him with delicious anticipation. His mouth watered—it would go perfectly with the brandy.

2

Eva Janssen looked up at the incline in front of her. She'd read the map right, she was sure, so up there had to be the only structures. The rest of this part of the forest surrounding the coordinates she'd been given was pretty much just trees.

The path, virtually a straight line up, looked slickly muddy. It would be easier to go around, but the deadline the kidnapper had given for the ransom or a dead hostage was approaching too fast.

She checked her holster was fastened and took her first step. She made it almost halfway up before her boot tip slipped and she belly-flopped onto the steep path. Last summer's dead ferns to the right of her mud bath invited her over. The vivid green moss that patched the carpet of brown leaf-fall would make the climb easier, drier, warmer. But picking her way through the storm damage litter of twigs and branches would be like ringing a bell when she got it wrong. The target could be planning a deadly welcome for her just over the top of the rise.

She pushed herself up in an awkward press-up, her foot

slipping while she tried to get traction. They should have included crampons in her kit. Grabbing what holds she could, hands and feet giving her four points of contact now, she crab-crawled on up.

Out of breath and sweating beneath the layers under her camouflage jacket, just below the top of the slope, she stopped to listen. The chorus of birdsong continued uninterrupted. That was good, right? She wiped her right hand down her trousers to get the worst of the claggy cold mud off, flexing her fingers to warm them up. Some Spring this was.

A spider scurried over the rock she gripped, running over the alien intrusion of her muddy fingers. It jumped right off, the skein of silk it spun its Tarzan vine as it let the wind carry it towards the other side of the path.

Just do it. Eva pressed her weight down into her boots, pushing herself up enough she could peer over the top. No guns pointing at her. She still had a chance to do this.

Cover, where? The trees had been thinned to one every few metres, and those were young, their trunks too skinny. She scanned the area with binoculars. A shallow ditch, a dip in the ground was her only choice. Drawing her gun, she crawled over the rise, crouch-running until she could press herself into the meagre cover.

Stilling her breathing, listening.

Just her.

Ahead of her were two, no three structures; calling them all buildings would have been an estate agent's optimism. The hut on her left looked like it would fall down if she sneezed near it. Maybe a reason for the kidnapper to choose it? The cabin to the right would give them more protection and security, surely the best choice?

She pulled out her binoculars to double check, but

nothing she could see ruled either place out. Come on, decide. She had to stop analysing the scene, be more spider.

Her binoculars showed her the one she'd have chosen. A lean-to type construction propped up against a weathered-to-grey wooden shed beyond the main cabin that might have been a shelter for pigs or a log store. One window on this elevation, all in the kidnapper's favour, able to see her coming. And the choke point between the two front buildings was the perfect place for a booby trap.

That's what she would choose. But had they?

Decide already, which one?

Binoculars away, she picked up her gun. Now the real test. In an elbow over elbow crawl, she pulled herself out of the ditch to the not much better cover of a skinny holly bush ahead of her. A shout reached her from behind. Eva froze, barely breathing, holding everything tightly still. So worried about what was in front of her, she'd let her rear guard down. Stupid, stupid, stupid.

"Wait up." A teenager by the sound of her, not a hostile Eva didn't know about. She strained to place where her shout was coming from.

"Told you girls can't do this one, change up," a cocky guy called back from further to Eva's right, behind the girl?

Eva turned slowly, so slowly she hoped she stayed unnoticeable. Then she could see them, the neon yellow of the girl's bike making it easy.

"I know how to ride a mountain bike." she snapped.

Her friend was ahead of her, both biking far too close to the edge of the slope. The mum in Eva couldn't help hoping they weren't going to ride down the path she'd come up.

Her camouflage helmet hid her bright blonde hair, and her extra layer of mud only helped make her less visible. If she stayed still, they probably wouldn't realise she was there. But the girl had stopped to adjust her backpack. Go on, get out of here. Eva didn't dare move to check her watch, but the pressure of the deadline ticking closer with every breath pressed against her.

"Eat my mud." The girl barged past the guy, knocking him flying. "Told you girls are better." She biked off, leaving her friend in a tangle, screaming as though he'd lost a limb. His falling silent was worse. The quiet of the forest smothered everything again. He lay on the leaf litter carpet, his body all wrong angles.

Nothing to do with her, that's what Eva's trainer would shout at her. Ignore distractions, stay laser-focused on the mission objective. And recovering the kidnapped victim was her target, not playing paramedic.

She looked at the structures, back at the kid. No change on either side. Still silent, that wasn't good. Eva shook her head. But how could she ignore him? He was someone's son.

She crawled back to the ditch through the soggy mud. Crouch-running then to the teenager.

"You okay?" She reached to feel for a pulse, "can you hear me?"

His arm was moving from underneath him. It snapped out, and he shot her in the chest.

Eva dropped to her knees, rolled onto her side.

"Woo hoo," his shout echoed through the clearing, negating all of her subterfuge. "Kill shot. She's out. You're supposed to stand up with your hands over your head." The guy untangled himself from his bike.

The door to the cabin on the right, not the lean-to structure, opened and two men came out, one walking in front of the other.

The teenager bent over Eva. "Sweet shot, got you good."

"Not quite." She whipped out the knife from her trouser

leg pocket and stabbed him with what would have been a quick jab to the heart if it weren't for the retractable blade on the prop knife.

"I got you, you're cheating." he whined.

"Not at all, not even close." Eva rolled onto her stomach, pulling her gun out, targeting the second man. It was a long shot.

"You lost. You can't do that." the kid insisted.

"So you say, but, stab wound to the heart, you're definitely dead, so shush."

"Whatever." The teen sulked, dropping back onto the ground. "Least I won't get in trouble for cheating."

The men had got close enough. She fired. Her splurge of yellow, not dissimilar to the bright colour of the girl's bike, splattered across the chest of the kidnapper, making him oomph in surprise. Her second shot, more by luck than anything else, splattered paint on his chin. Kill shot.

She shouted at the first man, the one she'd been tasked to rescue. "Reggie Wallace, Trainee Agent Janssen, consider yourself saved."

Eva unzipped her jacket to show the kid the flak vest she was wearing underneath it. "Not everything is always what you see. If you'd shot me in the chest in the real world, I'd have been winded but alive enough to stab you and save the hostage."

"Don't mean nothing." Still sulking.

"Real life doesn't follow rules." She told him the one thing her soon to be ex-husband's actions last year had taught her.

Eva wiped a strand of hair away, smearing mud over her face. She hoped they had decent showers there. It wouldn't help her dragging along half the forest with her for the most important test of the day.

3

Eva's harassed minder stopped in her headlong charge along the corridor and accused her. "The meeting's about to begin."

Not really a meeting, was it? Eva wouldn't mind attending a meeting. She kept her slower pace, pretending it was because this was the first time she'd been summoned to the Houses of Parliament, and not that she was rehearsing answers again to whatever they might ask her.

"Here we are." The woman knocked at a wooden door and opened it, ushering Eva in.

"Eva Janssen." She announced, closing the door as if she thought Eva might bolt and be unaccompanied in the hallowed corridors.

Eva squared her shoulders against the room's intimidation. Dark green-edged tables mirrored its squareness, making the space claustrophobic despite the ridiculously high ceiling. Maybe it was all the wood panelling that reached above her head and the heavily patterned orange wallpaper far above that which made her feel insignificant rather than the weight of the room's history.

Four faces looked up at her entrance from one side of the quadrangle table. The fifth was focusing downwards on the tablet he was holding.

"Afternoon, Eva." Gordon Stamford, head of the unit she wanted to join welcomed her. She smiled at her ally as he made the introductions, gesturing with his glasses at each of the people sitting with him. "I think you know Julian Fairweather."

Knew of was a better way of describing it. Few in British Intelligence had probably met the Deputy Director of MI6, even though most knew his name. He was the only person, apart from Gordon and herself, who knew it was The Society she was asking to join.

"Nice to meet you." She smiled at the man on Gordon's right whose leanness made Gordon appear even broader than he was. He nodded back.

"Edward Markham," Gordon introduced the Foreign Secretary, a pudgy man in a black suit still entranced by his reading material. It was odd seeing him there in front of her, not on a TV screen. He'd been in the news non-stop since his appointment, so she felt like she knew him.

"Sandra Locke, Thomas Pryor." Gordon completed the introductions with the other woman in the room and the man representing something of diversity compliance.

Eva returned their nods of greeting. The last trials were held in this building in the early nineteenth century, she reminded herself, it just felt like a firing squad today. They couldn't hurt her, except by denying her the future she wanted. As she reached for the chair placed in the middle of the floor space, she pulled her hand back. With an awkward side-step she turned and sat instead behind the table opposite the panel.

Fairweather began. "A reminder for those not privy to

meetings here that what is said within these walls stays here." He looked at Eva, but he didn't need to reinforce the secrecy. She'd signed the Official Secrets Act twice now.

"Ordinarily, your application would have been dismissed, given recent events, but you have quite an ally in Gordon. He can be very persuasive, hence we find ourselves here."

Where she had to shine. She flashed a thank you smile at Gordon, but he was watching Markham.

"Why Eva Janssen? Why didn't you take Charles Buchanan's name when you married?" Edward Markham looked up from his tablet.

How was that relevant?

"A lot of women choose not to, I was one of those." She wouldn't tell him that keeping her father's name was a way to stay closer to him. That was nothing to do with anyone there.

"Did you have a good relationship with your husband?"

"While he was my husband, of course." Eva realised where this was going.

Markham went straight there, for the kill. "Can you explain then how it's possible you had no idea of his intentions towards the former President of the United States and most of the G20 leaders?"

Perhaps he was so abrasive so no one would remember he was young to hold a ministerial post. Maybe it was just an unfortunate personality. She could understand why Gordon didn't like him.

"Are you married, Mr Markham?"

He shook his head. "Only to my career."

"Do you have a significant other?"

"I'm not the one being questioned here." His hand reached up as though he was going to run it through his hair. His slicked back style was held in place by so much gel it was almost the glossy blue-black of ravens' wings. As if thinking better of it, he instead patted the back of his neck.

"They're rhetorical questions." Eva said. "You can be as close as partners to someone and not know everything about them. Trust is an important element of every relationship. I trusted my husband was the man I thought he was. And, yes, I made a mistake that he wasn't. He never told me our supposed ally had trained him to activate against us and why would I ever think to ask *that*?"

Fairweather leant around Gordon to address Markham. "As a point of clarification, we've ascertained that it was a personal vendetta that made him act, rather than him being activated against us."

It probably wasn't the best time to point out that it didn't matter to the thousands who'd died. "Because of what happened last October," Eva rushed past the catch in her voice, hoping the panel hadn't noticed it. "I've identified a pool of sleeper agents trained in America's so-called charm schools. We can't rule out that these agents won't be activated to act against British interests at some point. They're very well hidden, there will be others I've not yet found."

"It's difficult to stomach," Markham said, "far-fetched one might say."

"As is the idea that India and Pakistan would sign an accord agreeing with each other over their border, yet that's what they've just done, thanks to you."

"Are you trying to flatter me into voting for you?"

"No, Foreign Secretary, I'm stating fact. It's a remarkable achievement, something many had said was impossible to realise, far-fetched even."

"How are you going to cope in the field being a single mother?" Sandra Locke joined the questioning.

Was she allowed to ask that? Play the game, Eva reminded herself, but still she challenged it.

"Do you ask that of fathers in their application process?"

"If it's applicable, yes."

The panel didn't need to know about Eva's sleepless nights, the frantic arguments she'd had with herself. The guilt she already felt over Lily, for wanting, needing, to make some kind of atonement for what Charles had done. For wanting to make a difference in the way her own father had through his journalism. For still wanting to make him proud of her.

"Do you have a significant other to look after your daughter?" Locke insisted.

Eva had to hold her mouth closed. In the four months since her husband had betrayed her, she was supposed to not only have wanted to find a new partner, but one she trusted enough with Lily? She might be eleven and believe she didn't need looking after, but letting her go back to their flat and be alone for the tiny window between her getting out from school and Eva getting home pushed the boundary of what she felt comfortable with every day.

Her reply was clipped. "I have childcare in place for my daughter."

"You were an analyst before, why not return to that post?" Locke nailed it.

"I know I can make a bigger difference in the field. I have a lot of skills, I'd like to use them in that way."

"Why do you think we're reluctant to appoint you?" Markham gestured at Gordon, his honesty a dart in Eva's hopes. "Stamford here talks an excellent case for you, but we only have your say so that you had nothing to do with your husband's genocide."

And the fact she'd got the word out to warn the people

of Marrakech that Charles had poisoned the water. And that she'd orchestrated handing him over to the US Marshalls to answer for killing their President.

The panel didn't need to hear the safe words she'd been practising. She had to win them over as her otherwise the offer would mean nothing. Be more spider, it was time to jump.

She held his belligerent gaze. "I imagine you're reluctant to appoint me for the same reason your opponents argue that you have no chance in the leadership race to become the new Prime Minister."

One panellist let out a small gasp, loud in the stunned silence.

"You're untested in that position," Eva pushed on. "A good record as Foreign Secretary won't mean much at number ten when you have to be decisive and act. Past performance is no judge of future and that's why we're here. You know you can do that job, I know I can be good in the field. We're both in the position of trusting that those making these decisions about us will honour our self-belief, take our past achievements as a guide that we can do better."

Eva could feel the weight of the panels' increased scrutiny flushing her face. Gordon studied his hands resting on the table in front of him. Probably wishing he had a whisky.

As Fairweather drew breath, Markham cut across him. "The most extreme scenario I'd face as Prime Minister isn't the same thing as putting your life on the line for your country. You're prepared to leave your child an orphan?"

Were they really so worried about Lily's welfare, or was it a handy way to reject her?

"As my father did me. I managed, I got past it." Eva kept her gaze away from Gordon, sending him a psychic message to not call out her lie. "Obviously I don't wish that for her, but I almost lost her when she was in the care of her father. I could as easily be run over by a bus," a tiny falter. That was a bad example, Charles had nearly made that happen to her. Eva swallowed, making sure her words stayed unemotional. "We can't let our better selves not act out of a fear of what if or maybe."

Markham gestured at the file in front of Fairweather. "What do you think your psyche evaluation says about you?"

The pages and pages of psychometric tests and online assessments she'd completed had been the easy part. More off-putting had been the people who'd watched from the back of the room during fight training, while she shot so many bullets at targets that she fired guns in her dreams. She'd like to think it all reinforced that she was worthy of their trust and confidence.

"Foreign Secretary." Julian Fairweather fired a warning. "Those results will remain confidential." He looked at Eva. "What do you think of your performance this morning in the hostage scenario?"

"Are you familiar with Star Trek?" she asked.

He shook his head. Eva looked at the other panellists. Thomas Pryor was the only one nodding.

"Then you'll have heard of the Kobayashi Maru?"

He smiled, his teeth very white. "I have. You believe the scenario was as unsolvable as that?"

"Am I wrong?"

He laughed, a high-pitched delight. "The Kobayashi Maru is a no-win scenario given to test the mettle of prospective captains in the sci-fi series Star Trek. After failing it twice, our intrepid Captain Kirk, realising it was unwinnable, changed the computer program to give him an option to win. That was what your flak jacket was?"

Eva nodded at Pryor's question, aimed her answer at Sandra Locke. "To reiterate, I understand a field agent's job can be dangerous, it's in everyone's interests for me to mitigate that risk as much as I can. I intend to give the Intelligence Service a good return on the time and money invested in my training so I can be an asset for a long time. I intend to come home to my daughter after every mission."

"No one told you to wear a flak jacket?" Gordon asked.

Eva shook her head. "No one told me I couldn't."

"Some might call that cheating." Locke said.

"Others might call it being prepared." Eva tried to make it sound light-hearted, not a retaliation, nothing desperate there at all in her defence. But she could hear it behind her words.

Julian Fairweather wrapped up the agony. "Thank you, Eva. No need to wait, you'll know soon enough."

4

———

Eva walked back to Gordon's unit. No need to wait, did that mean the obvious? Did she just need a simple majority? She knew she could count on Gordon's vote, maybe he'd get Julian Fairweather onside too. But the others? She'd managed to alienate the Foreign Secretary, and the woman. Thomas Pryor, had there been a connection there so he'd vote for her? Never suppose, her father's words reminded her.

At the top of St George's Grove, she hesitated. Nora would want to know how it went. Eva wasn't ready for those questions yet. She walked on to Vauxhall Cross instead. Approaching the boxy building that squatted alongside the Thames, one of the most overt intelligence headquarters in the world, always thrilled her. Today she felt it more desperately as she swiped through security. But they hadn't taken away her temporary access yet.

In the lift she sagged against the wall. She should have stuck with the answers she'd rehearsed.

Eva jabbed at one of the lower floor buttons. Hiding in plain sight, it was a genius move, the surreptitious addition of floors below ground level far from public scrutiny. Most were harmless, a gym where they could train without attracting attention in the combat classes, studios in which to practise weapons training. She still had the bruises from her last session.

But -3 was fast becoming her favourite.

Movement sensitive lights welcomed her into the austere space. Eva pressed the doorbell beside the series of heavily locked cabinets that flanked one wall.

"What will it be?" A disembodied voice asked.

"Glock 17 please." Eva's choices were limited to two and a rifle wouldn't do what she wanted today.

One of the locker doors popped open, giving her safety glasses and ear defenders and the Glock with thirty bullets. Enough to work out her stress.

She swiped through the door to a longer space, colder in there beneath bright lights. Cut into half a dozen cubicles, the open ends led to a run of what could have passed as bowling alley lanes. Apart from the lack of polished wooden floors and the human figure cut-outs at the end.

Someone was in the far lane, so Eva took up position in the middle. The first time she'd held the preferred handgun for use in the field, the weight of it had surprised her. Now it felt good, solid. But she hadn't had to trust it to save her life yet. She took up a two-handed stance.

'You'll never be in an optimum firing position in the field' her instructor's most repeated advice was her mantra.

She shot and clipped the edge of the cut-out.

'Your blood will be pumping' she hit the cut-out.

'Your heart will be racing' another shot, closer.

'You'll probably be being fired upon' better.

'Add to that adrenaline spike the pounding of the life-or-death split decision you'll have to make, it's nothing like it is here' a closer hit.

'Fire, don't fire, kill shot or not' Eva emptied the magazine and reloaded.

One-handed this time, she shot almost half with her right, switched to her left.

She shouldn't want this.

Left was improving. She looked to have scored a couple of body hits close to the heart.

She should be happy at a desk, for Lily's sake.

Her best shot yet with her left hand.

But it was her life, too.

A bullseye through the paper heart.

Two bullets left. Would this be her last time in there? A good time then to nail the shot her instructor had told her was a visual effects cheat in movies. Hitting the return the cut-out button, she ducked down, counting. She sprang up and fired in one motion, one shot, her last.

Still missed. Dammit. She ripped the cut-out down and tore it into three.

In the ante-room a slim guy in his mid-thirties with brown hair and hazel eyes, wearing a black shirt and expensive suit, waited.

"That's a tidy score. I wouldn't look so upset about it, you've only been at it five minutes." Luke Fox grinned at her.

"When did you get back?"

"Last night."

A locker door popped open, and she pulled out the empty magazine of the Glock and laid it on the cloth inside.

"That looks sore." She nodded at his face.

He shrugged. "Just a scratch, I've had worse. Perks of the job. How's it going?" He gestured at the space around them as if that was where they worked.

"I'm about to find out." Squeezing on the bar that held the slide in place, Eva pulled it forward off the top of the handgun and laid the bottom half alongside the magazine.

"If it helps, I gave you a glowing reference."

"They called you as a witness?"

He nodded. "I was on the ground with you in Marrakech. I saw your reaction to everything that went down, that's what they wanted to know about."

"Why can't they just believe I had no idea what Charles was planning, what he'd do to get back at Jed Carson? It was only luck Lily wasn't poisoned, after all." She pinched out the spring that held the barrel in place, disengaged it and laid the parts beside the others, then pressed the door closed.

"I'm sure the new US President thanks you, as will whoever gets the PM position and all the other leaders new in post. They just can't say so out loud." He looked more serious. "They're not what you expect as a master, the government. You'll see."

Tiny matter that they had to accept her first.

5

"Good morning, sweetheart, you sleep okay?" Eva put Lily's favourite breakfast in front of her, a plate of pancakes drenched in lemon and sugar. "You're in a good mood."

Eva's pretence was working. No messages from Gordon or his right-hand woman, Nora, had more to do with her being up early enough to make them both a decent breakfast than good intentions. She hadn't been told not to go to St George's Grove so she would, hoping it wasn't for the inevitable debrief if they were kicking her out, something else to sign, her pass to give back.

But she smiled at her daughter, they didn't need any more strain on things. "I'm my usual sunny self."

Lily grunted, tucked her long brown hair behind her ear and put in a headphone. Eva gestured for her to take it out. "You know the rule." She pretended not to hear Lily's muttering, not to notice her jabbing at the pancake stack. "So, what's on at school today?" She put a forkful of her pancakes into her mouth. Tart yoghurt, sweet strawberries, delicious.

Lily shrugged. "Nothing."

Eva cocked an eyebrow, pretending Lily was just being eleven, not deliberately trying to hurt her. "Seven hours of nothing? Easy day then." She pointed her fork at Lily's phone. "What're you listening to?"

"Nothing."

Eva resisted sighing. "What were you listening to?"

"Interview about climate change."

"That's cool."

"It's not cool, Mum, climate change is terrible, it's an emergency that no one's paying any attention to."

Another of Eva's attempts to bond with her daughter spectacularly failing.

"You want to play it so we can both hear?"

Lily hit the play button and a man's voice filled their kitchen, warning that the best time to have done something to halt the climate emergency was twenty years ago.

"Who's that speaking?" Eva asked.

"Carl Rubin, he's head of the Futura Energy company. He's proving that the world only needs green energy, but the rich people won't give up the oil. It's simple, no more oil equals no more wars, no more pollution, more jobs in cleaner technologies. But the people in power won't listen. They're so stupid, they're killing our future."

Oil could be blamed for more than that. From what Eva had pieced together of Charles' past, the so-called black gold had first justified him committing crimes.

"His company's signing an energy deal with our government to help us meet our renewable targets." Lily speared her pancakes as though they were to blame for the climate crisis.

"You know a lot about it." Eva tried to keep the surprise out of her voice.

"We talk about it in Environmental Studies."

She did Environmental Studies? Eva was becoming as out of touch with her as Charles had been.

She glanced at the clock. "Can we listen to the rest of this together later? You can educate me."

Lily smiled. "Sure, it's up to all of us to do something to stop it." She shovelled in the last mouthful of her breakfast. "Yummy, thanks," pocketed her phone and headphones. "Gotta go."

"I won't be late," Eva said. "Have a good day."

"You too." The door slammed, Lily gone. Eva wished she'd grabbed her and held her. They used to be so close. Maybe this could be the way to break through the wall Lily had put up around her. It would just be a relief to not feel the blame for her father being gone with every glance her daughter gave her. And she didn't even know it was Eva who'd had him arrested and imprisoned.

Her words to Charles when she'd handed him over that whatever happened to him was nothing to do with her haunted Eva more than she wished they would. Her conscience had a loud voice. But he shouldn't have done any of it, lying, deceiving, poisoning, destroying her charity, marrying her, pretending to love her.

While they were waiting for their house to be rebuilt after it had been blown up, the two bed flat she was renting for her and Lily had been a refuge. Now it was beginning to feel claustrophobic. Eva hadn't realised how much she relished the postage stamp garden at the back of their tiny house, the knowing and trusting their neighbours. She hoped the blank slate the new inside would give her would help lay to rest the memories of her failed marriage, the mistakes she'd made.

"Do you think so, Daddy?" She asked the photo of her

father that used to sit on her desk at her charity, Every Drop, before Charles had destroyed it. Her father smiled at her, his hand raised against the glare of a strong sun that high-lighted the colours around him: sand, sky, washed out khaki clothing, the corner of a red daubed building.

She picked up his photo. "You think that's all I need?" It wasn't, she could almost see him shake his head.

"You know, lilla gumman, what it is." he'd have said.

She still missed hearing his pet name for her. At thirty-two she was closer to being the 'little grandmother' he'd teased her it translated to than she was to the 'sweetie' he meant.

"What's your heart thinking?"

"That I really want this job, beyond wanting to impress you. Is it wrong of me?" She traced his face with her finger-tips. "What about Lily?"

This side of him captured behind the glass might have told her she should put her daughter first, like he'd doubt-less wanted to do for her. The other photo of him in storage, when he'd been Time Magazine's Person of the Year, serious in army fatigues and a microphoned headset on his helmet, might say the opposite. She sighed, she'd give anything for him to be there with her, a grandad, how he'd have loved that. Twenty-five years this year since he'd left her. It was a long time to self-guide; it was one lonely heartbeat.

Eva ran up the shabby stairs at St George's Grove two at a time to the top floor, where she knocked at Nora's office door. It buzzed open and Nora waved her in with a flash of her trademark red nails.

"Was that Arabic?" Eva asked when she'd finished her phone call

Speaking Russian had always opened doors for Eva, but Arabic and Chinese were probably the languages people got excited about now.

Nora laughed, took off her glasses. "I'm not so old if I can learn new tricks now, am I? My cunning plan is to make myself indispensable, so they won't put me out on my pension."

"Impressive, you know they'd be too lost without you, they'll hang onto you until you get fed up and demand to leave."

"It's a hard game, we're in, even behind a desk and you're far too young for the which bit's falling apart today club. My right foot, my left wrist, my neck, all of those I can ignore. As long as the most important muscle's working as it should." Nora tapped her temple. "Enough of that, my Andrea tells me I need to focus on how good I feel, how young I am. Better get my roots done then, eh?" Nora's big blonde hair always looked as if she'd just stepped out of the hairdresser's chair, today included. "How are you?"

Eva skipped the question. "Any news?"

"Gordon's in his office, go and see."

There was no way Nora didn't know, but Eva understood the hierarchy, that things had to be done the way they had to be done.

"Sleepless night?" He asked when he released the door lock and invited her in.

"That obvious?"

"Shows me I'm right. If you didn't care, you'd have slept well. Sit. Tell me who voted which way."

"Markham and Locke voted against me, you," she looked

the hope at him, "Pryor and the Deputy Director voted for me?"

"It was two for and three against."

"Oh." Eva winced. That was it then, she was done before she'd even started. Her Plan B was a good salvage. "Can I go back to being an analyst?"

Gordon shook his head. "That's not on the table."

Eva blinked, she was hard up against a brick wall. She hadn't expected to fail completely.

"Because," he went on, "the panel decided to give you an unprecedented test mission."

Eva's insides lightened, unwound, her relief a mini euphoria.

He held up a warning finger. "It'll be tough. You can't fail your objectives. The panel can't be told specifics, but you'll have clear-cut goals you must hit for them to agree you should be appointed."

A delay of execution. A chance to show them they'd underestimated her. "I understand, thanks for what you did for me."

"Don't let me down."

She shook her head. Not a chance.

"Thank you, for vouching for me."

"I know I've got the measure of you, if I didn't think you'd be an asset, I wouldn't have asked you to join us. You have to have a mentor on this one though, someone to oversee you on the ground. Ready?"

She really was. Finally, it was time to see exactly what she'd got herself into by agreeing to join the unit masquerading behind the former assassins' group named The Society.

6

"You sure?" Luke asked. A dark navy suit today, always dressed ready for the job.

Eva nodded, waiting for him to explain why they'd met on the ground floor of St George's Grove underneath the scruffy staircase.

"In the words of The Society 'dare you'? There's no going back."

"I'm sure."

He held his access card up to one of pictures hanging on the wall under the stairs and the outline of a door opened beside them. "I give you S."

"S?"

"No one's come up with a decent name for us. S for Society, St George's Grove, Sword—"

"Sword?"

"Yeah, don't remember whose idea that was. We're really scraping the barrel here, competition's wide open if you have a better suggestion."

He pushed the door and Eva stepped after him into a small room clad in dark grey panels. Low-level lighting ran in thin strips where the walls met the floor and ceiling.

Luke closed the door behind them and it disappeared. No handle, no interruption in the uniformity of the panels, nothing to mark it was there at all. He crossed to the opposite corner and held his access card up against a panel and a click disengaged another hidden door.

S for slick, Eva wondered. "This is unexpected, compared with what's up top."

"Yeah, hiding in plain sight, oldest rule in the book. When MI6 bought this building, it took a year of modifications before we could move in. The contractors thought they were building underground car parks. Our maintenance people finished it, made it definitely not a car park."

The same lighting lit their way down a wide spiral staircase. Eva's boots clanged a warning that she was coming down each metallic step. She followed Luke through another hidden door at the bottom into a huge space surprisingly bright and airy, given the lack of windows, and warm considering all the white and chrome.

"Wow."

"I know." The woman standing at one of several iMacs and more computer configurations that looked custom built, looked up. "I am that and more."

Eva felt her face flush. "I—"

"Eva, right?"

She nodded. Of course, she'd have been briefed. The whole building would have to know who she was, to not challenge the stranger.

"Eva Janssen, meet Sadie Baldwin, she's our Q." Luke explained.

Eva made it worse. "You're Q?"

"This bi-race fineness not white and old enough for you,

girl?" Sadie gestured from her spectacular afro, black eyes, down her red jumpsuit to her white converses.

"No, I meant, we have a Q, it's not a rumour?"

"You saying I'm not all that?"

"I mean, I—I should just shut up, right?"

Luke laughed. "I told you to go easy on her."

"Officially, Q's a rumour," Sadie clarified, "and if they exist, why Quartermaster? Should at least be Quarterperson."

"Which sounds wrong." Luke pointed out.

"I'm not Q, no one here's Q, we're a department, Provisions. And according to the accounts for HM Government, you lot are hungry." She drew out the last syllable, looking at Luke over her black-framed glasses. "You, especially."

"I can't help I'm so good at what I do. Sadie sorts us out for going into the field." He peered at her monitor. "What you working on?"

"That's the question of the hour. You hear about the triple shooting couple days ago in Denmark?" She looked from Eva to Luke, who both shook their heads. "Nice non-aggressive country, nothing extraordinary about their crime rate. Suddenly three people assassinated."

"Does it fit with the annual figures?" Luke asked.

"Assassinated at the same time."

"Mass shooter?"

"Impossible, look."

Sadie moved her mouse around, drawing blue circles around the two bodies on the pavement in the image. "See this?" She wiggled the cursor over the front of a dark glass building at the top left of the screen, then pulled up a second image at the bottom. "There it is again, same building." She ran the cursor up and down the tiny portion of reflective glass visible in the new image on the right-hand edge this time. "Same street, only this photo," she pointed at the second one, "is taken from further down." A bright blue circle this time around one body slumped on a bench.

"I could make those shots, why're you puzzled?" Luke asked.

"At the same time?" Sadie asked.

"Clear shot in all of them?"

She nodded.

"Double tap, sure," he pointed at the two victims, "but with the change of direction, it'd be a lucky shot even for me to get the last target cleanly. The rifle would still be in motion when the trigger was pulled for the third time. It'd be more of a carving into," Luke moved his hand across the screen, "rather than a straight shot." He jabbed at it, then peered at the photo. "Definitely one shooter?"

"Preliminary reports suggest one gun."

"Ballistics not back yet?"

"Oh, they're back, you tell me." Sadie maximised another window, zoomed in on three small masses of metal and melded wire. "These are the bullets they fished out of the bodies, some kind of electronics. Never seen anything like it. I've requested one to analyse but I'm not sure how much it'll tell me."

Eva could feel Sadie studying her. "If it's the same gun and it can't be the same shooter, you have two gunmen, or women, with identical weapons. A field test?"

"That's a good hypothesis."

"Is anyone looking at overlap of victims?" Eva asked.

"Eva used to be an analyst." Luke explained.

"I expect the Danish police are." Sadie said.

"Could I take a look?"

"Sure, extra eyes on this wouldn't hurt. I'll make it available to you." Sadie stood back from the monitor. "But you didn't come all the way down here to help me with my curiosities." She picked up a tablet, tapping on it as she walked to the opposite side of the room. Behind the door that opened for her was a much smaller space, a duplicate of the room upstairs with its dark grey panels and low-level lighting.

"What's your mission? Need these?" She pressed on a panel and when it swung smoothly open, Eva could see a collection of sub-machine guns.

"That'd be some first mission." Luke said.

"What about any of these beauties then?"

Behind a different panel, quite the assortment of knives, daggers, even swords that Eva was sure any Anime hero would be proud of.

"One of those, definitely." Luke pointed at the longest sword that looked like it had been picked up from a movie prop department.

"You never know, Eva might be an expert." Sadie looked the question at her.

"Sorry to disappoint."

Sadie laughed. "Boring handguns then. Where you off to?"

"Norway." Luke said.

"Norway?" Away from the UK already? What would Lily think? Eva was certain she'd be only too happy to spend the night with her best friend, Anya, but would her mum, Tricia, mind Eva calling in the overnight stay favour so quickly?

"First mission, we want something easy. A there and back with only one overnight, break your daughter in gently." At least he didn't say break her in gently. "A husband and wife spat, should be easy."

A spat? One of them had ordered that the other be killed.

"What handguns have you shot so far?" Sadie asked.

"Glock 17." Eva said.

"That's what you get then."

"We're taking guns to friendly peaceful Norway?"

"Like friendly peaceful Denmark?"

Luke had a point.

7

———

"What's happened?" Lily rushed up to Eva where she was waiting in her school's reception.

"Nothing, nothing's wrong. I just wanted to let you know you're staying with Anya tonight, I have to go away on business."

"You got me out of class for that? You could have texted."

"I'll miss you too." Eva held out the bag she'd packed for her.

"When are you back?" Lily looked at Eva's overnight bag on the floor by her feet, go bag Luke had called it.

"Tomorrow. It's only one meeting. Do what Tricia tells you, okay?"

Lily rolled her eyes. "I'm not a kid, Mum."

Still only eleven, yes, she was. "I know, but you're precious." Eva checked the corridor, Lily was the only kid in it. Safe to hold her arms out. "Hug."

Lily looked up and down. For a second, Eva thought she'd refuse, still punishing her about Charles, but Lily took the step she hoped for and wrapped her arms around her.

Eva held her tightly. Let this be the end of hostilities over why she couldn't see her dad.

"Be safe and have fun. See you tomorrow."

"SEE how brave I'm being here, no hard hat." Luke let Eva precede him through the door out of the London RAF Northolt terminal building onto the airfield tarmac. Their hi-vis vested escort gestured for them to follow.

The memory of the first time they hadn't got on a plane together, when Eva's husband had knocked Luke out and taken off without her, clouded the moment. He kept a high profile in her thoughts for someone who was apparently out of her life.

"Just messing with you. Pop quiz," Luke stepped closer to her, dropped his voice. "what's our number one rule?"

She matched his tone. "That we preserve the integrity of The Society's reputation."

He nodded. "It was hard won. Everything we do on mission has to be from the standpoint that we're ruthless assassins. No one must ever find out the link between us and MI6."

It had been the overriding message throughout her training.

"What about the plane?" She nodded at the number painted on the tail of the jet they were approaching.

"Shell corporation owns it, shell corporation owns that, another owns that. No one's going to figure out its provenance, it's as shady as The Society is to anyone looking and we hide in those shadows."

"A private plane though."

Luke laughed. "You sound like Nora. Overall, it works

out cheaper in terms of use of man hours, it's faster but most importantly it's more secure than flying commercial. We're subject to minimal security checks, no questions asked about whatever we're carrying. The payoff is sometimes we share, stuff gets taken in and out of countries in the diplomatic bag on here, including people. Sometimes we have to wait for our ride or drop everything to take it. The pilots and co-pilots are cleared at top level but not for anything 'eyes only' or to do with our specific brief." She didn't need his emphatic look. "Just us today but, going forward, no passenger on here, no matter who they are, how much they pretend to already know, should hear anything from us about anything, not even your name. Same for any air crew."

"Got it."

He checked his watch. "Let's get on board, we're taking off."

For the biggest test of her life. She squared her shoulders and followed Luke up the steps into the cabin.

"We only carry stewards if we have additional people on board." Luke closed the door, pointing at the instructions beside it. "If it all works out, you'll learn how to do it all. Buckle up, wherever you like."

If it all works out? Didn't he think she'd pass the test?

Eva chose the seat facing forward at the table, Luke took the one opposite her. The plane's smooth taxi-ing increased to take-off speed, pushing her back in the cushioned leather seats.

"Every cabinet in here is fully loaded." Luke said. Eva looked around at them, locked by digital keypads "You'll get the combinations if you're taken on. You don't share them with anyone or open them in front of others. Guest luggage goes in the hold."

Out of the instructions he was giving her, the one thing that repeated over and over reinforced that her being there, part of this, wasn't a done deal.

When the plane levelled out, he got up.

"Coffee? So you know all about Norway, what can you tell me?"

"I'm half-Swedish, not Norwegian."

"Isn't being Scandinavian the same," he chinked real cups and saucers from the unit at the back of the cabin.

"Not quite. And that's like asking if you like being a Great Britainer, no one says that. Norway has the fjords, beautiful to kayak in, sail around, not so hot to swim in unless you have a good dry suit. You can camp anywhere you want, they love the outdoor life, the brown cheese is to die for."

Luke wrinkled up his nose. "Brown cheese, that shouldn't be a thing."

"Tell me that after tasting it."

He brought them what looked like lemon cake and a pack of dark chocolate ginger biscuits with a pot of coffee.

"You make a pretty good air steward." Eva teased.

"You can be mother." He put the cups down. "Nora's uploaded everything we need to know for the mission to the server. The usual protocol here is that we fake kill the victim and then the spouse is arrested on some other charge to keep our reputation intact. The fake death photos are uploaded to our portfolio."

"Who gets to see them?"

"Potential clients. They big us up, consolidate our reputation as the best, cases all unsolved. We practically guarantee no comeback on the clients, strict anonymity, which is what they're looking for."

"But all the clients end up in prison?"

"Something like that. Any new client never thinks to look at that, they only ever want to know about the 'victims' as proof we can deliver."

"What's our mission?" She felt ridiculous calling it that as if the laptop would spontaneously destroy itself at any moment.

Luke pulled up a photo of a lean brown-haired man in his mid-forties on the screen.

"Carl Rubin. CEO of Futura Energy, a renewable energy company."

"Lily was telling me about him this morning. He's an advocate for climate change. He wants to kill his wife?"

"Best piece of advice I can give you for this job, actually for life, is never assume."

Eva's father's words coming out of Luke's mouth rapped at her.

He gestured at the laptop. "Rubin's business partner was shot the day before yesterday, while he was standing right next to him. Something I've learned in this business, there's usually no such thing as coincidence. We believe that his lovely wife," Luke clicked through the information and Carl Rubin's image was replaced by a stereotypical Scandinavian woman, slim, long blonde hair, blue eyes, just like Eva. "Agnetha here paid a novice and the guy missed, got his partner. She's now stumped up for The Society to bump him off properly. He's a self-made billionaire so she can afford us."

"We're expensive?"

He sipped his coffee. "Every person is billed according to what we know they can pay because we don't want to scare them into going elsewhere. They're ordering a hit on someone, we like to get them to face the justice of that. But, yeah, for those who can afford it, we're not cheap." He gestured around them. "We have a few more overheads than a guy in a hotel room. It weeds out people who might not be serious but are just pissed off at that moment. Those who follow through, well, they don't get exactly what they were expecting."

"What's her motive?"

He shrugged. "Motive doesn't matter to us, that she hit the button to instruct us, despite our warnings, and we give them plenty of chances to stop, does. Ordering murder for hire makes her a criminal so that's how we treat her. Her husband can probably give you an idea if you ask the right questions. You'll be surprised at how petty some of them are."

"What happens to her?"

"Local law enforcement will deal with her, we have no powers of arrest." Luke hesitated.

"What is it?"

"We'll have to see what happens. This is your mission, I'm only here to witness what you do."

Eva nodded. She was glad it was him. Someone she kind of knew, someone she felt safe with.

He took a second slice of cake, offered the plate to her.

"No thanks, don't like it."

"Don't like cake?" He looked as if she'd said she was going to step outside.

She shook her head, stopped herself saying not eating it had saved her life last year because it had cost her former colleague his.

"How're you feeling about this, into the field?" Luke asked while she poured more coffee for them.

Eva put the pot down. "Honestly, bit nervous, I'm not fully trained. This is like the hardest job interview ever." She sipped the coffee, hot and strong. She imagined she could feel the caffeine zinging through her body. "And I'm carrying a gun, that makes me more nervous than anything."

"That's good. No nerves is a bad thing, time to get out."

"You're nervous?"

He shook his head. "Not on this one, it's your show. On mine, sure, at some points, helps the get it done mentality." He adjusted his cup on its saucer, looked at her, intensity burning in his hazel eyes. "Don't get caught up blaming your perceived lack of training, no one can teach you to be prepared for everything. Sometimes all the training isn't enough."

He handed her a leather wallet which she opened to see her face on an ID card for Erika Miles.

"Interpol?"

"We use them as cover a lot, people have an inflated sense of what they actually do, think they're some kind of continental police. It's a Hollywood ideal that Interpol Agents waltz around the world, gun on hip, arresting bad guys."

"Like us, you mean?"

Luke laughed. "Exactly."

8

———

Eva touched the flap of her hip holster.

Luke noticed from the driver's seat in their hired 4 x 4. "It won't just fall out and the holster won't spontaneously undo itself."

"Just checking."

"Think you got it the third time."

He steered the big SUV past what would probably be a grassy knoll the rest of the year, but was a snow-covered mound now.

"What do I do if someone asks about it?"

"Who are you?"

"Erika Miles, Interpol."

"Who are you really?"

"Eva Jan—"

"No, Eva Janssen doesn't exist on this trip. You're a nameless assassin pretending to be Erika Miles." Luke parked in the visitors' section in front of a two storey glass-fronted building. Every space had a charging point in front of it, but only three cars were parked, two of which were plugged in. The engine of the third was still running. "That's why you didn't come on your passport. Your Interpol ID is sufficient for anything on this job. Eva Janssen is in the UK at her boring meeting. And how can you be an assassin without your weapon?"

She looked at the boxy building in front of them. If her nerves were tightly strung before, they were positively humming now.

She could do this. She was just asking a man some questions. No need for the gun there at all. She rubbed her hands together, pulled the door handle.

"Check it." Luke said. "They taught you that much, right? Before entering any new situation, you check your weapon. Even one as innocuous as this."

Eva did as he said, clipped it back into her holster, checked its fastening.

Getting out of the heated car, the icy air sucked away her breath. She'd never inherited her father's immunity to the cold, something he'd never lost, despite spending much of his life in the desert areas where conflict made itself at home.

Everything felt heightened: the weight of Luke's gaze on her back as he followed her up the snow-cleared walkway; the vast emptiness beyond the glass building they approached; the flatness of the white landscape making it hard to differentiate between the horizon and the colourless sky. Sound was deadened, muffled, and every breath crystallised against the back of her throat with a rawness coughing didn't dislodge.

Someone waited outside Futura Energy's main entrance, head bowed, their long blue padded coat a splash of colour in the white on white on grey surroundings. Eva and Luke's footsteps made them start, look up, brush past them, dabbing at their face hidden beneath a large fur-trimmed hood.

"Are you okay?" Eva wished she knew how to say it in Norwegian.

The coat-shrouded person shook their head, flapped a gloved hand at the doorway where half a dozen bunches of flowers lined up beside each other.

"We're very sorry for your loss."

Luke tried the door, but it was locked to them. No sign of anyone inside who might have heard and apparently was ignoring his knocking.

"Excuse me," Eva called after the figure. "Do—"

"The company is closed until tomorrow as a mark of respect." The woman sniffed.

"Would you have any idea where we can find Carl Rubin?"

She shook her head, disappearing further into her coat.

Eva flashed her ID, "International police."

The woman took a slow step towards her, another, until she was close enough to ask quietly. "Is it true, the rumour?"

"Which one?" Luke asked. As if realising he'd taken the lead, he stepped backwards, away from the conversation.

"That Mr Rubin was the target." the woman said.

"What makes you think that?" Eva asked.

The woman turned towards the car with the running engine.

"We want to bring the killer to justice. Mr Willander was obviously well-liked." Eva gestured behind them.

The woman looked at the shrine outside the building and nodded. "He was, he was a lovely man, keen on educating people, helping them to see things with new eyes."

"And Mr Rubin?" Eva prompted as she fell silent.

"Mr Rubin is not not nice, he's just not the same, more distant, removed from people, more focused on the company's mission. He'd notice you if you were a seal or an elk."

A sob got the better of her and she hurried to her car, blowing her nose for a long time before driving off.

Luke had the car heating on full blast before Eva got her door shut. "Cold out there."

"Glad now we've got decent outdoor gear?" she asked.

"Yep, successful mission as far as I'm concerned just on that. Though all the survival gear's a bit OTT, we're only here one night and in a city."

"Where are we now?" Eva looked around at the remoteness of the building. "Not seeing much in the way of city things. Better to be prepared and not need it than underprepared and die."

"You Scandinavians, you're brutal."

"All this blonde-haired blue-eyed business makes us look like pushovers but we're Vikings at heart."

"Next step?" Luke asked.

"Rubin's house." She hated that it came out as a question.

"Address."

Eva connected to their secure server and thumbed through the dossier summary. "It's in Bergen at the top of Mount Floyen. I'll call." She tapped the number into her phone.

Luke put a hand on her arm. "Same as the weapon, one thing we do if we have time before making contact?"

Eva had nothing.

Luke pressed call on his phone and their surveillance and tracking expert's deep voice filled the car.

"How's it going?" Iago sounded so clear he could have been in the back seat.

"Too cold here for you, mate. You're on speaker with Eva and me, got a job for you."

"I love how you never think I have anything else to do, that I just sit here on the end of the line waiting for you to call me up to deploy my genius."

"That's exactly what we think you do." Luke agreed. "Gonna try a target's mobile, any chance you can hack in and trace it for us?"

"Now you're insulting me."

"We're in the middle of nowhere, not sure how good the signal is."

"Details, details." Iago tapped at the keyboard controlling his system back in London. "Patching through to you, acquiring you."

"That sounds all wrong." Luke said.

"Careful, you'll owe me a forfeit in a minute."

"Haven't seen a doughnut here, not even a bakery."

"Mental note never to go there, I'd starve in five minutes. Okay, you can try it. Keep them talking as long as you can."

It took five times of trying before Rubin's mobile was answered.

"Am I speaking to Carl Rubin?" Eva asked.

"No, but I can help." The man said.

"May I ask who you are?"

"May I ask who you are?"

Eva had to try hard to not do a Lily-like rolling of her eyes. "I'm an Interpol Officer, should we start again?"

9

Luke pulled up behind the Tesla 4 x 4, the only vehicle they'd seen for miles parked on the snowy verge, just where Rubin's bodyguard had said they'd be. "That's some paint job."

"It looks like paua shell." Eva said.

The pearlescent white of the body changed as they walked past it, fluctuating flashes of green, silver, pink.

She looked from the Tesla to the trees. "Better than directions."

Luke followed her onto the disturbed snow where footprints went down the slope between the widest gap in the trees.

As they got closer to the bottom, they thinned enough to give them glimpses of something spectacular, but as they left the cover, Luke summed it up. "You know, I don't do outdoors much but that is something."

"It's stunning, isn't it?" Eva agreed. But she wasn't marvelling at the snow-covered mountains on the opposite side of the fjord that soared from the deep blue water towards the white sky. Her gaze travelled from plateau to outcrop to recess. They'd be camouflaged in white, any potential assassin, and prone, so still that she'd never see them without a thermal camera.

The slope she and Luke had come down levelled out onto a wide, flat shelf of snow-dusted rock. A low white tower with a red roof stood at the far end. The man directly in front of them bundled in a heavy-duty parka, a black holdall near his feet, turned as he heard them. Sean Finch presumably, Rubin's bodyguard.

"You're up." Luke said.

It had to be the most picturesque place a test had ever taken place.

"Rock's probably slippery," she warned Luke, not altogether delaying coming out from the cover of the trees.

But she wouldn't pass anything hiding. Eva forced herself to take one step, another, as tentative as walking a tightrope between two skyscrapers. An eddy of snowflakes meandered around her.

A man in a black helmet and jacket kayaked towards Sean Finch in strong, decisive strokes.

"Good paddle?" Finch's question sounded loud over the water, the English surprising, but then he probably was. Sean Finch didn't sound very Norwegian.

Rubin's kayak bumped gently against the natural jetty. "Too many down the end and a cruise ship, it's unbelievable."

He stepped up out of the boat.

"Interpol officers." Eva said. "Can we have a word?"

"Is this about Goran?" Carl Rubin looked more vibrant than he had in his photo, beyond just having exercised.

"We're sorry for your loss. It must be quite a shock." Rubin couldn't have heard her, for all the notice he paid to her sympathy. She pressed on. "We're here about you. Could we talk in the trees?"

He looked up the spectacular fjord. "You don't like the peace, the stillness?"

"I don't like that the person who took a pot shot at you a couple of days ago hasn't been caught."

"I think we're quite safe." He followed her gaze at the mountain opposite. "You think there's someone up there? You do realise they'd have to be a serious mountaineer to climb that side at this time of year. Sean, ready?"

Finch grunted, and they lifted one end of the kayak each, placing it up on the rock shelf. Rubin took off his helmet and dropped it inside the boat, stripped off his jacket and the top layer of his dry suit.

Eva glanced behind them. Rubin noticed.

"The trees themselves probably are easier cover for an assassin right now." He looked amused, taking and putting on the thermal base layer, fleece and bulky parka that Finch handed him from the holdall.

"You should take extra precautions for your safety until Goran Willander's killer has been apprehended."

"Sean here has my back."

"The assassin could as easily take him out." Eva pointed out.

Movement in her peripheral vision distracted her, had her reaching for her jacket zip, but she wasn't as fast as Luke, who had his Glock out already, prescribing the arc for his target. In the water the would-be assassin was dark grey, a small head, large eyes, regarding them curiously.

"I sincerely hope you're not about to shoot it." Rubin said.

"Of course not." Luke retaliated, "just doing your body-guard's job."

More seals popped up, bobbing around the first, watching the humans.

"Biggest raft I've seen for a while," Rubin said, "I hope they're gone by the time the cruise ship moves."

Finch zipped away the layers Rubin had discarded and dropped the bag into the kayak.

"On three. One, two, three." They lifted it above their heads.

"Mr Rubin, we have evidence that proves your life is in danger."

But they walked away from her with no acknowledgement, crossing the rock like it was a gritted pavement.

Eva and Luke followed more gingerly, but Rubin and Finch charged up the slope as though outrunning a bullet.

Panting along behind them, when she burst out from the tree cover, only their silver hired SUV remained parked by the road. No sign of the distinctive Tesla or Carl Rubin.

Great, her first crack at this had gone nowhere. Objective one, failed.

10

———

"You're on speakerphone with Eva and me," Luke advised Nora as he drove carefully away from the fjord. The windscreen wipers kept up with the patchy snowfall on their slowest setting. Eva peered up at the clouds. They were underperforming.

"How's it going?" Nora asked.

Eva looked at Luke, he didn't answer and she didn't know what to say.

"That good? You heard the news? About the new PM?"

"Don't tell me," Luke said, "Edward Markham got it."

"Won't tell you then. Eva, Edward Markham got it."

Being abrasive, cock-sure and bolshie worked sometimes then. Eva hadn't warmed to him even before she'd actually met him. But that had to be a good thing for her. It'd be the new Foreign Secretary on her review panel.

"Gordon was right," Nora went on, "Markham's ordering reviews. Which gives you both a little down time; we haven't rinsed the fraud case against Agnetha Rubin yet and now our accountants have to prioritise budget reports."

"Likely timescale?" Luke asked.

Nora sighed. "Yours is low priority."

"Does that mean we have to stay here until she can be arrested?" Eva's question wasn't exactly mission-oriented, Lily was expecting her to be away for only one night. "Isn't that a waste of resources?"

"Perils of an easy case." Luke said. "I'm guessing you didn't put us up in a spa?"

"Chancer." Nora said. "I'll be in touch. I'm pushing to get it done asap."

Luke hung up. "Let's see where they've put us."

"What's rinsed?"

"When we pass the case on to arrest the client, we have to be doubly sure nothing can be traced back to us. Trails have to lead away from MI6, we can't have anyone associating The Society with us, or word getting out that everyone who instructs us is then mostly arrested."

"Mostly?"

He nodded. "You'll understand. Word spreads fast in prisons where Agnetha Rubin will end up. We have to be absolutely sure our fingerprints are nowhere near anything we give to law enforcement."

He pulled into the well-cleared car park of the hotel. "I've stayed in worse, anything with a roof on is good." He burst out laughing. "Your face, we don't get the five-star luxury the Bond movies would have you believe but they do look after us. I've got an errand to run which'll give Rubin time to cool off then we can try speaking to him again."

Eva's room was all blond wood and white, an arctic landscape reflected indoors but the shower, huge and powerful, was right out of a hot spring. She let the water pummel her, focusing on the tropical rain sound of the man-made waterfall, the warmth of the drops on her skin.

And inspiration found her in the form of her father's

wisdom, words he'd quoted often in his interviews. The story doesn't start when you become aware of it, you need to go backwards to find the origin. Thank you, Daddy, backwards it is then.

In the hotel bar, she laid her snow parka on the chair beside her, checked again that her suit jacket was still done up.

The coffee she ordered was artfully made, a frond of white in the chocolate topping, but the size of it wouldn't warrant her sitting there for more than two minutes.

She logged onto the servers at S, searching for Agnetha Rubin in the dossier. Nothing stood out in her family background, she'd been average at school, married Rubin at eighteen, had no children. Quite the socialite, lots of photos of her at events all over Europe and the Middle East where she really dressed the part. If her jewellery was real, it was no surprise she could afford to hire The Society.

Eva extended her search to include Carl Rubin. The photos told her nothing, too staged. A search of hospital records showed Agnetha hadn't been in the emergency department since she was fifteen, after a fall from a horse. Neither had he.

No police reports on or from either of them. Why couldn't she just ask him for a divorce? Even if it split his personal fortune, they had more than enough to go round. What was driving Agnetha if it wasn't money?

No contact with the client, her trainer's voice in her mind was loud. The Society was far more fearsome as an anonymous group.

But if she could talk to Rubin again now, as soon as the backend stuff was sorted out, they could get Agnetha arrested and fly straight back to London.

Eva signed for the coffee, remembering as she wrote the

E of Eva to extend it to Erika. She scrawled Miles so it was less recognisable as a name, hoping it didn't differ too much from what she'd signed in at check-in. Showing initiative, that had to be a plus, using less resources, another advantage. Surely the panel would recognise that? Shrugging on her coat, Eva stepped outside where everyone walked quickly, minimising their time spent out of the warmth of the inside.

A train was waiting in the funicular railway station, ready to speed her up the side of Mount Floyen as though it was giving her its approval. Getting out at the top, Eva headed for the road where the Rubins lived. The houses were understated, coloured clapboard with car ports and perfectly landscaped gardens, doubtless designer fitted out interiors that were perfectly co-ordinated in a flow from graceful minimalist room to graceful minimalist room.

Their view, wow, that was what made these places a CEO draw. Eva could have watched it all day, even today when the sea borrowed its colour from the sky, grey and ominous-looking. Bergen spread itself out below her, the sprawl of low buildings reaching almost to the waterfront where two cruise ships waited patiently in the harbour, one dwarfing the other.

A woman came out of one of the houses, crossed the road, walking away from Eva. Blonde, petite, her white fur coat and headband almost glowing in the dim daylight, looked incongruous with her black skin-tight trousers and black trainers. Swinging her arms, the woman power-walked, checking behind her before crossing the road. Agnetha Rubin.

The origin of the story sped up. Eva reached their house. No psychedelic Tesla anywhere to be seen. Maybe Agnetha was meeting her husband. Seeing them together might help

Eva understand. Not part of your remit, she could hear Luke telling her. But not willing to talk to police officers, Rubin was clearly going to be hard to reach. And there was no way she was failing this test.

Follow her, let her go. Which choice?

None at all really. Eva sped up behind Agnetha who walked steadily down the steps and steep pavements, following signs for Bergen centre. Eva was just going to watch, if she could see them together it might give her ammo to get Rubin to agree to do what he was supposed to so she could claim this mission a success.

On a switchback, Agnetha shot a look behind her. Eva had to fight the urge to hide, pulling her phone out instead, taking a photo of the fabulous bolts of colour knitted around the trunks of the trees close to her. Lilac, yellow, red and blue, they fruited rainbowed pompoms on their lower branches, their bright pops of colour welcome.

She gave Agnetha more distance as they paced down the hill, but she didn't look back again. Into the town Agnetha marched past the row of market stalls skirting the edge of the wide pavement curving away from the harbour front.

A guy in a dark parka over which he'd tied a blue and white striped apron held a tray out to Eva.

"You want to try?"

"No thanks." Eva flicked a glance at the white coat almost at the entrance doors to the fish market building.

Seal," he gestured down first line of bites of dark meat, "whale, reindeer."

"I'm vegetarian," she shrugged it like a confession, rushing on.

A steady stream of people hurried into the fish market through the glass entrance doors, log-jamming against those who dawdled to leave it.

A swarm of Japanese tourists congregated around one of their number who was shouting, gesturing furiously at one of the men in their group. Eva crossed to the second door, slipping past a woman in a bright blue scarf.

At that moment, the woman stepped the same way, barging into Eva who knocked into a vision of white. Little more than a tap contact, but suddenly Agnetha Rubin was flying backwards. She landed right on her back, her perfection squelching on the concrete floor where the melting ice and water sprays from the fish stalls had accumulated in pockets of dirty water. Glaring up at Eva.

11

―――――

Barely pausing, the woman in the bright blue scarf muttered something in Norwegian, but the universal tone of 'what the hell are you doing' was easy to make out.

Agnetha Rubin still glared at Eva. So much for no contact. She could hardly just walk away now.

"I'm so sorry, she pushed me too." Eva held a hand out to help.

People rushed past them on every side, coming into the warmth and noisy bustle of the fish market. As delicious as the wafts of fresh coffee and warm pastries were, they weren't strong enough to mask the sharp fishy odour.

"You want to look where you're going." Agnetha twisted behind her, looking at the back of her coat. "My coat's ruined."

Eva argued with herself. There'd be time enough to rationalise the right or wrong of doing this. The one that won was Luke's own: this is your mission. How could she pass up this gift?

"Agnetha? Agnetha Lundstrom?" Eva asked.

"My name is Agnetha Rubin now."

"Well, congratulations. I'm just getting divorced, couldn't quite manage the whole happy ever after thing."

Agnetha scrutinised her. "Who are you?"

"Erika Jakobson, wasn't that at school but, you remember me, we were in the same year for a while, until my parents had to take me out and put me in international school. I'm just as hopeless at Norwegian now as I was then. How about we get a coffee, it's the least I can do and, of course, I'll get your coat cleaned for you."

"Okay, but I choose where."

Agnetha breezed out of the building, long strides across the square without checking if Eva was following. Not that one. Eva sent a psychic instruction to Agnetha that she didn't get. She pushed open the door Eva didn't want her to because it led into a smoked glass fronted champagne bar that, in an expensive city, oozed Krone signs.

A middle-aged man welcomed Agnetha with a double-handed handshake and a greeting Eva couldn't understand. She checked her phone, hoped its refinements were as good as Sadie had told her they were, and put it in her suit jacket pocket.

Eva watched the unintelligible back and forth between the man—the manager, she guessed—but didn't need to understand it to work out he'd introduced Ralph, who was presumably waiting tables while his modelling career got going. Agnetha waved a hand behind her at Eva, and Ralph bent his head sightly. That smile, Eva couldn't help wondering if he worked on the side for the books that had bare-chested men draped on the covers. He'd be good at that.

He caught Agnetha's coat as she dropped it. "Hang that

somewhere else, it's not had the best day." She said it in English as a dig? "There, we want to sit there."

Agnetha smiled at the manager as she chose the table at which a couple sat talking over each other then pausing awkwardly at the same time.

"Of course, Mrs Rubin. In the meantime, if I may suggest you wait just here," he gestured at Ralph who pulled out one of the leather armchairs for Agnetha at a low table two along from the one she wanted, "with a drink of your choice, on the house, of course."

Agnetha smiled, folding herself into the chair as though she were a dancer. "This will do nicely."

Eva felt clumpy beside her.

"That strawberry one I had last time, you have some still?"

The manager nodded. "And for you, madam?"

"Coffee would be lovely." Eva said.

Agnetha looked at her, "you do know this is the premier champagne bar in Norway?"

Of course it was.

"I'm not much of a drinker," Eva excused herself. "Alcohol gives me a headache. Caffeine's my god."

"We'll have a bottle and two glasses," Agnetha instructed. "Upgraded. Coffee later. And Ralph to serve me."

One glass of champagne would be okay. Eva could handle that and, with a bit of luck, it would soften Agnetha up to answer her questions.

The ice bucket was a masterpiece of gold and black, placed on Agnetha's side of the table. Watching her, Ralph withdrew the bottle slowly from the clutches of the ice cubes. It was like a magic trick. The ice had made the gold-labelled bottle grow to twice the size of a normal one. Droplets of water ran down the glass as he presented the bottle to Agnetha for inspection. She smiled and nodded, pulling off her headband, ruffling her hair, basking in his attention. She didn't quite pout at him, but her eyes were definitely giving him a come on. Whatever she purred at him in Norwegian made him smile, slowly.

"You're new." She accused him in English.

"I am," he replied.

"I will thank your manager." She toasted him, turning to Eva when he went to serve someone else.

"Skol." Eva wet her lips while Agnetha downed several swallows. "This is lovely."

Soft relaxing music, subdued lighting, it was a place to spill secrets.

"I haven't seen you around that I recall. You didn't stay here?" Agnetha asked.

"I work for an international company, nowhere really feels like home anymore."

She snapped her fingers at Ralph, who almost fell over his feet in his scramble to refill her glass. She talked to him as though Eva wasn't there, her smile was definitely an invitation.

"How about you?" Eva tried to ask it innocently when Ralph left them to it, but it landed between them sounding like the set-up question it was.

Agnetha tossed back the rest of her drink, stared at the empty glass. "I wanted a role in the business but I'm only good for wining and dining, apparently."

"Is it Carl Rubin your husband, the CEO of Futura Energy?" Eva said it as if she'd just realised, ignoring her phone vibrating with an incoming call.

Agnetha topped up her glass.

"His partner was just shot, wasn't he? I'm sorry for your loss." Eva tried not to stare, not to be obviously gauging her reaction. But it was as surprising as her husband's had been. A careful nothing beyond a study of her drink.

Eva waited.

"It's very sad." Agnetha said finally. "He was a lovely man. They're quite rare, I'm finding."

"You must have been so worried. I heard your husband was right beside him when it happened. It must have been scary for him."

"I suppose so."

"Does it worry you, that he has such a high profile?"

Agnetha laughed. "He seems to have nine lives, or at the preparation for them at least."

Eva's phone vibrated again.

"Sorry, I just need to check." Not Lily. Pierre, Luke's cover name calling, again. "Think my boss wants his report badly." She slid her phone back into her jacket pocket. "Can I ask you something personal?"

Agnetha gestured at Eva's glass. Eva sipped the pink champagne, feeling the bubbles fizz against the roof of her mouth, but Agnetha wasn't having sipping.

"I'm not drinking alone." She finished hers and looked expectantly at Eva, refilling both glasses, when Eva copied. "Now you can ask me."

"Did you have a pre-nup when you got married? Only I didn't and now my husband is saying I'm only entitled to the half of the assets we had when we got married."

"Any decent lawyer will have that thrown out before the judge can read the statement. I can give you the name of one. Here's to your freedom."

Another toast. This wouldn't have a happy ending. Eva could already feel mellowness spreading through her.

So money wasn't the reason for Agnetha's assassination order. What else could she learn? She sipped at her drink.

"What's the secret then for a happy marriage?"

Ralph interrupted, bringing over a beautifully presented tower of seafood, but there was nothing on there Eva could eat. Was that caviar? Ouch, her expenses.

"Do you have any bread?"

"Of course, madam, would you like salmon mousse with that?"

"No, thank you. I'm a vegetarian. Bread will be fine, with brown cheese if you have it."

"Don't know what you're missing." Agnetha patted her mouth with the thick napkin. "Best way to soak up the alcohol, want to be with it later." She smiled, flicked a glance at Ralph.

The brown cheese, a similar sweetness to it as a Caramac bar of caramel chocolate, took Eva right back to childhood Christmases spent with her godparents, magical in the snow and enveloped in the unconditional warmth she'd never really felt from her mother.

"Do you have children?" she asked.

"No." Agnetha's answer was prompt, practised. But then the champagne prised loose a further truth. "I'd never seen myself without them but we were so busy building the business time ran away with us. It has its advantages, I'm always free to pursue what I choose, go wherever I want."

Ralph's ministrations with the champagne upended the bottle for the last of it to dribble out into Agnetha's glass. She said something to him in Norwegian; he replied and she ordered something else that he tapped into his phone. A lot of something else, an Amazon jungle fruit to be flown in while they waited and drank the bar dry? Chocolate topped gold bars?

"I have to go." Agnetha cut Eva's wondering short.

"But–"

"Another time."

"It's been great to see you," Eva said. "Fancy bumping into you here, of all the places you go, you have such an exciting life."

Agnetha stood up. "Life's only exciting if you're leading it."

12

"Hungry?"

Luke swung himself into the seat opposite Eva in the hotel restaurant. The two slices of pizza left on the black plate gave her away.

"It's Margherita, help yourself."

Luke gestured at the nearly empty bottles of water and lemonade, the coffee pot.

"Thirsty, too?"

Eva nodded, straightening up in her seat.

"Where've you been?" He took a slice and bit into it.

She leant in towards him. "I met Agnetha."

"Have you been drinking?"

She held up her thumb and index finger a couple of centimetres apart. "Teeny bit, just to keep my cover," she whispered the word.

Luke chewed the pizza. She poured the dregs of coffee into her cup, screwing her nose up at the bitter smell. Maybe that was the bit that would work, the rest of it didn't seem to have done much good.

He reached for another slice. "When we're on mission,

we don't do that. You can order a non-alcoholic version of almost everything now, a mock-tail—"

"She had champagne, out of a bottle." Eva's reply was snappier than it needed to be. "I tried to have coffee."

"You should've answered your phone." Luke ordered a coffee, gestured at her pot. She shook her head; the thought of anything else to eat or drink made her feel sick. "I could have reminded you we don't have contact with the clients."

"It was kind of an accident. It's not like there's a field manual for me to follow, I thought she might lead me to her husband. I wanted to see them together. How was your errand?" Eva tried to change the subject.

"You were told that's not protocol."

"I know, but it's my mission." She clapped her hand over her mouth, looked around her. "Mission," she whispered.

"Did you have your phone tracker on?"

"Course."

Luke paused while the server deposited his coffee order on the table.

"You have to weigh the risks of every step you take on a case. Risk versus reward, the reward has to be worth the danger factor every time."

Eva burst out laughing. "The only danger was to my expenses and I'm afraid to report it was fatal. Agnetha had caviar, on top of the champagne."

"If you've blown it, at least you did it with style."

"She bought my," Eva had to force herself to lower her voice again, "cover story. I'm not an idiot."

He sipped his drink, put the cup down carefully on the saucer. "People rarely tell you they don't believe you to your face, they're far more likely to give you disinformation."

"Well, we can see. I recorded everything she said,

including all the stuff she didn't want me to hear in Norwegian."

NORA'S CALL cut through the moody silence in their SUV.

"Hey, Nora, you're on speaker with Luke and me. Any news on us being able to close things up here?" Eva sounded like she knew what she was doing. Had to love that champagne confidence, even if it was making her mouth dry, and feeding a growing ache behind her eyes.

"Not yet, other than Agnetha Rubin is an impatient lady. She's messaged The Society to find out why her husband's still breathing. Offered more money to bring forward his demise. He's going to Denmark later tonight and she wants us to bring down his jet."

"Wow, that's cold." Agnetha looked like a model, led a desirable life with everything Rubin's money could buy, yet she wanted him killed in a fireball, along with the cabin crew. This side of her didn't marry up at all with what Eva had seen of her. "What did you tell her?"

"We haven't replied, no one has The Society dance to their tune."

"Let us know when we can hand her in." Eva disconnected.

Luke slowed the car and pulled off the main road onto an unsignposted lane. The tyres crunched on the gritted snow. The trees on either side of the narrow turning leant over the car as though they were trying to hide it. Their headlights burrowed through the deepening shadows. A blaze of security lights jabbed at Eva's eyes as Luke drove out of the natural tunnel onto a flat paved area, banked by shovelled drifts of snow. Behind a mostly open garage door, one of a block of four, the pearlescent Tesla was charging.

The house didn't suggest a billionaire lived there. Nestled in the dip where the ground sloped downwards away from the drive, it looked more like an extended cabin.

Luke turned the SUV round, so it was facing out the way they'd driven in. "Always want to be thinking about your exit. Ready?"

"I'm guessing I don't tell him his wife is planning on having him killed?"

"It's your call. There's no set thing we do, it depends on so many factors. Is she in danger if he knows? Is it the only way to save his life? She seems desperate to get rid of him quickly. What might she do if we don't deal with her now? She might have broken the law but we don't know what's going on in their marriage, who they are to each other."

Luke was a surprising guy, like a kaleidoscope Eva was never sure which side of him she was going to see. He withdrew his gun.

They were going in weapons drawn?

Luke checked his and returned it to his holster, looked at her.

She had hers in her hand, checking. "Every time before going into a scenario."

He took hold of the door handle. "Ready?"

Not really. She nodded.

Outside was lit up like a TV studio, dazzling them under spotlights from every direction. Carl Rubin took security seriously.

Her feet had just touched the ground when Sean Finch appeared.

"You need to leave."

Eva shut the door. "We need Mr Rubin to answer our

questions and then we will. We won't take up much of his time." Out of his parka, Finch was as muscular as she'd expect a bodyguard to be. Dark blond hair, tall, he had a calm demeanour about him that was probably his biggest asset in his line of work. It was more threatening than if he'd been screaming in her face to get out of there. There was something about him, his restless gaze, the vibe he gave off that he could take on and beat anything. She straightened up, channelling the authority the fake ID gave her. "My partner's desperate for dinner, trust me, it's not worth it for me to be anything other than quick. And, unless you want us to bring local law enforcement out here as well, you'll co-operate."

Tensed against a hand stopping her, she crossed the courtyard, the soles of her boots crunching on the salt laid to stop overnight snow freezing.

The inside of the house continued the outside surprise, more log cabin than luxurious country spread. Rubin was standing in front of an enormous picture window in the lounge, but the view was lost in the darkness behind the various lamps that threw muted pools of light over the comfy furnishings and warm rugs. The view must be quite something in daylight.

"Can you close the curtains?" Eva asked.

Rubin picked up and pointed something at them. They swished together. "You're very jumpy for an Interpol agent."

He pointed it at the blank, uninviting fireplace. Flames instantly ignited, making the room perfect, if she paid no attention to the yawning blackness beyond the fabric at the window that could hide any number of assassins.

"Biofuel," he explained, setting the remote down. "Burning wood, apart from being the worst thing we can do to a tree, takes the planet years to recover that carbon."

"I've heard it's not so good for us to breathe in either." Eva said.

"How did you find this place?" He asked.

"We're Interpol, Mr Rubin, we can find a lot of places."

"But this one?" He shot a look at Finch. Eva wasn't going to tell him she'd recorded his wife giving the address to Ralph for a booty call when he'd left for Denmark. "IDs." Rubin held his hand out.

He inspected the unassuming cards in their fake leather wallets, apparently reading every character. Eva forced herself to stand still, look relaxed, not snatch it back, repeating Luke's assurance to herself that they were as good as the real thing.

"You sound very British." Rubin observed

"Interpol officers are drawn from all over Europe." Eva repeated the spiel that was included in her dossier.

"You don't say much." He gestured at Luke.

"She's the lead on this investigation."

Rubin returned Luke's ID, looked at Eva. "Forgive me, Ms Miles, but you seem familiar. Have we met before?"

"Not that I'm aware."

Eva and Luke's phones both sounded. A text from Nora, Agnetha at the end of her patience, she'd take matters into her own hands if they didn't complete the job that night.

"How did you know I'd be here?" Rubin asked.

"An educated guess," Eva said. "The quicker you answer our questions, the sooner we can let you enjoy your evening."

"You haven't asked any yet. So what can I help you with this time?"

"Well, you didn't help us earlier, let's hope we make more progress now. Who do you suspect was responsible for Goran Willander's death?"

Rubin spread his hands. "As I told the Norwegian police, I have no idea. Goran was well-liked, a good partner, supportive, not as innovative in his thinking as me, but that's why our partnership worked. It's been a terrible shock. Why is Interpol interested in a domestic incident?"

Tell him or don't. Eva flicked a glance at Luke but he was watching Rubin, not her. A vision of a jet exploding, raining fiery globules of burning aviation fuel and charred body parts loosened her tongue.

"We believe you were the target, but the perpetrator missed."

Rubin looked surprised. "He shot Goran instead of me?"

Eva nodded. "We would like to take you into protective custody for your safety until we can catch the perpetrator."

"Do you have any idea who it is?"

Rubin waited for her to fill the silence. He couldn't know she could out stubborn Lily, she stared right back.

"Let's speed this up." he said. "If you're looking for enemies, I have many and they are legion. I've broken the mould of what was before. The oil and gas companies, the people behind those, are probably all my number one enemy. Others in the green energy field, jealous of Futura Energy's success. No one, I would say, locally, we're a definite benefit, we've brought wealth and jobs to the area and I've rejected every suitor trying to woo us away with tax incentives and a lower operating cost. Here," he waved at the view beyond the closed curtains, "you can breathe, you can feel the power of nature in this vastness. It looks empty, doesn't it, but you'd be surprised at what's out there."

Eva found herself nodding, she knew there was life hiding within the snow. Her godfather had shown her how to spot it, seek the footprints she'd delighted in identifying with him when her parents had taken her to stay with him in Sweden. Per, such a sadness crushed her at his death.

"We're playing catch up," Rubin was on his soapbox now, "we need to get faster at it. There are those who believe we're too late to save the planet, but I don't subscribe to that theory."

"Is it true there are enough resources for everyone, they're just badly distributed, hoarded by people with wealth and power?" she asked.

"It depends on the metrics used to measure them. We're an overpopulated planet, that much is certain. We should never have got to this point where we're jeopardising our survival, but humankind is selfish. Our populations are out of control, expanded beyond the point that a slowdown in the birth rate can save us."

"Save us?" Eva asked. It sounded over-dramatic.

Rubin's stare was righteous. "We can't carry on as we are."

"Getting back to you, we need you to lie low for a while."

"No."

"Mr Rubin, I don't think you understand—"

"I understand more than you're aware of." He looked at his watch. "I have somewhere to be."

Eva's imagination made his plane crash worse by the imaginary addition of a single high-heeled shoe and a captain's hat strewn at the top of a debris field on a scarred landscape.

Six o'clock. Ralph was driving there after his shift at the champagne bar, but Agnetha could arrive at any minute. "Your wife is the person who ordered the hit on you." She blurted.

"My wife?" Of all the ways he might react, she didn't expect him to laugh. "You're mistaken."

"She's instructed another, better operative, who won't miss. What we're asking you to do is—"

"Impossible. I have responsibilities here and abroad."

"I'm talking about your life here, Mr Rubin. Surely nothing is more important?"

"There you are, another human with an inflated sense of self-importance. I'm not going into hiding, if that's what you're implying." He gestured out the window behind her. "That's important, we're not, we're just here for the shortest time, a ship passing."

"I'd like to make sure you reach your port."

"I've no intention of altering my plans. Sean will show you out."

Eva could see the members of the review panel shaking their heads, ticking the box on her first objective—fail.

13

"What?" Luke watched the windscreen but the blasting heater of their rented SUV hadn't cleared one ice crystal from the outside. "I can hear you thinking from here."

"What do you do if the potential victim won't cooperate?"

"Doesn't usually happen."

"Rubin's reaction was odd, wasn't it? Who laughs when they find out their partner wants them dead?"

"You'd be surprised at how some people deal with it."

"But why would he think that way if she's saying she'll kill him if we won't."

Luke peered through the clear sliver at the bottom of the windscreen. "What else?"

The security lights lit him up from behind, so his face wasn't easy to read. Was this a test?

"He's not impressed we found it, this place, he seemed more surprised about that than anything."

"What makes you say that? Maybe he's late to get wherever he's going. Plus, as far as he's concerned, we're law enforcement. No one gets to be where he is without a few skeletons."

Luke released the handbrake and drove forward slowly.

Maybe the house was the origin.

"This address not being listed in his or her name," Eva persisted, "means it's hidden by a front company. Why? What doesn't he want us to find here?"

Luke reached the end of the drive.

"What you said about risk versus reward, how does waiting for Rubin to leave and then taking a look around figure?" Eva asked.

"You want to break into his house?"

She rubbed her hands together, warming them up while the heater focused on the windscreen. "He closed the curtains as soon as I asked but at the fjord, right out in the open, he wasn't bothered about an assassin?" She let Luke catch up to her hunch.

"There's something out there he doesn't want us to see."

Eva ignored the tap dance her insides were doing. "No need to break into anywhere if it's in the back garden. What do you think?"

"You did the training part about stakeouts, right?"

"I did, boring, cold, boring, tiring, boring."

"And you still want to do it?"

They were approaching the end of the tree tunnel. To the right was Bergen, the hotel, dinner, sleep, warmth. To the left an uncertain time in an inhospitable environment waiting. For nothing potentially. Eva nodded to herself. "I do."

"Okay, it's your call." Which made her think it was the wrong one again. "Just in case they have cameras out here." Luke indicated right and turned toward Bergen. He drove until he passed the first bend and did a rapid three-point turn. Back past the Rubin property line, he did the same again to park on the verge, turning off the headlights and engine.

As their night vision kicked in, the winter scene resolved into varying shades of white, grey, blue, black. With every degree the temperature in the car dropped, she wondered if she should just tell him to go back to the hotel.

"You got cereal bars or something in your survival kit?" He asked after a while.

"Better."

Eva fished around behind his seat and pulled out a small bag, handed him a can. "Open it, wait a couple minutes."

He did as instructed and she knew exactly when he felt it getting warm. "What magic is this?"

"Self-heating coffee. It's not bad either."

"Whoever dreamt that up deserves a knighthood."

The first sip of her own was very welcome. She handed him a cereal bar. "Your wish is my command."

Only ten minutes after they finished their second bars, the side of the road ahead of them lit up, long headlight beams parting the darkness from Rubin's driveway. "And there he goes." Luke pointed out the obvious.

The Tesla turned right, away from them in a smooth motion, the driver apparently untroubled by the realisation they were there.

Luke turned the engine on. As the heater blasted away the long fingers of arctic night that had wormed their way into the car, Eva's shoulders relaxed into the warmth. She unclenched her gloved hands in her pockets, breathed out all the way.

"How do you want to do this?" he asked.

"So many security lights, what's the betting the untrusting Mr Rubin has cameras outside his house?" Eva thought aloud. "But, given how remote he is there, maybe not out the back."

Luke gazed at the pristine snowy fields leading back to the Rubin property. "That's quite a trek, don't suppose you have snowshoes in that survival gear?"

"Better."

"CAN YOU PUFF ANY QUIETER?" Eva waited for Luke at the top of the small incline where she waited. "They can probably hear you in Bergen."

"These are some kind of hideous torture instrument." His words rushed out with his breathing. He leant forwards, leaning on his ski poles, sounding like he was on the summit of Everest without oxygen. "I class myself as fit, but. . .seriously, why did you think to bring these?"

"Being stuck once without them. Cross-country ski-ing gets everyone when they first try it but trust me, it's way harder walking through deep snow." She wasn't going to tell him her thighs were burning, her lungs sore with the exertion of breathing the cold air, that the residual champagne in her system was making her head ache. Very out of practice. "But you're warmer now, though, right?"

"Wish you'd brought snowshoes."

Eva pointed to their diagonal left. "That way, those trees are definitely on their property. The house must be thirty metres to the north of them."

"Up that hill?"

"I'm so tempted to say yes. But that bump will make us visible, round it would be safer. Also, we don't have skins on our skis."

"Skins?"

"Strips that go on the underside that allow you to slide forward on the snow but not go backwards. You need them for inclines, these," she gestured at the landscape, "don't count but no sense making it harder for ourselves."

"Glad I brought you along, handy knowing all this stuff." He seemed to have forgiven her for her faux pas with Agnetha and the champagne.

"It's kind of my element, the snow. Don't know how much use I'd be if we were in the desert. Ready?"

The time it took to reach the double bank of trees at the bottom of Rubin's property gave Eva plenty of opportunity to argue with herself. How would this look to the panel? Breaking and entering was going to be hard to justify, particularly if her instinct was wrong.

"That little voice inside your gut," her father had told her when he came home after the assignment where he'd been kidnapped, "listen to it, do what it tells you. If I had, I wouldn't have gone out without an escort and, if I hadn't, I wouldn't have dropped my gear that led them to find me."

What had that voice been telling him when he'd saved that little girl's life that cost him his own? Had it been screaming Eva's name?

"Eva," Luke saying it then made her start. "We doing this, or what?

"Just checking."

The vastness of the vista behind them was stunning. A landscape of pristine snow that would sparkle in strong moonlight, broken by sparse runs of trees at the edge of her vision. The Northern Lights from there would be phenomenal. Rubin's house was higher than where she and Luke stood but he'd let the firs grow to a natural height, probably double Eva's five foot three. Why then would Rubin, who was all about the beauty of nature, make a landscaping choice to curtail his view? Was it a case of what kept him in would keep others out?

Looked at like that, the trees were a good deterrent, planted as they were in a dual overlapping band especially tight at the corners where they turned in soldier-like precision to skirt the sides of the property. Eva unclipped her skis and slid them underneath the trees.

"Thank God." she couldn't help smiling at Luke's relief as he did the same.

Near the middle of the barrier, she got down onto her belly, slithering past the low branches that would snag and hold on to her.

Elbow over elbow, she dug her boot tips into the ground behind her and pushed.

"You forgetting something?" Luke dropped the question on her.

Was she? They'd hidden their skis for their route back to the car, if Agnetha was waiting for Ralph to finish his shift they'd be out before she even got there. The snow would be the only giveaway of their presence.

The slide of a gun behind her sounded like a shot. She hadn't checked hers. Again. Eva's head dipped to the ground, a what an idiot gesture. Then she heard something else.

She froze. "Pull me out."

Luke grabbed her ankles and yanked her backwards over the powdery snow.

She rolled up to standing. "Thanks, something's electrified in there."

"In a tree-line? I'm no engineer but wouldn't that be impossible?"

"What else would hum out here?"

He squatted in front of the natural barrier, in the

disturbed snow where Eva had begun her creep forwards. Breaking a low twig off the fir tree in front of him, he threw it further in than she'd crawled. It fell to the ground noiselessly.

He repeated it, throwing the next one higher. "Not seeing anything to suggest it."

Wood wasn't a great conductor of electricity but these trees were damp, they should have triggered some kind of interference. But they were touching the wires all the way along the boundary.

Eva walked along to the next weakening in the treeline, to where she could push herself through. On her belly she listened. It was there, just above her head. Up on her knees, she listened again, another humming about shoulder height.

"I can probably get in between the two. You want to wait here?"

Luke gauged it. "I'll follow, ladies first."

She pushed at the fir tree to dislodge the snow on the upper sides of its branches. Upplega, the Swedish word for that type of snow. She remembered her godfather, Per, making a rhyme up out of the fifty odd words for snow they'd sung together to get her resisting seven-year-old self to ski back to their cabin when she was so tired all she wanted to do was lie in the kornsnö, her favourite one of those words.

Eva lifted her leg to step over the lower wire and a snapping crack hit her. She recoiled so fast,she fell back faster than Agnetha had in the fish market. Grasping her leg, she swallowed the swearing she wanted to scream.

"You okay?"

She flexed her foot, stretched, rubbed at where it hurt like hell. "Definitely electrified. How did it do that?"

"If you still want to go in, we're not getting in that way. Would you rather go back to Bergen, regroup, figure out another way to get this done?"

Was that Luke's way of telling her she was making a terrible choice? Finding whatever Rubin didn't want them to see was the only way Eva could imagine having leverage to get him to comply with her first objective.

If Luke hadn't been there to cast doubt on what she was doing, she'd be doing it. She looked at him. "There's a run of buildings up each side of the property after the trees. I can climb in that way."

"Not happy about putting those contraptions on my feet again." Luke sighed.

The ground sloped upwards towards the house, it'd be a harder ski. "The snow's probably shallow near the buildings, we'll be okay to walk in boots." She hoisted her skis up onto her shoulder. Going from slipping between trees to climbing over a building was a whole other layer of explanation for the panel. This had better get her something to offset everyone's disapproval. Channelling her father's ghost might cost her dearly.

The moon blinked away behind a run of dark clouds as they reached the first building.

"You're sure about this?" Luke murmured. "It'll have to go in my report."

"Yes." She looked at the roof edge. It seemed a long way above her.

"I can boost you."

Eva stepped into his cupped hands. He hoisted her as though she weighed nothing high enough that she could lever herself up onto the flat roof. Not so flat lying on it though, a surprising incline towards the front of the building. As she scrabbled up it, her boots shuffled the snow, clanged on the freezing metal.

From up there she could make out the lighter outline of the house beyond the rise of the land, every window a screen of blackness in the dark. A bowing dip creaked beneath her as the metal flexed. She froze in a starfish shape. It wasn't far, the front edge. Roof, please hold.

Wriggling more slowly, Eva reached the compound edge and peered down. A couple of trees cast the ground between them and her into a blackness she didn't want to drop into. It probably wasn't as high as it looked, nothing to be afraid of. She wouldn't fail this mission because of something that wasn't even a phobia.

She pushed herself to the left; the roof protested.

Another shove with her heels and pull with her hands and she was above where the drop was more dark grey than pitch black, light enough to be sure there was nothing to hurt her other than the distance to the ground itself. Sweating beneath her technical layers, she worked herself round until she could get up on her elbows and lowered herself over the edge, as though she were just getting into a cold swimming pool.

It seemed a long way down. As she was about to lose her balance, she dropped on to the gritted snow.

Too late she wondered at her knee, or rather her ACL ligament, sprained in a collision with a cyclist last year. A jar on the soles of her feet as she hit the ground, heart pounding. She straightened up, flexed her legs. No other damage. She checked her holster, its contents where it was supposed to be.

"I'm down." She hissed at Luke. "Stay there, I'll be quick."

A gentle breeze teased at her with icy fingers, pointing

out the wet patches on her jacket, down her wrist where the snow had settled in a poorly tightened glove.

Eva tucked it under her arm, wringing her hand dry, and prised out her phone. Wooden fingers, clumsy with the cold, texted him.

She tested the outbuilding door. Solid in its frame, locked in part by a securely fastened padlock and what looked like an iPad attached to the wall. Eva jumped at the shattering crash of metal onto concrete on the other side of the door.

Then a low growl reached for her from behind.

14

Eva held her arms out to her sides, turned to face it.

The lynx was beautiful, face impassive, tiny tufts of dark fur on each ear stuck up, the contrast with its well-camouflaged body that rippled in and out of Eva's night vision as it prowled through the ribboned shadows of the trees towards her. Its partner joined it, approaching from the bottom end of the property, giving the same warning.

Eva tensed, forcing herself to not run, pushing herself as tall as she could make herself. But how long before they realised she was no threat and pounced? They stopped a distance from her, watching, gauging what she was. Or were they?

She took a careful step towards the cats, all while her brain screamed at her to run in the other direction. They didn't move, she took another. As though communicating telepathically, they stayed still. Another step forward and Eva caught it, a snatch of a hum.

More closely spaced than in the back tree-line, lines of

almost perfectly camouflaged wires ran from beside the tree spans. As she held her hand out to the one at her shoulder height, a hum grew louder, as she withdrew it, the sound melted to virtual silence. To her left the wires were secured to the metal edge of glass panels that extended high enough to dissuade the lynxes from climbing up the trees and jumping out.

Rubin's reaction to the seals in the fjords didn't equate to a man who kept wild animals caged. Nothing about that man added up. Maybe it was Agnetha, she seemed to like her fur.

A faint banging reached Eva.

The crash—Luke.

She rushed back to the building, knocking, shouting at the door. "Are you okay?"

Nothing from inside. Grabbing out her phone, her call went straight to the automated voicemail.

He was conscious, at least, if he was knocking.

Pulling on the head torch from her inside jacket pocket, she studied the door and held her hand up to the iPad-sized panel. Handprint entry. What the hell was Rubin keeping in there?

And the door, not dissimilar to how solid the one at St George's Grove was, top security. She pulled on the padlock. A flash of a locked door in Marrakech behind which she'd found Lily when she thought she'd lost her, and her husband's unknown about brother's decomposing body, disoriented Eva. Luke had dealt with that locked door, she could take care of this one.

Her ski gloves wouldn't let her pull out her Glock. She took them off and stuffed them in her pockets, and, holding the gun by its barrel, lined up the handle with the padlock. She smashed it down, but the padlock held. They made it look easy in the movies. She tried again, but it didn't budge. So she did what Luke had done in Morocco.

The shot reverberated from building, to tree, to house, to field beyond the tree-line, cracking through the silent Norwegian landscape. The lynx would have taken refuge as far away as the electric fence would let them.

Eva pulled the hasp. It held. What was this made of? Side on to the padlock this time, she shot it apart.

Scrabbling at the hasp, she pulled it open, but there was still the matter of the access panel.

The door opened.

Eva's heart leaped. She pointed her gun up.

"Bang. You need to be faster. Take cover first before exposing yourself." Luke was standing at the side of the doorway, putting away his weapon.

The lighter blackness of the sky filled the space above her head where the roof had been. A tumbled slide of metal sheeting filled the middle of the floor space. "I told you not to follow. You're okay?"

He moved his shoulder round until he winced. "Yeah, won't do that. Strained something."

A pile of tarpaulins poked out from under the metal, extended in neat rows to the opposite side. The stacks of flattened cardboard along the far back wall had been half buried and crushed by the imploded roof.

"That's a lot of security for some cardboard."

"It's camouflage." Luke pushed the tarps to one side at the opposite corner to the cave-in and her head torch beam picked up a large rectangular outline cut into the wooden floor. He lifted the trapdoor up. "Your hunch was right. Don't put your head below the opening, haven't checked for booby traps."

Eva peered into the darkness from a careful distance.

Her light glinted off shiny guns, long-barrelled rifles, an open wooden crate filled with some form of grenade nestling in foam packaging and cylindrical black metallic objects with a trigger that could have belonged in a beauty product display. Everywhere she looked, something different met her gaze, boxes taking up the entire hidden floor space beneath them.

"Carl Rubin's quite the paradox," she said, "wanting to save the planet with his green energy and blow it to bits. That's Agnetha's why, he'd never divorce her, she knows too much."

The darkness in the hut blazed away, the overhead lights almost blinded her.

"I suggest you step away from the trapdoor. You do not want to fall down there." A man's voice boomed into the space behind them. "Hands in the air."

15

───────

Eva pulled her Glock out as she whipped round. Sean Finch stood in the open doorway holding a gun on them that looked as if he'd picked it up from a space station.

He laughed. "You think you're taking me on with that kid's toy? This is a Scorpion, with a serious sting. Watching this fire's like watching a blowtorch through ice cream. You want me to demonstrate? Say goodbye to your partner."

"No, wait." She raised her hands in surrender. He wasn't that far away, she could definitely hit him. But no guarantee she could incapacitate him before he pulled the trigger and he was pointing the gun unwaveringly at Luke.

"Put it down."

Eva could have screamed at the 'why don't you try this' scenarios her brain was feeding her. She wasn't good enough to risk Luke's life. She placed her weapon on the floor.

"And you," Finch pointed it at Luke, who did the same. "Mr Rubin's not going to be happy." He looked at the space where the roof had been, then back at them. "Strip."

"What?"

"You heard me."

"You're a big man." Eva said.

"You're not my type. Strip, I'll let you keep something on."

That wasn't what worried her. Being naked in front of him was neither here nor there in the circumstances. It was the lack of layers of warm down and technical fabric that did. Her face and fingers were already feeling it. Norway in winter wasn't the time to be taking off outer layers unless you were beside a roaring fire.

Luke seemed unfazed at how their day was going. As Eva pulled off her second fleece, she was already shivering, even in her merino wool base layer.

"That'll do." Finch said. "Boots off."

She sat down to unzip them.

"Stuff in a pile in the middle, trousers, phone, keys. Any other weapons."

She placed her phone on top of her salopettes, the frigid air rushing around her, stealing away her warmth.

"Move." He stepped aside, nodding at the open doorway.

"Are you mad?" Eva asked. "We can't go out there like this."

"You'll go out there naked if I tell you to. Don't make me take those off you." He gestured at her with the barrel of the Scorpion. "Move, left out of here, last building on the right."

Towards the house, on the opposite side of the property. Figuring that out didn't help her, it was a long way to walk through snow in socks.

"Any tough guy tactics and I'll shoot. I'll probably get a bonus if I do, so, go ahead, try something."

As though it had been waiting for them to come outside, a gentle waft of tiny flakes, snow breadcrumbs, the kornsnö

Eva loved, drifted around them. That wasn't so much the problem as the snöfyk, the very wet snow on the ground. Eva's toes grew numb in only a handful of steps as the icy liquid squelched up through her ski socks.

The wind had dropped, but the air sucked at her core temperature like a hungry vampire.

The hut to which Finch directed them was a twin of the one Luke had crashed into. An enormous chest freezer lining this back wall was all Eva noticed before Finch slammed the door and the lights went out.

The access panel on the outside bleeped.

"Take off your socks, them being wet is worse than wearing none." She told Luke. "Rub your feet to warm them up."

She laid her socks on the floor beside the wall so she could find them again in the pitch black, patting at them to pull them straight.

"I'm wishing I'd stayed at the consulate." Luke said. "Or we'd just gone back for dinner."

"This isn't how I thought my first mission would go."

"If you'd have shot the idiot, I'd have given you top marks. Now? You've got some ground to make up." Having discounted doing anything to the door, Luke was walking around the inside perimeter, running a hand over the walls, pushing and knocking at the panels.

"You'd have shot him?" Eva moved the stiff tarpaulins and fingertip searched the floor beneath them. A grooved cut out of another trapdoor which disappeared under the freezer. He probably didn't use that one.

"Of course. He had a gun on us and, judging by what we found, he's not shy of shooting if he has to. More paperwork but I'd take that."

"You're probably a lot better shot than me."

"One on one, you never put your weapon down. Did they not teach you that? Think of holding on to it like breathing." Eva shut her mouth on pointing out that he'd surrendered his gun too. "Three or more against you, probably then, but always be thinking of a back-up plan. And how you're going to get it back."

That her instinct had been right was no comfort as the frozen air crept obscenely into the tiniest chink in her base layer, feeding greedily on her numb toes, her nose and chin.

She steeled herself to open the lid of the freezer. The light jabbed at her eyes, making her squint at the white labels on the top-facing cuts of meat wrapped in cling film, arranged Tetris-like to fit in the space. Blue ink spelled out words in Norwegian close enough to the English that she could understand 'reindeer', seal',' whale', 'beef'. She held a leg joint out to Luke.

"I'm hungry but I'm not that desperate yet."

"It could be a passable weapon, in a caveman kind of way."

She took one for herself; it thunked onto the wooden floor. There was enough in there to build a barricade of meat in front of the door which might slow Finch down when he came back for them but did she want to help him keep them in the cold? Not really. Instead, she placed a couple more in the corner behind it and beneath the tarpaulin, then closed the freezer lid to preserve the little warmth that remained. It made the darkness bleaker.

"We need to keep moving, to stay warm." she said. "I'm pacing on the right, you do the left, your left, so we don't collide."

Up and down, bare feet slapping on the wooden floor as she marched, her hands tucked under her armpits, listening to Luke do the same. She could feel the tension of her body bracing against the extreme temperature across her shoulders, down her spine, in her jaw, her neck. She focused on breathing out all the way, but her breath in was too icy to help.

"Aren't we supposed to huddle together for warmth?" She could hear the smile in his voice.

"Glad you haven't lost your sense of humour. It might come to that. Unless you have something in your boxers that you could get us out of here with?"

"Not this time. I'll have to have a word with Sadie, she's left me sadly lacking. But I have a little something, a knife. Nothing to get excited about but up close it could be enough to get us away from the bodyguard."

"If the roof would fall inwards, you think we could do anything to get it to lift upwards?" Eva asked.

"Gravity was helping. Watch your eyes."

He opened the freezer, releasing a cloud of below zero air into their space and balanced on its corner edge, using the light to check where the roof met the walls. "Nothing doing, we're not making any impression on that. Its weakness is clearly its straddle."

He closed it and they paced in silence again, Eva swinging her arms across her body and out. "Does this find redeem me from earlier?"

Luke took three laps of the building to reply.

"Depends how it plays out. There's no redemption in any of this right now. I've always thought the worst of people, that way I'm not disappointed." Luke said. "But I didn't see this coming."

The dark silence stretched until Eva's question burst out of her.

"Agnetha's a target now, isn't she, now I told him?"

"Probably, but hard to feel sorry for her, under the

circumstances." He walked up and down a few times, then added. "Sadie would love to get her hands on some of the stuff Rubin's hiding. Reverse engineering things, rebuilding, redesigning, that's her happy place."

Eva matched his pace. She was completely sober now, but the pizza and cereal bar felt like yesterday. Even her shivering wasn't keeping her warm.

She could feel Luke running through her chain of failures leading to their current mess and the likelihood they'd freeze to death in an outbuilding in remote Norway with no one knowing what happened to them.

Lily. On Eva's first time out of the country she was placing her in exactly the same position she'd been in when she was eight years old and her father didn't come home from assignment. There had to be something she could do, it couldn't be that she wouldn't make it home. But the pacing didn't give her any brainwaves. Were her thought processes failing already?

Up and down, up and down in a failing attempt to fight the all-pervading cold.

"Can I ask you something?" She wouldn't have been able to do it if she could have seen Luke's face.

"Go for it."

She pulled in a breath that scraped at her throat. "Why do you think I can't do this job?"

Before he could answer, a muted beep stole the silence. No time to grab any of Eva's carefully placed frozen weapons before the door opened and the overhead lights stabbed at their eyes.

16

Eva blinked away the blinding intrusion of bright light. She wrapped her arms around her body, trying to buffer herself from the blast of air that pulled its way inside.

"You realise you're in serious trouble imprisoning Interpol officers." Luke was right on the offensive.

"I didn't imprison you." Rubin was back. "Unfortunately, my bodyguard's rather zealous about my protection, he didn't know who you are. Breaking and entering is something I'm certain your superiors don't condone. I've come to let you out, of course."

Dressed in a dark blue parka and black hat, Rubin clumped up to Eva, his snow boots on the wood thumped like he was wearing the weighted metal shoes deep sea divers used to wear to hold them on the seabed. Sean Finch filled the doorway, holding the Scorpion.

"Hello, Eva Janssen."

Eva tried not to give away her surprise, but her own name was perhaps the last thing she expected to come out of his mouth. He shook his head at the start of her denial.

"I knew you were familiar. Your husband, Charles Buchanan, now he's a kindred spirit. His outside the box thinking is truly revolutionary. I can only hope to emulate him in my field."

"Gunrunning?"

"I prefer the term arms dealer. Gunrunning is a little restrictive."

Eva shivered, a shudder at what Charles had become, at Rubin, a concession to the plummeting temperature. The frozen air hurt. Her lower jaw juddered.

"I have a proposition for you. Because of my admiration for your husband, I'm prepared to give you the chance to live. Him," he gestured at Luke, "he won't be so lucky. But it's a shame for you to follow."

"Are you prepared for the fallout on you, the microscopic examination of everything to do with you if we don't report back? Our superiors and back-up know where we are." Eva spat. "You're not a stupid man, the only sane choice is to let us go."

"Are you accepting my offer?"

"Go to hell."

He tutted. "Eva Janssen, is that any way to treat a gift?" And then he said the worst words. "What about your daughter?"

"You shouldn't make a child an orphan," Luke said. "Let her go, this can be between you and me."

"Didn't you tell me she's the lead on your investigation? Doesn't the fallout of any decisions land on her as your superior?" Rubin asked.

Luke laughed, an unexpected sound in the tenseness. "You think she's my superior? This is like an extended job interview where I'm watching her, and she's failing, I might add."

Rubin shook his head. "Women just can't do certain things, as I've tried to show Agnetha when she wanted to have her own clients. Men trust men, it's that simple."

Luke nodded. "Have to agree with you there."

"So, Eva, you want to go home to your daughter, or shall I send flowers?"

"You have my answer." She got the words out through her juddering jaw. Now she'd started, it'd be hard to stop.

He stepped away from her, closer to his bodyguard. "Where are my manners? I'm not a barbarian. Sean, help these people out." The bodyguard picked up a black holdall and threw it at Luke. "Eva can tell you about the dangers of hypothermia being caught out in the snow without adequate gear. I'm actually doing you a favour, what you were wearing wouldn't last five minutes out there." His voice tightened. "Of course, it's nothing like it should be. This winter the Arctic ice is at a record thinness, its coverage less still than it was last year and it was a colder year then. Did you know scientists believe that the thinning of the ice at the poles is actually changing the Earth's axis? People are tipping the balance beyond recoverability." He shook himself, gestured at the bag. "Put them on."

Luke hadn't moved, braced against whatever unexpected either of their enemies would do.

"Sean won't shoot you, while you're doing what I ask." Rubin laughed, sounding delighted. "But you should see the Scorpion in action, it really is quite something." It was scarier that he didn't sound deluded, irrational, or even a bit mad.

Luke unzipped the bag as though there might be a live one in it. When he tipped it out, it turned out to be white snow suits, with fur-edged hoods and dry ski socks.

"One set for both of you." Rubin said.

Eva didn't need to be asked twice. Grappling the socks on with numb fingers twisted them. She rubbed her toes, the soles of her feet wishing Rubin's benevolence extended to two pairs each and their fleeces back. But the snowsuit zipped on, hood up, would help.

"Better?" Rubin asked, standing over her.

Eva stood her ground.

"Your mind is made up?" he asked. "I can still save you."

From what? He'd given them warm clothing, was he just now going to shoot them anyway? What kind of sick joke was this? A trick to win their confidence and still he'd dispose of them?

"I'm not abandoning my partner." Eva ground out. "It's human decency as well as Interpol protocol. As is investigating missing officers. The alarm will already have been raised because we missed our check-in." That wild gamble had paid off for her before, but this time her opponent was apparently less easy to fool.

He lifted a hand and caressed her cheek. The brown leather gloves he wore were soft, but didn't mute his touch enough. She stepped backwards, beyond his reach.

"Pity." He said.

Rubin walked over to Luke. Grasped his chin, pushed him backwards, away from him. Eva wondered where Luke's knife was, Rubin was close enough to take out. But the bodyguard, the Scorpion. "I can't see it, the reason she would sacrifice her life to save you. You're a lucky man."

"And you must be stupid." Luke retaliated.

Rubin adopted a meek position, looking down at the floor, hands clasped in front of him. "I'm so sorry to hear about your missing officers, yes they were here, but they left after just a few moments. The roads around here are quite dangerous in the winter, if you're not used to driving on them." He straightened up. "We'll drive your vehicle off the road where it won't be found until the snow melts. And that discovery just corroborates my story. Of course, given that this isn't Erika Miles," he gestured at Eva. "I've no reason to suspect anything else coming out of your mouth is the truth."

He strode towards the door, staying out of the Scorpion's way, retrieved something from outside and threw a succession of heavy things into the middle of the floor. Their ski boots.

"I'm not a maniac. I'm letting you go, as you wanted, reasonably equipped. You have a chance."

He took off his gloves, turning them inside out and laying them on the floor by the doorway as though they were his firstborn. He took the Scorpion from Finch. "Give them the gloves. Again, you see, I'm really on your side."

Finch approached Luke and handed him a pair of white gloves, held out a pair to Eva. She'd like nothing more than to tell him where to shove them but, right then, keeping her fingers trumped short-term one-upmanship.

"Give him the walkie-talkie." Rubin instructed Finch. "It's only short-range and, as you'll have noticed, this property is very remote. There's no one to hear you if you use it to call for help."

Luke put the device Finch handed him in his pocket.

Rubin gave the gun back to his bodyguard, clapped his hands together. "Right, I'll deactivate the fence for, let's give you five minutes. You can get through the trees if you're motivated enough. Did you like the fence, by the way? It senses body warmth so it activates to keep the lynxes in, if they ever got out of their pen. And if they keep worrying at it, the voltage increases. It can pack quite a punch.

'I assume that's why you decided to go over the building.

Not a bad choice but you were unfortunate to have selected the one with the weakest roof. And, of course, now I have to resite everything and get it repaired. All an inconvenience, I should probably bring that to the attention of your bosses at Interpol." He laboured the word with heavy sarcasm. "More ingenuity, the fence, a by-product of something else. It's how nature teaches us, to take advantage of the synchronicities. And that's exactly what I'm doing with you. Off you go. You have five minutes to get off my property. And then you're helping me test my new weapon, the Lynx Assassin."

17

Luke went for Rubin.

Eva grabbed up one of the slabs of frozen meat and threw it at Finch.

"Stop!" He roared. "This weapon will kill you both in one pulse."

Eva paused in her dive for another of her makeshift defences.

"Drop it," Finch shouted at Luke who had Rubin in an awkward grip, his tiny knife held at Rubin's neck.

"You've got no play here," Luke said. "One jab and your boss is history."

Finch pointed the Scorpion at Eva. "One more second and your partner is."

There was nothing she could do, nothing to use to distract him. Unless.

"You let us both walk out of here and I'll tell you who's coming after you." Eva blurted out.

"They won't get him." Finch stated it matter-of-factly.

"That's what the US Ambassador Hunter Malone thought until they blew him up in Moscow." His hadn't been a The Society kill, but the men after Eva and her family last year had blamed it on them. It had made a big enough media splash Finch might have seen it too. She didn't know the names of anyone else to throw at him. "That's what all their targets think." It was a weak finish.

"They didn't have me." Finch said. "I won't say it again, put it down or say your goodbyes."

Eva snagged Luke's gaze. He wasn't happy with her, but he'd save her, wouldn't he? He'd put down the knife.

"Don't think she's a mind reader." Finch said. "Five."

Luke wasn't moving.

"Four."

She was too far from the open door to make it in the second she had when he pulled the trigger.

"Three."

Eva's desperation distilled into two syllables tearing her apart.

"Two."

Lily.

"Okay, okay," Luke pushed Rubin away from him, put his hands up in surrender, flat palms empty.

Rubin adjusted his parka. "You've got five minutes to get off my property. At five minutes and one second Sean will fire the Scorpion."

Luke shot out of the door before Eva moved. Ignoring the pins and needles in her toes and fingers, she charged after him, hurtling past the lynxes, slipping on the slushy snow as she hit the incline down towards the trees. She crashed onto the hard ground. One of the cats shot over to her, keeping the tiniest of distances from the wires on its side, close enough to intimidate her. It pawed the ground, dislodging the snow from a small pile of bones. Eva stared in horror; she'd fallen near its dinner table. The lynx bared its teeth at her in a snarl.

She scrabbled up onto her feet, slipping, sliding, dragging her focus away from the long bones settling on the trees, her goal.

Luke cut across to the middle of the boundary and was on his belly, halfway out to freedom by the time Eva got there. She followed, diving headlong onto the track he'd carved in the snow.

She kicked herself forward. He grabbed the shoulders of her snowsuit and yanked her through as though she were on a sled, pulling her halfway to standing.

"You okay?"

She nodded.

"We need to collect those god-awful skis and get back to the car. Hug the boundary, keep low, keep moving, so he can't get a clear shot at us."

"Right behind you."

They'd tramped only halfway to the corner when the walkie-talkie in Luke's pocket crackled at them.

"Tick tock," Rubin's voice taunted. "Your skis are gone, the way back to the road impassable for you, allow me to demonstrate."

The boom resounded in her chest, made her throw herself on the snow, copying Luke's quicker reactions. Her ears weren't ringing, the explosion hadn't been so close.

"Rats in a maze, get moving, but not that way." Eva was beginning to hate the sound of Rubin's voice. "Nor down the other side of my property."

"He's mined the safer routes." Luke's voice was flat. "Seems we're going out into the open. Zig zag, try to be unpredictable in where you run—"

"If the snow's as deep as it looks, we won't be running anywhere."

The moonlight, fainter again now, helped them understand how hopeless it was. Untouched by footprint or animal print, the snow glistened at them, taunting, daring, but Eva knew the nightmare it'd be. "If you can, shuffle rather than run. You'll tire really fast pulling your legs up enough to get out of it."

"You casting aspersions on my fitness again." Luke's attempt at humour was the most valiant thing Eva had ever heard. "Ready?"

Not at all.

"Tick tock." Eva already wanted Luke to smash the walkie talkie.

"Trees opposite, zigzag," Luke confirmed, "then we'll cut back to where we parked. He can't have mined the whole place."

It was hard to take that first step, even though it was the safest one, protected by the trees as they were. Out from their cover, Eva pushed herself faster, harder. Move. She shuffled through the snow. It wasn't the pudersnö, the powder snow, she'd hoped for, but at least it wasn't as wet as it had been in Rubin's compound.

She pushed herself forward. The rise had looked low from their starting point but felt like a mountain. Lily was expecting her mum to come home from her boring meeting and she would. It wasn't like she was standing by an exploding building as her father had been. There was no way she died by being shot in the back by a madman.

"How far do we have to go?" she panted.

"Further."

"How far?"

"You don't want to know."

Over the rise the ground levelled out, no dip downwards to give them coverage. Too far away from them was a line of snowy fir trees. The level of snow undulated off to the left, away from their car, a gentle curve up and down in the landscape, harder going but offering them some sliver of cover. To their right, towards the car, the ground looked flatter; the snow giving the opposite of cover. But then why had Rubin given them white snowsuits? Was he using a weapon that relied on thermal imagery?

The walkie-talkie woke up again. "How're you getting on?"

Luke left it in his pocket. "I'm done talking to that sick bastard."

"As you're so kind as to help me out, I thought you might like to know a little about this weapon, what makes it so special."

Eva tried to use Rubin's voice to galvanise her, to pull on her anger at him to give her a burst of energy but the cereal bars they'd eaten in the SUV felt like breakfast last week, her body long used it up trying to stay warm.

"It's revolutionary, obviously."

Before she'd met Rubin, Eva had had a guts full to last beyond a lifetime of a man professing his genius. Charles had a lot to answer for.

"I don't need to follow you, or locate you from the sound of your voice," Rubin went on, "it's much cleverer than that. You can talk back to me. In fact, if you do, I'll give you another minute on the clock."

She gestured at Luke for the walkie-talkie.

"You want to engage with him?"

"Not the smallest bit but a minute is a minute. Plus he can maybe tell us something useful for Sadie if I flatter him enough."

"On the off chance he might then be too busy to remember to shoot us?" Luke handed her the device.

Eva dredged up a smile from somewhere. "I hate an unanswered question." She pressed the transmit button. "Me talking to you depends on whether you have something to say that I want to hear." She waited so long for his response she thought she hadn't pressed the right button.

Then Rubin laughed. "What do you know about lynxes?"

"That they shouldn't be kept as pets." She snapped back.

"And?"

"I defer to you as an expert."

"They're beautiful creatures. This weapon, I call the Lynx Assassin, is an homage, if you will. It's the same, streamlined, well-camouflaged, powerful, a lean killing machine, unable to be called off once it's set in motion."

"Ask him how far it can shoot." Luke puffed.

"You're asking the wrong question," he said when she did. "How far away are you?"

"About two hundred metres." Eva wildly underestimated where they were, pushing herself harder, trying not to puff out her increased exertion when she spoke.

"You're nowhere far enough away yet. How far are you going?" He asked it as though they were on a treasure hunt he wanted them to win. Eva's thighs were burning, her shins ached viciously, the raw air scraped at her throat, her airway. Another shuffle, another.

"How far?" she rapped to Luke.

"Longest sniper shot on record's just over 3,500 metres."

Eva mis-stepped, her ankle almost twisting over itself, but her boot held it where it should be. "Three and a half kilometres?" she hissed.

"On record, set in 2017, Rubin's clearly got further."

She stumbled on. They had to get four kilometres away from Rubin's property to be safe. Four kilometres in the snow. She didn't know she had that in her.

"Satisfy my curiosity," Rubin asked, "how far?"

Eva gripped the walkie-talkie but didn't reply.

"I'd guess four kilometres," he answered for her. "In that snow, that's quite a feat. Pity you won't be safe then."

18

"He's bluffing, isn't he?" Eva looked at their tracks in the snow. Diagonally out from the tree-line their jagged zigzag cut to their right and then at an almost 90° angle, pitifully less than one kilometre in distance, let alone four. Rubin could shoot on the diagonal, making it all simpler, pulling them closer.

She'd answered her own question.

A tiny copse straight ahead but looking too far away, the flat ground back to their car, or the slight depressions in the land in the opposite direction. Not much of a choice.

She charged over to one of the undulations in the snow, sliding into it, lying against its gentle rise like she had in a wet and muddy ditch in England when she'd only been at risk from a paintball bruise and the words "You failed".

Luke slid down next to her. "It's not deep enough."

"It's not, but we only need to be out of his sightline. Bullets only curve in movies."

"He's too much in control in this scenario. We can lie here getting wetter and colder while he's in his warm house deciding when to shoot us. Always better to be a moving target than a sitting duck."

The siren lure of hypothermia and a gentle sleep to death was strong.

"That's an interesting move." The walkie-talkie spoke to them.

Was he tracking them or watching?

"It's not distance." Rubin taunted.

Eva keyed the transmit button. "Go on then, impress me."

"I'm tracking you, or rather my tech is. And you're both providing a powerful signal."

"Thermal?"

"That's unimaginative, so last century."

What else? "The signal from the walkie-talkie?"

"Not even warm. Excuse the pun. And lying on the snow isn't going to change the outcome."

Then she understood. The sound travelled across the silent landscape ahead of it, the angry buzzing of a drone.

"We need to get in those trees." She pushed herself up, scrambled out of the dip, which now felt like it was two miles deep, heading east towards the thin copse, Luke right beside her.

Eva keyed the walkie-talkie. "Nothing cutting-edge about that, just your over-inflated sense of ego. Teenagers in America have been fixing guns to drones for years. Even in the UK they've been messing around with laser pointers on them to disrupt airports. I thought you'd have known about that given that you're all about fighting the climate emergency."

"It's not what you're thinking. There's no weapon attached to that drone, it's a rather grandiose transmitter. Is that enough of a clue?"

Eva's legs were shaking, her breath shuddered out. A clammy wave of sickness slowed her. She had no idea what he was talking about.

"I'll give you a fighting chance, I'm nothing if not fair. What do you know about RFID chips?"

That's what he was using? The drone shot up into the sky and she lost its lights amongst the stars the clouds had peeled back to reveal. The buzzing grated at her.

She pushed herself harder still.

Rubin's voice came from Eva's pocket again. "Those trees aren't enough though."

She wasn't pandering to his ego anymore. Apparently he didn't need her to.

"You should see the weapons I have coming online next," he crowed. "Taking my inspiration from nature has been the making of my business. The Lynx Assassin is laser-like in its focus, just like the lynx. Yellowstone, that one is quite something. I nearly called it Mars. I still might because it's more fitting on every level. I'm at the leaving the Solar System level of spaceflight while my, and I use the word loosely, competitors haven't yet left planet Earth."

The copse loomed, but as she approached it her ramming heart dropped. Just a couple of trees thick, not the wood they needed. Rubin was right, not nearly enough cover.

Eva began unzipping her snowsuit before she reached its meagre shelter. "Take your snow suit off. That's how he's tracking us, it's literally a target on our backs."

"If you wanted me undressed, I wish you'd told me when we were somewhere warmer."

Eva threw herself into the trees. Her mind screamed at her to hurry, even as her body rebelled at the painful cold.

She undid the ankle zips and pulled the snowsuit off over her boots. "Hurry up."

She threw hers on to the ground, laid it out as though she was still wearing it, making sure it was more under the pitiful cover than not.

"He's using RFID tags must be in the suits. They only work over a short distance so the drone must be reading them and he's relaying the signal from the drone to wherever he is. There has to be a camera on it, don't let it see you take it off."

Luke was shovelling his suit into the snowdrift.

"That won't help, cold doesn't drop the signal."

"Let's get away from here."

Eva grabbed his arm. "We don't know what distance is safe, our best chance is to stay right beside it."

"But we can get further away through these trees."

"No, trust me. I know about this stuff, Lily had to do a science project and she did one on RFID tags to spite Charles. He wanted to do something more difficult, bask in reflected glory." She had to stop doing that, stop running him down at every opportunity because it was going to slip out to Lily one day. The past should stay there, it couldn't fix the present. Except Lily could. After the project she'd made Eva buy a protective wallet to keep all her credit cards safe and, even her own bus pass went in one, just in case. But Eva and Luke had no metal on them they could use to confuse the signals.

Eva laid his snowsuit beside hers then stood close to him.

"Do I have anything on my face?" He looked down at her, still slightly out of breath after the snow shuffling run. She pointed at her cheek.

Luke leant closer. "What'm I looking for?"

Eva shivered. "I'm not sure."

He tilted her chin up towards him. "Can't really say, we need more light. Why, what're you thinking?"

"He touched us both on the face, then how carefully did he take his gloves off? No reason to do either unless he was priming us with the tags."

She ran her hand over Luke's chin, her fingertips didn't pick up any foreign objects but depending how small they were, they could have been caught up in his stubble. She did the same to her face but couldn't feel anything.

She grasped up a handful of snow, rubbed it on her cheek. It was so cold it felt like it was burning. "Water confuses them, in case, it could help, wipe your chin where he touched you."

"And there I was thinking he liked me." Luke copied her, scrubbing at his chin. "Is it a bad thing it doesn't feel cold?"

"It's not good. There's one other thing we can do. Too many tags get the readers confused. We have to hope he hasn't been able to get past the inherent disadvantages of using them. That's why the drone, he can't pick up the signal from more than a couple of kilometres away."

"What I said about presenting a moving target still holds. Staying here is insanity."

"Exactly, he won't be expecting us to do it."

"Don't like it." Luke hesitated. "We should be running."

"Where?" Eva challenged him. "We can't outrun a drone, you know how fast those things can fly. Its camera will tell him we're not wearing those snowsuits. You heard Rubin, he has other more deadly weapons. What if he tries one of those on us that don't need the chips to target?"

Luke looked through the trees away from Rubin's house,

where Eva had already discounted. More the same through there, snowy fields divided by tree banks. Deep snow to navigate and they were both exhausted.

"How do we do this?"

"Not easily, I need a box to stand on. Let's try you sitting and me kneeling."

Luke gave her a sideways look but got down on the ground. Eva knelt beside him, too tall. Shuffling onto her bum, she leant in against him.

"Put your chin on my cheek," but the leaning forward made her back ache. "Do you mind if I sit on your lap?"

"Go for it."

"Only my bum's now wet, so you'll get it from both sides."

"The things I have to do for my country."

Eva wriggled up onto his lap, stretching her legs out on either side of him. "If you put your chin on my cheek, I hope this'll confuse the signals for those we didn't wipe off. As a bonus, we won't die of hypothermia quite so quickly."

"I knew you knew Norway." Luke's chin tickled her face as he spoke.

"I've gone right off it. Next mission better be somewhere in the Caribbean." Her joke was hollow, but Eva would trade being thrown out of SIS for getting home alive.

They waited. She focused on the warmth of Luke's body on her front, pretending her back wasn't freezing.

"Not that this isn't a great way to spend a night but any idea how long?" He asked after a while.

"It's all guesswork, I could be completely wrong about all this."

"Just wanted to get up close and personal, I get that a lot."

Eva laughed, an edge of hysteria to it.

"It's going to be okay." He added, squeezing her closer to him.

Unless Rubin didn't make his move soon, then the cold would take them and he wouldn't have to.

19

———

Time stopped. Eva and Luke waited.

Waited.

"You okay there?" He murmured, his chin warm against her cheek.

"I'm good, though maybe need to apologise to Mrs Fox, sitting on you like this."

Eva felt Luke's chuckle deep in his belly. "You're good, there's no Mrs Fox."

"A Miss hoping to be?"

"Not currently. And the whole freezing wet nether regions isn't the turn on you'd think."

"Nether regions?" Despite everything, Eva almost laughed.

"Plus the real possibility we're about to be shot kind of hijacks the mind." He shifted her to the left a touch. "Throwing you in right at the deep end of your first mission, pretty impressive mentoring I'd say."

"How am I doing?"

"I'll let you know, when we get out of here."

Waited.

Eva shivered. Was her hunch wrong? Over Luke's shoulder, filtered into tiny specks through the tree branches, the green and purple of the Northern lights was fading up from black. Somewhere beneath their flimsy shelter and Rubin's house, the drone's mad insistence raced back towards them. Was this it?

Luke tensed against her.

Should they have sat further away from the snow suits? Trying to stay hidden from the drone's camera's probing lens, the ribboned camouflage from overhead wasn't wide enough for much of a distance. Should they have run as Luke wanted? Too late now.

A thwacking hit their snowsuits.

Eva held her breath, Luke did the same.

Rubin had fired at them. He'd really intended to kill them. How could he? He was every bit the monster his weapons cache suggested.

The drone's insistent buzz hovered on the house side of the trees. She didn't dare move. Luke's grip on her back tightened. She had to remind herself to breathe, the shallowest breath in.

Then it whipped away, its buzz fading to silence.

They both waited beyond the point the sound had ceased to register.

"That it, do you reckon?" she murmured as though the drone might overhear.

"Only one way to find out."

Cautiously they got to their feet.

The shimmering waves of the Northern lights hadn't bloomed beyond a whisper of colour. The moon dominated the sky now, huge and icy blue, turning everything around them into a Christmas card scene. No sound other than their breathing, nothing moving other than the plumes of frosty air they gulped in and out.

Eva retrieved the bullets from their snow suits, her hand trembling just a little.

"Souvenir?" Luke asked.

She held them out on her palm. "For Sadie, the Danish authorities. They look a lot like what she'd got from those murders in Denmark. It was him, these prove it."

Luke poked one of them. "Good thinking, I can't imagine they're standard. Think it's safe to say our mission's changed. We'll need to report in, get clearance as to next steps."

"Is losing my weapon on my first outing a bad thing?" Eva hesitated to put a foot in the snowsuit. It looked all white and innocent but it felt like she might be putting on a suicide vest.

"It's not ideal."

"We have no powers of arrest but Rubin doesn't know that."

Luke laughed. "I like your thinking, but him not knowing we survived is a good advantage. I'd like to keep it, for as long as we can, you never know when we might need it. What's your plan now?"

"It's 10:04, and Agnetha was definite about bringing the waiter here when Rubin wouldn't be here."

"That might have been the case before I brought the house down." Luke pointed out.

"Fair point but he was going to Denmark, if he's gone we could have time to look for our weapons and IDs."

"You mean breaking and entering this time?"

"Probably but if he's got rid of our hire car, we can't walk back to Bergen, the chances of hitchhiking from out here are zero. We need to find our skis." Luke grunted. "Or he might have a skidoo or something. How're your hot-wiring skills?"

"I can give you a masterclass."

"I was hoping you'd say that."

Now she'd totally blown her mission, Luke was being the Luke she'd met last year, the frosty edge had melted away entirely. Had he wanted her to fail?

They trudged back through the snow, retracing the tracks they'd made earlier, as an extra precaution.

Usually getting back from somewhere felt faster, easier, but this was only harder. They could probably assume a rifle wasn't targeted on them, but their adrenaline rush had faded, leaving them exhausted, wet, hungry and thirsty and probably on the edge of hypothermia. Bodies running on near zero.

"Is this normally how it goes?" Eva asked as they reached the tree-line at the bottom of the property.

"Not always. Sometimes it's hard."

She listened for the hum. "It's back on. Looks like we're going the long way round."

"What're the chances of all the roofs being so weak?" Luke looked beyond the end of the trees to the outbuildings they knew were there. "It's a bloody long way to walk from this end to their driveway, and time's not on our side."

"I'm not the one who fell through it. How's your shoulder?"

"I'm willing to give it a shot."

Dropping into the Rubins' compound from a different outbuilding, Eva strained to hear Luke. The metal roof they'd chosen this time creaked a warning, but he made it over, wincing as he landed beside her. They hugged the shadow of the outbuildings as they approached the house.

One foot over the rise and security lights snapped at them. No disguising their intentions now. Eva forced herself to not freeze, if she'd been seen, she'd been seen. Standing there like a deer wouldn't help anything.

They reached the back of the house. Nothing, no one shouting or shooting. Just like it was when they climbed into the compound the first time.

20

Every door to Rubin's house and each of the four garages at the front were locked electronically, a hand access panel beside each one. Even if Eva and Luke had a pick gun, there was no getting into any of them.

Luke peered through a window at the rear of the house, then tapped at it. He pulled out his knife and placed the handle in the bottom corner of the window. The glass crazed into a psychedelic spider's web that he elbowed into the room.

"That's impressive." Eva said.

"Safety feature in triple and double glazing. Also, doesn't hurt to get your knife from Sadie. This little punch has saved me probably more often than bullets."

He levered himself in through the window, and the alarm screamed at him. Eva followed, feeling the crunch of broken glass beneath her boots, rather than hearing it above the racket of the clamouring siren.

"You search in here, I'm in the next room." Luke ordered.

She drew the heavy curtains before switching on the

light. A long sideboard and a sparse bookcase were the only places they could be hidden in what was the dining room. The drawers had apparently been organised by someone with OCD. It made for easy searching.

The kitchen was the same, everything gleaming and in its place. The warmth of the house was draining Eva's reserves. Exhausted after their runs through the snow, at the wrong end of the champagne effects, she wanted to lie down on the sofa, put the fire on and just sleep.

Luke was standing in front of a closed door at the end of the hallway. "Nothing in the. . ." the blaring alarm snatched her words away. "Nothing in the. . ." yelling got her nowhere. She touched his arm. Luke whipped round, his fight stance softening when he saw her.

"Nothing in the kitchen or dining room." She shouted right at him.

He nodded and gestured at the access panel, leaning closer to her. "This must be his office, he's either put them in there or in our car to give credence to his story about us."

Eva's turn to lean close to him. "Your punch no help there?"

"Not unless I don't mind being electrocuted. If he hasn't taken his sat phone with him, it's in there."

"If we can turn the power off, could you break the panel?" She yelled.

He shrugged. "Probably but I'm guessing he has other safeguards that'll kick in then. He could have a generator, solar powered batteries, he's got enough panels on the roof, he could be off the supply entirely, which probably means no transport back to Bergen."

Eva didn't need to hear his last words, swallowed by the alarm as they were. "Then we eat something and walk it."

"I knew this mission would be trouble," Luke shook his

head. "Should never have taken it." Then she understood, because she'd failed it, so had he. But she was losing more.

"As I failed every single objective, it's safe to say you won't have to work with me again," the yelling was easy now, "once I get us back to Bergen—"

"You don't get it," Luke shouted.

"So you keep telling me."

The alarm stopped and the silence that collapsed on to everything made them both start.

"What the hell are you doing in my house?" Agnetha, a picture of righteous fury, demanded.

"Looking for your husband."

"By breaking in? How did you find this place?"

Eva could see the moment she realised she'd understood her giving the address to Ralph. "You said you don't speak Norwegian."

"I don't," Eva agreed, "but Google Translate does."

"You can call the police." Luke held his hands away from his body, showing her he posed no threat. "They'll vouch for us, we're Interpol."

Agnetha looked him up and down, even though his snowsuit was no tux. Her fury softened a little. "You're with her?"

He nodded. "Partners. You calling us in?"

"That depends. How good are you at the sweet talk?"

"What do I need to sweet talk you about?"

"He's obviously not here, my husband, since you triggered the alarm." Her look changed when she added, "we have an open relationship. I'm free to pursue whoever I please."

"Or pleases you?"

Was Luke flirting with her? Whatever got the job done, Eva supposed.

Agnetha smiled, dropped her fur coat on the floor for a maid to pick up, and sashayed into the lounge. Not the coat that had half the fish market on it, this one looked like a lynx, ready to pounce.

She pointed the remote at the opposite side of the room and ambient lamps turned on in two corners. Then the flames leapt alive again. It was all Eva could do to not rush up to them.

"I'm having a cognac, for you?"

"Our IDs and service weapons, would be a good place to start." Luke said. "Your husband took them from us."

"That was a little careless on your part." She chinked the decanter against a heavy glass and the spirit splashed into it.

"Agnetha, is what's outside the reason you can't divorce Carl?" Eva asked.

"What're you talking about?" Agnetha snapped. "The lynxes are better cared for than if they were in the wild. Ours never go hungry."

Eva looked at Luke, reveal their hand? He gave a slight nod. "I'm talking about what's inside the outbuildings. I'm guessing you don't divorce an arms dealer."

Agnetha turned away, staring at the curtains as if she was looking right through them at the view outside.

"Who said anything about divorce?"

"You're unhappy, I could see that when we talked—"

"You don't know the first thing about me." She gripped the drinks cabinet.

"There might be some room to make a deal for you," Luke said, "if you help bring in your husband and give us information on who he's been selling the weapons to. We can use that as leverage for your future."

"My future's well assured, thanks very much. I won't be telling you anything about his agenda." She picked up the remote again, pointing at the cabinet this time and the door popped open. She turned to face them and Eva recognised the only handgun she knew, her or Luke's Glock.

"I wouldn't do that if I were you," Luke said as calmly as if she were just offering him a drink. "Shooting an Interpol agent will bring heat on you that you really can do without."

Eva glanced around the room. What could she use as a weapon? The cushions on the sofa were too big and unwieldy, the china coasters on the coffee table? Agnetha would have shot her before she grabbed one.

"If you hurt us, we can't help you." Eva tried for reasonable.

A man's voice behind them interrupted. Eva snapped around. A gunshot filled the space.

21

———

The stunned silence erupted as Luke ran at Agnetha. She fired into the ceiling and he stopped as though she'd shot him.

"I didn't say move. Now you know I'm not afraid to use this and we have a dead civilian, shot by one of you two, I won't have any trouble, will I?"

"Can I. . .?" Eva gestured at Ralph, lying on the floor.

"No point, I'm a crack shot. I meant him to be dead, he's dead." She sighed. "Look what you made me do. Such a waste of that pretty face and body."

She was like a different person to the one Eva had spent time with in the champagne bar. This was the Agnetha who had pressed the button to confirm her husband's assassination order. She laughed. "You look shocked, but married to an arms dealer, it's just makes sense to be a better shot than he is." She hefted the Glock on her open palm. "Who does this belong to?"

Eva glanced at Luke. She had no idea.

"It's mine." They said it together.

Agnetha laughed again. "How noble. Well, Erika and?" She raised her eyebrows at Luke.

"Pierre," he gave his cover name.

"Pierre, we could have had such fun, but maybe you're not enough of a bad boy for me. I'll give you a head start before I call Ralph's unfortunate demise into the authorities. But not a long one, I want them to catch you after all. What are you waiting for? Get out." She jabbed at the hallway with the gun. "Now."

The front door closed behind them with a solid thunk and the electronic sound of locking.

"Back in the window to rush her?" Eva asked.

"Unless you have a better idea. I'm so over this sodding cold and not a little fed up with the Rubins."

The security lights bathing the front of the house with their spotlights went dark.

Eva closed her eyes to help her night vision wake up. It felt colder outside now they'd been in the warmth inside. She could almost wish she'd grabbed up the fur coat.

"Now?" she asked.

"Give her a couple of minutes, let her think we've gone. Element of surprise is always best if you have it firmly on your side."

Eva's breath sighed out in a white stream. All hints that the Northern lights would play were cloaked now by the ethereally deep, dark sky.

And then she caught it. Luke snapped a look at her. He'd heard it, too.

"Is that what I think it is?"

The low growl came again.

She nodded. "Definitely the lynx, definitely not in its enclosure."

"You know anything about them?"

"A bit, they're in Sweden too, but they're usually shy of humans, not even as bold as the urban foxes in London. But these two aren't completely wild, they're used to humans." Eva tried to think of when her father and godfather had taken her out into the Swedish countryside. "Whatever you do don't run. Its instinct is to chase, if you run you're acting like prey and that'll make him a predator."

"Can we climb out of their way?" Luke was checking out the trees that ran the length of the driveway, looking behind him as though he was thinking about trying to get on the roof.

"They climb better than us."

The low rumble was closer.

"Hold your arms out, make yourself seem bigger." Eva added.

She saw it then, its beautiful fluidity, a weapon in motion, padding through its natural element. Stalking. Right towards them.

Eva yelled. "See it?"

"We doing this for a reason?" Luke shouted back.

"Being assertive. Showing it we're the boss."

The yelling was already exhausting.

The cat bared its teeth, Eva hoped it was just for show, it was apparently well fed going by the pile of bones she'd fallen beside. And she, oh God, it was–those bones; she realised what she'd seen. Human bones. They were in more danger than she thought.

"Behind the pillars," she yelled at Luke, shuffling to keep the far too thin wooden column between her and the big cat.

The lynx paused, head up, alert. Stared at her. Eva roared at it. She'd be dinner for sure if they were hungry, they were probably sizing her up already as easier to subdue than Luke. Holding her arms out further away from her body, she yelled, "Go on, get away."

The lynx stood still, watching.

"Let's get inside the house." Eva said. "Walk backwards though, don't turn your back on it. Go, I'll follow."

Luke's ski boots crunched on the trampled snow behind her, freezing now to ice. The lynx watched.

Eva's legs were tensed ready to run. Deliberately she took one slow step backwards, then another. Don't bolt, slow steps away.

A thud behind her, a hiss.

"Luke, is it the other cat?"

She couldn't turn around, take her gaze off the one in front of her in case her stare was the only thing holding it still.

"Luke, what're you doing?" She forced her panic-edged words out past her dry mouth. "Luke?" She shouted.

"Slight deviation from the plan." He gasped.

"Talk to me."

But he didn't.

"Luke?" Eva took two steps to her left, skirting where he was behind her. Past his boots, on the ground his feet flopped outwards. A snapshot of him having been knocked unconscious by Charles at the airport hit her for the second time that day. Damn him, he wasn't going to haunt everything she ever did. She had to let go of him and the hurt he'd caused.

Keeping her gaze on the cat, Eva slowly backtracked to Luke. He'd knocked himself out or fainted.

Nothing for it. She could only take care of one of them right then. Eva pulled in a frosted breath and, screaming, charged at the lynx.

22

———

Yelling like a mad woman, arms waving, slipping on the fast icing compacted snow, Eva chased the lynx. It wasn't what it was used to. In a sleekly fluid motion, it folded in on itself and bounded away, setting off the security lights.

"Yeah, you run." She shouted after it. "You keep going, leave us alone."

She squatted beside Luke who'd regained consciousness. "What happened?"

"I slipped, shoulder." He breathed.

"It looks like you might have dislocated it. That's a hospital trip. Unless you've done this a lot of times and popping it back in is a hidden superpower?"

He shook his head, hissed out the pain. "I wish, first time, not intending to do it again."

"I'm going to have a chat with the lady of the house, show her it's in her interests to help us. Up you come, I'll get you behind the pillar."

"Think I'm good here."

"No, the cat could come back. Come on." She staggered

beneath his weight as he struggled to standing, hissing out the pain, on the edge of fainting again. "Easy mission, right?" she tried to take his mind off it.

"No plan survives contact with the enemy." Luke gasped, playing along.

"That something in my training manual I should have read?"

"Chinese general. Sun Tzu."

"I'll look him up." He slid off her, onto the step near enough behind the too thin wooden pillar. He was paler than the snow. "You'll be okay here, I think I scared it pretty good." Neither of them mentioned the other one, though Eva certainly worried about it.

"I'll be as fast as I can." She was sure it wasn't much reassurance.

The curtains she'd pulled across the side window in the dining room were still closed. She nudged them, checking that Agnetha hadn't piled an obstacle course behind them. They moved as she expected them to.

Gathering the fabric in her gloved hand, she pulled it back. No one in the room.

She hoisted herself up onto the windowsill, stepped into the welcome warmth and listened.

Silence.

If she were a real Interpol officer, she had enough on Agnetha to arrest her. Eva heard something from deeper in the house.

Not easy to tiptoe across wooden and slate floors in ski boots quietly. Eva peered around the lounge door. The flames were playing only to Ralph, lying where he'd dropped. Eva leant over him, just stopped herself pressing her fingertips to his neck and leaving her fingerprints unnecessarily. His sightless gaze told her Agnetha had been right, he was gone. The top of the drinks cupboard was empty and the door locked, no sign of their weapons or the remote.

She followed the noises. Agnetha was in the bathroom bending in towards a Hollywood style mirror, lit around the edges by brighter than the sun lightbulbs, a tumbler holding a couple of ice cubes with a mouthful of brown liquid in the bottom beside her.

It was a palatial bathroom, taking Eva enough running strides across the tiled floor to reach her that Agnetha could snatch up the gun hidden under her towel and scream at her to stop.

"What is it with you? What part of get out don't you understand?"

"Holding an officer of the law at gunpoint, again, I'm adding that to your list of offences, and, believe me, they're racking up right now. Setting the lynx on us, that was stupid. That implies intent."

"From where I'm standing, you're the one in trouble: you shot an unarmed civilian. And what am I to do if my idiot husband can't keep his pets under control?"

"This," Eva gestured between them, "is also intent, we'll charge you twice for that, once under Norwegian law and once under international criminal law. You want me to go on?" Her bluff sounded believable enough.

Agnetha laughed. "I thought you worked for an international company?"

"Interpol is international. My partner's injured, if you help me get him to hospital, I'll ask the courts to be lenient."

Agnetha laughed harder. "You have a bigger pair of balls than Carl. You think skirting the law bothers me? Our whole life together has been one long," she drew a spiral downwards with the gun barrel.

Eva charged.

She collided with Agnetha, marching her backwards until she had her pressed up against the huge bath, her hands pressing Agnetha's gun arm back, away from her. Eva pushed harder. With nowhere for their momentum to go, Agnetha's legs buckled, and they crashed into the bath.

Eva scrabbled to hold on to Agnetha's right arm, forcing it upwards, keeping the Glock pointed away from her. Agnetha screamed and writhed like a wild thing. She wrenched her left hand up and grabbed her right, pulling it against Eva's one-handed grip. Moving the barrel closer to her face.

This was nothing like it had been in training.

Eva snatched up the shower head and swung it at Agnetha's head, as hard as she could. The blow reverberated into her hand, made Agnetha gasp. Her grip loosened on the gun. Eva pulled it upwards, twisted it.

She shuffled upwards on her knees pressing down hard, one knee pinned Agnetha's arm, the one in her stomach making Agnetha scream.

"Enough." Eva panted. "Let go or I'll break your fingers. And they won't heal well enough for you to want to show off your expensive jewellery anymore."

Agnetha screeched as Eva knelt down harder. She let go of the gun.

Eva twisted it away from her and held it in front of her face. "Now you're going to do exactly as I say, is that clear?" Agnetha stared. "Clear?" Eva bellowed.

Agnetha nodded.

"You're going to drive my partner to hospital. Got it?" Eva climbed carefully out of the bath, training the weapon on Agnetha all while she directed her to do the same.

"From shooting Ralph, you'll know this has a hair trigger." She pressed it up against the back of Agnetha's head. "Any movement I'm not happy with, anything that surprises me and it'll go off, got it?"

"Yes."

"I need our IDs and the other Glock. Slowly, don't make me shoot you." While she covered Agnetha and got her outside, Eva's heart rapped as if it was sending morse code to London.

"You okay?" she called to Luke.

He was still upright and thankfully not mauled. "Bit chilly."

"Agnetha's going to drive us to the hospital."

"Mighty kind of her."

Eva prodded Agnetha with the Glock to make her walk to the garage. Agnetha put her hand on the access panel and the nearest door whirred up. Inside the four garages were one huge space. Between the out-of-place convertible parked at the far end and Eva and Agnetha were two SUVs, one much bigger and beastlier than the other.

"That's mine." Agnetha gestured at the smaller of the two.

"Keys?" Eva asked.

She gestured to the end wall where a white slimline cabinet was also locked by an access panel.

"Open it."

Agnetha's palmprint clicked it open. "Those." She pointed at the sets on the right.

Eva pressed the unlock button at Agnetha's car and it bleeped open.

"Can I wait in there while you get your partner, it's cold out here." Agnetha shivered.

One less thing for Eva to watch while she helped Luke. She pocketed all the keys from the key safe. "Sure."

When the door clunked closed and she could be sure Agnetha wasn't about to rush her, Eva jogged over to Luke.

"You want to hold on to me?" She had him halfway to standing when Agnetha drove out of the garage, tyres crunching on the crispy snow as she roared away down the driveway.

23

———

"Should've taken the keys off her." Luke gasped.

"I did, they're all in my pocket." Eva shot back. "How did she do that?"

"Don't sweat it, we'll take the other one."

The shiny black beast loomed over everything in the garage like a dare. "We can't. I can't drive."

"Piece of cake," he said through gritted teeth, shallow breathing. "It'll have snow tyres, it won't be as risky as driving in London in winter."

"No, you're not listening. I can't drive that because I can't drive."

"How can you not drive?" His voice rose and there she was, failing all over again.

"I live in London, why would I need to? That's what public transport's for." It sounded too defensive.

He hissed out pain. "We should've made that part of the training clearly. It'll be automatic, it'll practically drive itself and it's not like it's rush hour out there."

Eva pointed the biggest key fob at the huge SUV, half-expecting it to snarl as she hit unlock.

She got Luke into the front seat, but he said no when she pulled the seatbelt out for him.

"I'd feel a lot happier if you'd wear it."

"No chance."

Eva got into the driver's seat. It felt very high up, and the bonnet was huge. It was like an American rapper's car. She had to pull the seat all the way in to reach the pedals as though she was a kid pretending to drive it. Big breath, she could do this. First thing, get the heater going.

She ran a finger over the fob, no key, at the side of the steering column, nowhere to put one. The few buttons, the blank screens surrounding her, none of them helped.

"Keyless, the round button." Luke breathed.

She pressed it, but nothing happened. The car was very helpful. Its LCD screen told her to press the brake pedal when starting the ignition. She looked down at her feet.

"Big one in the middle." Luke confirmed, "right foot for both pedals."

The engine roared to life, the complete opposite to the Tesla, its throaty growl reverberating in the enclosed space. Behind her the wall of the garage glowed red.

"D is for drive, press the button on the selector and move it to D." Luke said.

Eva hated this, hated that he'd got injured, that she couldn't help him enough, that he had to stay conscious of what she was doing. First thing back in London, she was booking driving lessons.

She turned the heater to high then fiddled with the satnav and, after two false starts, input the hospital in Bergen. The computerised voice ordered her to do something in Norwegian. She could follow the graphic.

"Take the handbrake off, button on the console." Luke said. "Keep your foot on the pedal, ease it off gently. It's power steering so don't overcorrect, just a gentle turn with the steering wheel."

Eva pressed harder on the brake, released the handbrake button. As she eased up the pressure on her foot, the huge vehicle pulled forward.

Out of the garage, a much slower turn than Agnetha's, Eva crawled down the drive.

"Don't slam the brakes on, too much ice. You need to stop gently."

They did. Several metres from the edge of the road.

"Maybe get closer to the road first." Luke suggested.

Eva got the car to the road, just two metres away this time. Luke could have walked it quicker, even in his state.

She checked right, left, right, left, though it was completely dark in both directions, then eased the SUV onto the main road.

"Any sign of our hire car?" Luke asked.

"I didn't see it." She hadn't been looking but Rubin didn't seem like a man to not follow through on what he threatened.

After a few minutes Eva's hands cramped, making her release her death grip on the drive wheel, just a bit.

Luke stopped watching where they were going, leaning his head against the backrest of his seat, closing his eyes, hissing out the pain. At least the road wasn't potholed and Eva was going so slowly he barely moved as she coaxed the enormous car round the bends.

She was almost beginning to enjoy it when she caught sight of a brief flash of Bergen's lights twinkling in the far distance against the darkness. The windscreen wipers shushed suddenly across the screen, wiping away snowflakes.

Oh, please, not now.

The wipers sped up in a faster back, forth, back, forth as the flakes drifted down like feathers escaping from a burst pillow. She dropped her speed.

The end of the headlights' reach was getting shorter, lost now in the whirling eddies of snow closing them in. The car dipped the headlights. It was amazing, there really was nothing to it, these new cars did everything for you.

Until she drove round a bend and saw a stationary car in front of her, angled half on, half off the road.

She pulled her foot up, away from both pedals, jerking the big SUV onto the other side of the road.

"What you doing?" Luke groaned.

"It's okay." Eva pulled the car back onto the right side. Corrected her over-correction and braked to a gentle stop. She selected R and the car's parking camera showed her a whirling mist of falling flakes behind her. She reversed slowly up to the stricken car.

"No sense wishing you'd just be a good Samaritan to me?" he asked.

"I'm not being a good Samaritan." Eva checked her gun and clambered down from the heated car. She opened the boot and checked inside. The two snow shovels she laid on the back seat. Blanket, she left that in place, rummaging through what Carl Rubin thought was necessary for survival in case of breakdown. She glanced behind her at the stricken car. No movement. She pocketed most of the contents from the smallest dry bag—the energy bars, the self-heating hand warmers and bullets. The handwipes and bag she placed on top of the blanket, the rest of the filled dry bags went on the shovels.

"Won't be long." She reassured Luke, conscious that his heat was escaping.

Clicking the video on her phone, drawing her Glock,

Eva took a deep breath. The frigid air rushing into her body was like an adrenaline shot. She approached the car, walking carefully, deliberately. The crisping snow squeaked beneath her tread, but she didn't trust the ground. Tensed against the unexpected beneath the benign-looking covering, she dug every step into the slope beside the road as though she were mountaineering.

In a regular climate Agnetha might have tried going on foot, but in this remote part of Norway in February, staying in her car was the sensible call.

Eva pointed her Glock and her filming phone at her, gesturing at the door. Agnetha shook her head. Eva gestured more firmly.

Agnetha placed her fingertip on the dash and the car started, but the angle she'd ended up at gave her back wheels no traction. She was going nowhere except further off the road. And down into the yawning blackness below them wasn't a ride Eva would want to take. Agnetha neither apparently as she hit the steering wheel with both palms, then switched off the engine.

"Out." Eva shouted.

Agnetha shook her head.

Eva fired into the air. The falling snow swallowed the sound, but not enough. A car door opened behind her.

"It's all under control," she called to Luke. "Get back in the warm." She knocked the gun on Agnetha's window. "Out."

Agnetha held her hands up and got out onto the snow.

"Need a lift?" Eva asked, as though she wasn't holding her at gunpoint.

"No."

"So you're going to wait for someone else to come along?

D'you think that'll happen before you freeze to death? We're going into Bergen if you want to join us."

Agnetha marched towards the SUV.

"In the boot." Eva said.

"I'm not getting in there."

"Enjoy your walk then."

"It's too high, I can't—"

"I'm sure you can manage. There's even a blanket in there to keep you warm. Use one of the wipes on the backs of your hands. There's always a choice," Eva pre-empted her, "price of the lift is you do as I say."

Agnetha reached into the boot.

"Just the wipes," Eva said. "You touch anything else, lift is cancelled. If you try anything, I will shoot you."

Agnetha pulled out a wipe and passed it over the backs of both hands. "Happy?"

"Ecstatic. Put it in the dry bag, do it up and drop it on the snow."

Agnetha did exactly as Eva instructed.

"Get in. Remember when I open the tailgate in Bergen, this'll be the first thing you see." She gestured with the Glock. "It's been a long day, *I'm* on a hair trigger."

Eva pressed the close the tailgate button on her captive. When it clicked into place, she holstered her Glock and put her hand on the car, took a breath.

Not done yet.

She zoomed the video onto the dry bag on the snow, "Agnetha Rubin's sample for gunshot residue in connection with the murder of Ralph. . ." Sorry, Ralph, she didn't know his last name. She picked up the bag, "taking it into the chain of custody," put it on the car's backseat and clicked end on the video.

Any lawyer would have this flimsy evidence thrown out, but she didn't want it for that.

She tried the key fobs in her pocket until Agnetha's car bleeped at her and the indicator lights flashed orange, there'd be gunshot residue in there too. Hopefully, no one would rear end it during the night and send it down the slope.

"How you doing?" Eva looked at Luke as she fastened her seatbelt. Not so good. "We're on our way to the hospital now."

But what to do with Agnetha?

Eva hit the number for S, stored as Sam on her phone, and someone from the night shift answered.

"This is Sam." The guy sounded as though he and Eva were close friends and she was calling him at a decent time with good news.

"Hi Sam, it's Eva, have a slight pr—"

"It's all normal," Luke snapped.

Dammit, she should have used the codeword first so Sam didn't say anything they didn't want Agnetha to overhear.

"Erika," Luke mouthed, closing his eyes.

She'd given her real name. She really didn't need any help with self-sabotaging.

"What d'you need?" Sam asked.

"Just hoped you hadn't left the clothes in the washing machine, that they're all rinsed off okay?"

Sam understood her clunky code. "Door's still stuck, got the engineer coming tomorrow."

"Hold on, texting you a number." Fingers clumsy with the cold and fading adrenaline, it took her two tries to spell her solution to the problem, so it was readable.

'Okay to hand Agnetha Rubin over to local police on a

drink driving charge? She crashed her car. Will it come back to us? Complication = she killed someone at her house with one of our weapons.'

She waited, watching the dance of the feather snowflakes whirling in the beam of the headlights. They'd looked exactly like someone had burst a pillow but now they appeared to be shrinking back to breadcrumbs. Sam's reply dinged on her phone.

'DUI's a good call, Norway's hot on that, they'll lock her up for three weeks, serves our timetable. Weapons are untraceable, just don't get caught with it on you.'

"You got it?" Eva ended the charade.

"Cheers, I'll get onto them tomorrow." Sam disconnected.

Now Eva just had to figure out how to get Agnetha arrested without her pointing the finger at her for Ralph's murder.

24

Eva kept her Glock pointed at the tailgate of the SUV as it opened. Most of the surrounding streets were quiet, but Agnetha hadn't screamed or kicked hell out of the boot when she'd parked. So, what did she have planned?

Eva gripped her gun tighter, took a step closer to the car. Agnetha glared up at the barrel trained on her.

"Out, don't try anything." Eva ordered.

Agnetha looked around as she climbed out. "You take me in and I'll tell them all about Ralph and how you shot him." She'd recognised they were two roads away from the police station.

"Go for it," Eva surprised her, taking her arm with her left hand, pressing the Glock against her side with her right.

"I mean it." Agnetha warned.

"So do I. It's your word against mine and my partner's and we're the ones with the Interpol badges."

"I'm someone around here, you're no one." Agnetha's hiss was loud in the quiet night.

They'd reached the street corner in their awkward walk.

"Let's test that out, shall we?" Eva frog marched her across the road. "You tell the police I shot Ralph and I can call the bar manager in to testify you were flirting with him and play them my recording of you giving him your address to meet later. Plus, you have gunshot residue on your hands."

"That trick with the wipe, my lawyer will have that thrown out in two minutes."

Eva steered her over the next road. "How about the lynxes?"

"It's not illegal to keep them as pets."

"Probably illegal to keep them to clean up your husband's kills though." Eva kept her tone even, though she still shuddered at how she and Luke could have ended up in the pile of human bones in the lynxes' pen. "Who will we find under the snow, in their stomachs? DNA analysis is so sensitive these days we'll get something."

Agnetha's reaction, the tightening of her body, pressing together of her lips, told Eva she wasn't wrong.

"I'm taking you in on a drunk driving charge. You'll be out quickly enough from that, unless you lie about Ralph. Then I'll tell them to shoot the cats."

"They're Carl's, do what you want with them."

The entrance to the police station ahead of them was warm and welcoming, lots of interior lights on, surprising given the time, contrasting with the coldness of the night.

"Then there's all the weaponry."

"Again, all Carl's." Agnetha snapped.

"Does he leave it to you in his will? His side business?" Eva asked.

"I don't know what his will says." Agnetha was an accomplished liar, apart from when something was extremely important to her, apparently.

"If I'm asked one question about Ralph, I'll be taking the police out to your house with sniffer dogs and a forensic team personally." If any of Eva's threats would work, she could hope it was that one, judging by Agnetha's expression. Maybe. "I suggest you own the drunk driving charge silently." Her grip on Agnetha's arm tightened as they crossed the threshold of the police station. "But like I said earlier, there's always a choice."

25

***

Eva steered Luke out of the lift towards his hotel room. His legs appeared to have forgotten how to walk in the same direction.

"Should have hung onto the wheelchair." She pulled him away from the wall. "What did they give you?"

"All the good stuff." He laughed, "Not painful at all, this dislocation thing."

"That's because of the good stuff."

She got him into his room. "You can do the bathroom stuff unaided, right? I'm sure that's not in my job description." Luke pulled a face. "If that's an eyebrow arch, it's not working."

"I got it."

"Good, I'll see you in the morning, later in the morning. Sleep well. Phone's right beside you, if you need anything call me, I'm just next door."

After sending an update to S, Eva sat at the dressing table in her room studying the bullets that, if Rubin had his way, would have been in her and Luke.

Definitely nothing ordinary about them or the system

that fired them. Presumably a rifle fired the bullets, the drone tracked the RFID-tagged victims, relaying the tags' signal to the bullets that then hit whoever or whatever the tags were attached to. It really was a smart weapon.

Beneath the harsh glare of all the bathroom lights, Eva checked her face in the mirror. There, just visible, half a fingerprint's width of slight shimmer above where she thought Rubin had touched her. She wiped it off with a tissue, inspecting what it picked up. It was hard to say, some kind of powder? He'd got RFID tags so small he'd put them into a powder? But how did they not muddle the signal as she'd tried to do with Luke's chin on her cheek? The man was clever, she'd give him that.

She folded the tissue in on itself and wrapped it up in the shower cap she found in the basket of bathroom treats. Re-boxed it and put it in her overnight bag. Another puzzle for Sadie.

Eva examined her snowsuit next, working out from where the bullet had ripped through it. If it was a powder he'd used, he could have impregnated the suit with it. She inspected the seams. There, something stiff in the zip seam. That was probably it, close enough to the ragged hole the bullet had left. She'd leave it for Sadie because how Rubin had the tags secured might teach her something. Folding the suit in on itself again, Eva put it back in the large dry bag she'd taken from Rubin's SUV.

So, Rubin, what was in Denmark? Why did you use this weapon there? Who were the victims to you? Before opening the file on the Copenhagen shootings, Eva ordered a pot of coffee and another pizza. It was going to be a long night.

Her room phone shrilled into her dreamless sleep. Morning already? Or did Luke need something?

"Hello?" she croaked.

"Eva, it's Nora, call in on your laptop."

Eva dragged herself off the bed and turned the camera off before she connected.

"You're in luck," Nora didn't waste any time with niceties, "we've got an extraction team for the armaments. Rubin's in Denmark so you've got a time window."

"The Norwegian authorities okay with that?"

"We're flying under the radar. Norway's an ally, we can't be seen to be sneaking in and stealing this cache out from under their noses."

"But we can do it behind-the-scenes."

"Not one nation is as friendly and altruistic as they make out on the world stage. That's what the diplomatic bag is for."

"It needs to be a big bag."

"Our hierarchy is prepared to take the risk of getting back what we can. I've sent you a file so you know who to expect. We're prioritising rinsing Agnetha Rubin's case so she won't get out of holding."

"And Ralph?"

"The team will take care of it. How's Luke?"

"Doing okay last night, I'm about to check."

"You're being picked up in an hour." Nora's voice became much less business briefing. "How's it going?"

Eva let out something she hoped could pass as a laugh. "It's been eventful."

After her breakfast, she took a tray to Luke's room, opening the door with the spare key card a fraction.

"Luke, it's Eva, I'm coming in, are you decent?"

"Always." He laughed, sounding very uninjured.

"How're you doing?" Not bad, judging by how relaxed he appeared to be, sitting up in bed. He'd got his shirt half off, tangled around his sling. "Breakfast is served. Wasn't sure what you liked, so it's pretty much one of everything. Hope you're hungry." She put the tray down. "You want some help?"

"Sure."

Eva sat beside him and unvelcro-ed the sling, holding his arm where the hospital had positioned it while she gently worked his shirt off.

"It's okay," he reassured her worried glances at him each time she moved his shirt, "painkillers are working, they're some good shit."

"You might get cold now, don't move, I'll just. . ." Luke's go bag was a bag for all seasons. "You brought summer things?"

"Never know where we're gonna end up. Good to be prepared."

"You're a packing ninja."

"Been doing this a long time. That smells good." He sniffed the air.

"Freshly baked muffins." Eva laid a jumper over his bare shoulder, tucking it down his back.

She put the sling back on him.

"Nah, don't need that."

"I was there with you at the hospital so I know you heard the doctor, two weeks."

"On average." Luke reminded her. "I'm a fast healer."

"Overnight? Today you don't need to be, you can stay here and watch TV."

"Where you going?"

"To collect the goodies from the Rubin's."

"I need to come with you."

"Okay, up you get then. Which way is up, Luke?"

"I have to watch you. How can I report back if I haven't seen what you've done?"

Eva's phone dinged. "It's not like I'm going in on my own, the extraction team can watch me."

"Seriously, I'm failing my remit."

"I won't tell anyone." Another wrong thing to say, going by the look on his face.

"At least take my knife."

"Okay, and I'll give you a full report, promise. You stay here and ride the lovely drugs."

It wasn't as if anything she did today could salvage what had already gone wrong.

The SUV that collected Eva was so well kitted out for the weather, it could have comfortably driven to the Arctic.

"Aren't you underdressed?" The driver, a broad man with a shaggy beard, looked at Eva's two jumpers.

"The target took our good gear."

"We'll have to see about getting that back. In the meantime so you blend in, that's your outdoor gear." He nodded at the black grip bag in the footwell in front of her. She was grateful for the white camouflage jacket, hat and gloves, exactly what the others were wearing.

A twin SUV peeled away from the side of the street as they passed it and followed them.

The driver caught her glance behind. "They're with us, Bennett, Jacob and Vance, in that one. You get so many of us because of the hot goodies. I'm Fisher, guy behind me," he gestured at the back seat, "that's Taz, Oscar next to him."

The guys greeted her.

"Eva. How are you doing?"

"Easy flight in, decent kit, can't complain. There's a phone for you in the glove box, yours could have been compromised when it was out of your possession. It's protocol. How's Luke?"

"Trying to come."

He laughed, his face creasing into well-worn lines. Rugged looking, he clearly spent a lot of time outdoors. "He must hate this."

"He's not happy about it."

"Got the coordinates. You have everything you need?"

"You've seen my report?"

Fisher nodded. "We've been debriefed."

The route back to the Rubins' cabin was much better with someone else driving. And the weather co-operated, no new snowfall but the overnight flurries had banked in the open garage door. The team assembled around the lead SUV, and Fisher introduced her to the other men. Looking at them, she was glad they were on her side.

"Threats on the ground, identified from Eva's report," he summarised, "potential security check from the alarm company, local police if hostile told them about the corpse inside. Homeowner won't be back while we're here, other one's in custody."

"His pet lynxes," Eva added, "they might come back because here is their food source. They could be unpredictable. The outbuildings are behind the house, each one biometrically accessed. The one closest to the house on the left as you look towards the tree-line at the bottom has nothing of value in it."

Fisher pulled on a black armband. "Let's get started. In, out, you know how this goes."

They crunched their way through the pristine snow past the house.

"Show me where you found the weapons." Fisher said.

Eva led them to the building that Luke had fallen into. Taz attached electrodes to the access control, and in a few seconds, the lock clicked open. He moved on to the next building's panel.

Oscar scoped it out. Came out, shaking his head. "Empty."

Eva and Fisher went inside. The broken metal roofing had been moved out, the roof now covered in a blue tarpaulin that Eva was sure wouldn't stand up to one half decent snowfall.

"They're under there." She pulled back the pile of tarpaulins.

"Okay, what toys have we got?" Fisher lifted the trapdoor and shone his torch beam into the space.

"Watch out for booby traps. It's all hi-tech stuff, you see?"

"Not so much. Looks like someone's had a clear out."

"What?"

The booby-trap wires that had been there last night weren't there now. She walked down the steps into the storage space. It was virtually empty, just a handful of weapons left on hooks on the walls, a few boxes of ammunition. Nothing to excite law enforcement, maybe more rifles than necessary, but every one could be explained away by living as they sometimes did with polar bears.

Nothing else.

Which made it their word against Rubin's about what they'd found.

26

"Rubin said about having to move the weapons, after Luke fell through the roof." Eva stared at the empty space around her and Fisher. "Maybe he was worried about them getting wet?"

She followed Fisher outside, where Taz had got more than half the doors open on their side. She ran through the events of last night. The gap of time between Rubin thinking he'd killed them and them tracking back there, had that been enough?

The guy in the big bobble hat, Bennett, she remembered, had moved beyond the lynx pen and paced backwards and forwards near the tree-line at the bottom of the hill, on lynx patrol.

Eva went into the outbuilding nearest the house, there had to be more weaponry here. Similar in size to the one in which she and Luke had been held captive, they wouldn't have been able to pace in there. Tarpaulins, snowshoes, sleds, a whole pile of them took up the floor space by the walls and, in the middle, stood unrecognisable shapes hidden beneath canvas covers.

She pulled the one off the tallest, broadest shape. The weapon on a stand might have its roots in machine-gun technology, but she couldn't recognise it. Beneath the next, another weapon, smaller but more identifiable. Under the next was the Scorpion that Sean Finch had held on them. Every weapon appeared different but somehow the more streamlined and less busy they were, the more deadly they looked.

Shouts from outside, but the trapdoor caught her attention. Remembering what Luke had said about booby traps, she thumbed the torch on her phone which picked up the dull shine of a thin wire, stretched from the opening end of the trapdoor to a small silver box at skirting board level in the wall.

There must be something worth taking down there.

Another shout, there seemed to be several other voices outside now. Was Rubin back? Eva crossed to the doorway, staying behind the wall, dropping to a low squat to look out of the door. She was quite happy being on his 'I've dealt with you list', she didn't want to make another appearance on the 'I have to deal with you' one.

To the side of the house leading to the driveway, half a dozen men had gathered. Dressed like ninjas of Indian or Pakistani descent, they were a vision in black. Stark against the white of the landscape, they looked more dangerous than her team.

"Where is Mr Rubin?" one of them demanded in a strong accent.

Fisher approached them, cautious, gun drawn, but held behind his back. "Who wants to see him? Do you have an appointment?"

"Do I have an appointment?" The man gave a quick laugh. "You know who I am?"

Fisher appraised him. "Can't say that I do, hence my question, who wants to see him?"

The men behind the leader stiffened, Eva peeled up to standing, using the doorframe as her cover. The roiling in her stomach was all at odds with what she was seeing. What would Luke tell her to do? This was her mission, she had to decide. She unclipped her holster, but her hand hovered over her Glock. How would she not be a liability out there?

The leader unzipped his jacket. His wingmen were adjusting themselves in a reach behind them, a hand passing under their coats. Getting ready for something.

She caught movement at the rear of the property, Bennett in a crouch on his way up the slope. Jacob and Vance were closer, peering out of open doorways on the opposite side to Eva.

"Gently does it," Fisher warned the leader, bringing his weapon out from behind his back, pointing it at the ground.

"What is this?" The leader demanded, gesturing at the open doors of the buildings.

"Stock-take." Fisher replied.

"I come to take delivery of my shipment." The leader said.

Taz and Oscar were closing in as his wingmen, weapons drawn. The new arrival's back-up trained theirs on Fisher and his. If gun size was anything to go by, they had the upper hand.

"What are you doing? This is against the rules. We don't use the merchandise on each other. You know this. Mr Rubin is most insistent."

The tension outside zinged around Eva's body.

"Tell your men to back down and we will too." Fisher reassured the guy, who rapped a command in a language beyond her understanding.

She could have Fisher's back from within the outbuilding, the sight of one of these weapons should be enough to send the newcomers on their way.

The biggest, most impressive-looking gun was on a wheeled platform, it wouldn't fare well in the snow out there, but Eva could get it to the doorway. They didn't need to know she couldn't shoot it. She pulled and pushed, manoeuvring it across the wooden floor. Jammed it up against one of the others so the stand it was on pitched alarmingly. She grabbed at it to stop it from crashing to the floor.

And then the outside exploded.

27

———

Eva threw herself onto the floor, covering her head with her hands. The roar of the initial explosion faded beneath gunfire and shouting. What the hell happened?

Hand on her Glock but she knew she wasn't accurate enough to hit anything from there. Maybe the Scorpion would do it, Rubin had boasted enough about it. Time to see what it did.

Its trigger was locked. She flipped a switch, knocked a lever, pressed a button. Nothing. Maybe it had been programmed to the user. It remained inert, a lump of metal that would only be useful if she threw it at someone or hit them over the head with it.

More bullets outside, the rat-a-tat of death knocking.

Eva studied the stand the gun was on. Finch had held it in his arms. Maybe that was the thing. She squeezed the mount and dipped the barrel down and the Scorpion was in her hands. It barely weighed more than her Glock.

Flicking the lever on its left up with her thumb, she

pressed the trigger at the same time and felt it give. Her heart thumped, she'd activated it.

She peered out of the doorway. Where were they, the men attacking them?

The lynx pen would shield anyone on the other side of it from her so she'd use it in the same way. The intermittent cover of the tree branches let her crouch-run to the top corner, where she trusted the angle might help confuse things, even though it was glass. It had to be toughened, didn't it? But bullet-proof? She hoped she wouldn't have to find out. The uppermost tree gave her a sliver of cover.

She couldn't see who was screaming from there, but the sound reached her from near the house. Hopefully not one of her team.

Fisher lay on the snow ahead of her on the rise, using its tiny lip as cover. Another in white ahead of him. The house gave the attack team a huge advantage. They fired the second anyone moved, toying with them.

A volley of shots on the other side of the lynx pen, pinning Bennett where he was.

The men in black didn't appear to have noticed her.

Eva swallowed. She could do this, at least scare the hostiles into moving backwards to give her team a chance to get to shelter too. The rest they'd figure out. She ran the scenario in her mind. She was thinking too much. Just do it, before she started second guessing herself. Let her instinct guide her.

She laid down on the ground beside the pen, too low. On her knees, Eva braced herself against the glass. Slow movements, let the white jacket keep her hidden. She flicked the lever and pulled the trigger of the Scorpion, aiming high.

The gun barely kicked. Its high-pitched whine was almost obliterated by the sound of chunks of building being demolished. It tore through the corner of Rubin's house across to the outbuildings near where the hostiles sheltered.

Like a blowtorch through ice cream.

She stopped firing. Listening, an urgent cry in a foreign language. Not one of her team. A shout in reply. Another. A moan, a wail.

Fisher still lay on the snow, but whoever had been ahead of him had taken cover somewhere else. Placing the Scorpion on the ground, definitely too big to run with, she drew her Glock and bent low, running from the shadow of the tree in the lynx pen, pressing herself into the snow beside Fisher. Red-soaked.

Oh God, oh, God. Eva rolled away from him, eyes closed. Forced herself to look, to make sure. No, no one could survive that. His gun was still in his hand, his finger on the trigger in front of him but his face—he must have been caught by the explosion. Eva tightened her grip on her gun to stop her hand shaking.

'You'll never be in an optimal firing position,' her trainer's understatement was so on the money she could feel hysteria filling her. Her safer position beside the lynx pen, in the outbuilding called to her. But it was her fault Fisher was there. She wouldn't dishonour him in that way. Another of their team might need her help.

One hostile was down, lying in a halo of red snow. Another, the leader, had taken refuge beside the first outbuilding. But it hadn't given him much shelter. He slumped against the side of it, his hand pressed to his abdomen, barking orders.

Something blitzed past Eva, again, and again. They'd noticed her.

Pretend she was in the firing range, that this didn't matter. That all she was shooting at were paper cut-outs.

She fired back, waited. A handful of bullets shot in her direction, she fired back. Come on, show yourself. She definitely couldn't hit a target she couldn't see. Where was the rest of her team?

In the silence, Eva heard a familiar grumble, felt the hairs on the back of her neck rising. She knew why it was there, marking out breakfast.

"Hey," she called. "Call your men off, there's a lynx behind us, it's hungry and the smell of all this blood will make it want to feed."

The man pulled his attention off his abdomen, turned it on her, his arm snapped up and he fired. Eva ducked behind Fisher, pulling his dead weight as hard as she could over her, pressing herself beneath him as far as possible. Sorry, Fisher, so sorry. Thwack, thwack, the jerks of two bullets hitting him.

The menacing growl sounded closer. Eva didn't move.

The man bleeding outside the building shouted. His orders were clear when a barrage of bullets was unleashed at her. She tried to burrow further under Fisher, but his dead weight and the frozen ground held her too much out in the open.

She watched, she tensed, she waited. Threats from the front, silence from behind her. Ahead she caught a streak of movement, someone making their way towards the leader, stopping behind a black vehicle, pulled up close to the house.

Eva held her breath. He'd come out to the right and he'd spot Taz trying to shelter in amongst the sparsest of hedges. She aimed. This was almost that impossible shot, but she had to get it. She took a breath and fired, altering her aim slightly, bringing her hand across to her left with each shot.

The curving Luke had talked about with Sadie. The hostile went down.

The lynx growled, right behind her. Lying here, she was game for the big cat. Standing up so he'd choose someone else, she'd be offering herself up to the gunmen. What a choice.

The air beside Eva moved, the snow gathered up, dropping off the lynx's back legs as it bounded over her towards the man sheltering beside the building.

He screamed, his gun clicked empty. Click, click, click but the lynx was on him, its target decided. Screeching, a blood-curdling screaming, then the man fell silent. Eva wanted to clap her hands over her ears to stop the chilling sounds of the cat tearing his flesh apart. But she waited, as still as she could while the coldness of the wet snow beneath her crept through her, or maybe shock made her shake.

She shuddered as the lynx prowled past her. They were nothing like the wild lynxes she'd encountered in Sweden, these had been trained to be killers.

The roaring of an engine and the rattle of snow chains on the other side of the house, someone taking off in a hurry.

She waited, cold, wet, stiff, but uninjured, remarkably.

"Roll call." A shout on her right, Bennett, leader of the second team.

A low whistle answered her, one alive, another, another, she whistled too.

Apologising again to Fisher, she rolled out from beneath his body and got her feet, stopping when the other lynx slunk in and fell on what his or her stablemate had left of the guy.

"It's all clear out front, hostiles gone. Two dead." Taz walked backwards from the house towards her. "Holy shit."

He pulled out the handgun holstered on his hip and shot at the feeding lynx. The animal whipped around from its frenzy and snarled at him. He gathered his energy, ready to pounce.

"Look out, he's going to—"

The lynx dropped, unconscious.

"Tranquilliser dart. Should give us enough time for us to sort stuff out, get out of here. These new tranqs work fast, but not sure how long they're good for. As I was saying, three dead hostiles, we've lost two." Taz walked towards her. "You okay? Thanks for the save. They've all gone, bailed, the ones walking anyway. Looks like you found the good stuff. We'll get loaded up and get out of here."

Eva called Luke. "Just checking to see if there's anything specifically I should do here?"

"How'd it go?"

"Sideways. We're two men down, a group surprised us."

"Show me."

Eva video called him and walked past each of the bodies.

"That one." Luke said when she got to the one she'd shot. "You need to make him look like a The Society kill, so, once we figure out who he is, it'll be a new image for our portfolio. Then the other guy's a bit mangled. You remember the sign?"

Her breath caught. She wasn't likely to forget the training where she'd had to engrave a T and S on a joint of pork, over and over, until it looked less like a mangled attempt at carving the meat and more like the message they had to send.

But that was about a million miles away from doing it to a person.

"That guy's a shell, like the pork you practiced on." Luke reminded her.

Eva knelt beside the body.

"I'm sorry." she whispered, turning Luke's knife around in her hand.

The man was still warm. She closed his sightless eyes. Took a breath. Practiced with the knife in the air. The rest of her team were loading up the weapons into their SUVs.

Eva turned the guy's head to one side. "Does it matter which ear?"

"No, take your pick."

She swallowed hard, reached out and, sending the man another apology, carved the downstroke. She turned away from him as her stomach rebelled.

"Don't let that come up unless you don't mind picking it all up." Taz said. "We're disinfecting the scene. You throw up, you sort it out."

Eva swallowed hard, fought her body. "I'm okay."

Taz said nothing about the knife in her hand. The things they must have seen.

"Where's the body inside?" he asked.

"In the doorway into the lounge," she wiped at her streaming eyes, "last on the left."

"Got it." He marched past her and round the side of the house.

Eva took a breath, letting the frigid air ground her. Focusing on its slow release, she carved the top stroke of the T and the awkward curves of the S. The man's skin was less resistant than the pork had been.

"There." She held the phone up to show Luke.

"Not bad, recognisable enough. Send me a close-up of that and another of him in situ from more of a distance. You'll need to open his eyes again for that one.Then get shots of the hostiles' bodies and anything else that might help us identify them. The teams know how to disinfect our presence, just do what they tell you."

Eva found Taz kneeling beside Ralph when she'd done what Luke instructed.

"Can I help?" She asked before she realised Taz's thumb and index finger were digging around in Ralph's chest.

"Sure, there you go," he threw something at her. "that's your bullet." He snapped a knife blade about three times the length of Luke's back into its handle, replaced it in his ankle holster.

"Doesn't it need to be—"

"No chain of custody needed, this'll never go to trial." He held a plastic bag open for her to drop the bullet in. "All potentially compromising evidence goes in here and we take it back in the diplomatic bag to dispose of it safely." He looked around the room. "Anything else?"

Eva couldn't think.

"Get the door." He grabbed Ralph's feet and pulled him out of the lounge.

"Shall I. . .?" Eva gestured at his arms.

"This is better for evidence. You wipe down anything you both touched." Taz dragged Ralph down the hallway while Eva wiped everything she knew she and Luke had touched without gloves on.

Taz was propping Ralph up close to the man on whom the lynxes had fed when she got outside. He gestured at the still comatose big cat. "Might get lucky and he'll have lunch on this guy when he wakes up, help destroy traces of us. You done?"

Eva nodded.

"We have to get Fisher and Jacob, you helping?"

"Of course."

She followed Taz over to where the remaining four of their teams surrounded Fisher.

Bennett took off his bobble hat, bowed his head. "Fisher, fallen but never forgotten."

"Never forgotten," everyone responded.

They repeated their ritual for Jacob.

Bennett lent over Fisher and took off the black armband he'd worn, put it on his own arm. "I carry the mantle."

Eva felt like she was watching something she shouldn't be seeing.

"Onwards, brother." He touched Fisher's shoulder.

"Onwards." They all responded.

With surprising care, they lifted him, Taz stepping closer to Oscar to leave space for Eva to take hold of his leg. Carried to the back of one of the SUVs, the men lifted him into the boot onto one of the canvas sheets that had hidden the weapons Eva had found. They did the same for Jacob in the other SUV.

"First time losing someone?" Taz asked.

Eva shook her head. "But first time on the job."

Taz nodded. "Never gets easier, as it shouldn't."

28

———

Wedged in the back seat beside most of their kit and the black grip bags containing half the weaponry they'd seized, Eva stared out of the window as Taz drove them back to Bergen. Had it been worth it?

With their haul they could reverse engineer the weapons and they'd kept them from the other arms dealers, though that was probably only a temporary thing. But for Fisher and Jacob to pay for that with their lives? It was too heavy a price.

And the man she'd killed, would his family even find out why he hadn't come home?

She'd done it before, last year in Charles' lab. Under attack, she'd thrown chemicals at the man throwing them at her but hers were pyloric, igniting the moment they came into contact with the air, incinerating him.

She hadn't meant to kill him, she just wanted to stop him from hurting her. This was a whole other level.

Eva sat on her hands so no one would notice them shaking, studying the back of Taz's head in front of her. The hostile would have killed him if she hadn't stopped him. She'd assumed if she was going to get him at all, it would be a wounding shot, not a kill shot.

She blew out a breath, shut her eyes, let the warm silence in the car lull her. But the man's sightless eyes, her fingers carving his skin, played on a loop in her mind's eye.

This was what she'd signed up for. The glamorous image of chasing villains across rooftops in sunny locations was nothing like this. Wet, bloody, using the man who'd come at her request as a shield, taking the life of another, using him as propaganda. This was the reality.

How many had Luke seen that way, sprawled at his feet while he carved their necks? How did he rest easy with that?

Could she?

Could she hold Lily and pretend nothing had changed in her? Pretend that she'd been at a meeting when the man's face was there behind her eyes?

The team dropped her at the hotel with nothing more than a 'nice shooting', 'be seeing you.'

"Hey," Taz called her back to the driver's side. "Thanks again for the save."

Eva tried for a smile. "Any time."

"Here." He held out a white something that turned out to be a wipe. "You've got," he gestured at her face and chest. "Don't want to go scaring the hotel staff."

She looked down at herself as the SUVs peeled away and drove off. She was a mess, her white jacket swirled with a red camouflage pattern of Fisher's blood. Pulling it off, turning it inside out on itself, the baby wipe got enough blood off her that Eva got her keycard with only a sidelong look from the receptionist.

After a very long, very hot shower, she ordered a double whisky in the hotel bar, remembering how the one Nora had given her last year when she thought she'd lost Lily helped unknot her enough to function. She still hated it, but the harsh warmth that spread through her was growing on her.

"Celebrating?" Luke joined her, sounding less drugged up and moving normally, apart from his arm in its blue sling.

"Hardly. You want?"

"Probably not with my pain meds. They've called us back to London. Jet leaves in an hour." She nodded. "First time out is the hardest." he said softly. "And you did the hardest thing."

She shook her head, short, sharp. She didn't want praise, she couldn't say anything about their case because she could feel tears too close. Crying on a mission would never happen, no matter how much it hurt. She swallowed the rest of the drink, placed the glass carefully down, and addressed the bar. "I'm going to get Rubin."

"We will."

"I mean now. What's the procedure on diverting the jet for a stop on the way home?"

"Depends, where do you want to go?"

"Copenhagen."

PERSUADING Luke to stay on the jet had been the hard part, Eva told herself. She scrambled out of the taxi that brought her to Balancia just as the trickle of staff leaving for the night swelled to a flood. The shouted goodbyes and slamming car doors were the normal but the silent moving off of the electric cars was weird, unsettling, just as it would be at Futura Energy.

As long as Rubin wasn't there, there was no reason for this not to go as she hoped.

No smile from the receptionist at Eva's late appearance, as she'd expected. "You'll have to come back tomorrow, we're closed."

Eva flashed her Interpol badge and gestured at the photo and huge display of flowers in the middle of the counter.

"You're here about Patricia?" the receptionist's perfunctory manner disappeared.

Eva nodded.

"It's been such a shock, I mean, to be shot, you don't expect that. Patricia was so nice, why would anyone want to kill her?"

Eva guessed that from the photo of her the company chose to display. She was smiling widely, her grey hair held off her face by a green headband, picked up by the blocks of green eyeshadow she wore. Patricia Dryant, a framed card in front of the enormous display proclaimed, sadly missed.

No victim overlap that S had found between Patricia Dryant, a Balancia employee, and the other two victims of Rubin's bullets in Copenhagen, two primary school teachers, had led Eva there. Why Rubin would shoot her with the Lynx Assassin she hadn't figured out yet, but she hoped something would shake loose by being there in person.

"How long did Patricia work here?" She asked.

"Forever, I think she was here from the start."

"She worked in accounts?" Eva clarified.

The receptionist nodded.

"Is Carl Rubin here at the moment?" Eva tried to not tense at the question, or rather against the answer.

"He was, he left at around three."

"Is he here often?"

"Sometimes, other times he doesn't come for a month or two. It depends on the project he's overseeing I guess."

"What position does he hold?"

"He's our Emeritus Chairman."

That was an odd title, he was clearly still working there.

"I couldn't find his name on the website." Eva said.

"I wouldn't know about that."

"And I'm right in understanding that Balancia invents and produces clocks?" Eva played devil's advocate.

"Time pieces," the receptionist emphasised, reiterating the website's insistence that their clocks were far above that mundane label. "And all associated components of anything needed to monitor and measure a specific and accurate scale."

"That sounds impressive." Eva acknowledged. "Who can take me to see Patricia's desk?"

Jurgen was the security guard tasked with looking after her and, after a cursory scan through the few things the Danish police had left behind, Eva asked him to show her around the building.

"It helps to get a sense of proportion," she bluffed.

"You know who killed Patricia?" He asked as he took her to the executive suite.

"We're making progress. Had she upset anyone here?"

He shrugged. "I'm just security."

"No one's just anything." Eva said. "Can I take a look at Carl Rubin's office?" Because that's apparently who Patricia had upset. She'd get Iago to look into that.

"He doesn't have one, he spends most of his time here in the labs."

Eva ignored the hitch within her. Just a lab, no one in this one would be trying to kill her because the man it belonged to wasn't there. "Can I see those then please?"

She stared through the safety glass in the door to the first one. Only a lab it might be, but it had a weight of memories behind it that still hurt. Charles had spent most of their marriage in his. Was what was going on beyond this door worse than what he'd done?

"I can't let you in there." Jurgen said.

"You do realise this is a murder enquiry?"

"Of course and I would, if I could, but only the technicians and Mr Rubin have access."

"What if there's an emergency? If a lone worker needs help?"

"No one works alone."

She walked down the corridor. Five labs, three of them with airlocks on the interior side. She recognised the static free floor and the symbols on the lone working labels on the door, even though she couldn't read the Danish words underneath them. Protective clothing hung up on racks. What in time piece manufacture was hazardous?

Large rectangles of equipment, still wrapped in its shipping packaging on pallets took most of the floor space in the third and fourth labs. Too opaque to see through and identify anything in the shipment, it was enough she understood that Rubin was refurbishing or changing direction. But to what?

29

___

It was Carl Rubin's one concession to something that didn't have the planet's recovery at the heart of it, the fulfilling of his childhood dream. But the super yacht he could see out of the helicopter's window was beyond anything he could ever have dreamt of. He smiled at it, as though it were sentient. Lit up beneath him it was such a beautiful thing, so sleek and streamlined, so refined. He could have had homes all over the world if he'd chosen to, but the Overwatch satisfied that itch with a smaller carbon footprint. The good he did—more than most countries were prepared to manage—outweighed the small indulgence of using his private jet and a helicopter now and then.

He'd had the yacht set up as environmentally friendly as he could make it. Solar panels on as many surfaces as they would fit helped ease the nudge of hypocrisy away, the helicopter he was sitting in wasn't his. His green gauge was within the limits he'd set.

"Mr Rubin." His assistant on board, long hair blowing in the breeze, looking as immaculate as he preferred, even though it was technically still more night than day. She shivered, greeted him as he stepped off the helicopter deck, nodded at Finch. "Welcome aboard, it's good to have you back." She handed him a tablet, which displayed all the active systems to which she had access.

"It's good to be back, Marai."

He scrolled down the menu she'd opened. "How's the water reclamation doing?"

"The facilities manager reports that the yield is higher than we expected, no issues with the unit. In fact, our bathing water has come entirely from the sea this whole month."

"Excellent, I want to see him in an hour." After he'd sampled the shower himself. Then he'd know whether it was time to move up to procuring cooking and then drinking water in the same way. The patent on the unit would be one of his richest sources of income, ploughed back into scaling up so that he could use it in his company buildings, sell it on.

"Has Mrs Rubin come aboard?"

"No, sir. Not yet."

The shower was good, his swim even better. The infinity pool had been worth every penny. He could almost imagine he was swimming in the ocean as he swam away from the back of the yacht, looking outwards. Not right then without a dry suit, the sea around the yacht was probably some 25° colder in the daytime at this time of year. The warm water, the privacy of being at the end of the marina, enhanced by him taking the two closest berths as well, the meditative rhythm of counting his overarm strokes, the repetitive tap at either end as he turned, worked its magic. He began to relax.

It was a shame it had been a cloudy night, watching the sunrise was always special, even in winter. This morning, just a lightening through the cloud cover but, it amazed him, as ever, how the earth tried to rejuvenate every morning.

Two messages on his desk in his study when he'd dressed, along with a hot toddy. He lifted the ceramic lid off the glass mug and inhaled the scent of fresh lemon. The hint of whisky was just right when he had business to attend to.

He called Agnetha, but she didn't pick up. It was early, but she was probably still mad that she'd had to fly commercial.

Tarik Shah being unhappy, underlined, had to be called next.

"Tarik, it's the Lynx Assassin." Rubin paused, let the shiver of exhilaration wash over him. Doing nature's work, it was a badge of honour. "I understand you're not happy."

"Not happy? I have lost good men today."

"And that has to do with me, how?"

"I sent men to your home to collect what is mine."

Rubin's hand tightened around the phone.

"You went to my house?" The question was quiet, low, a human snarl.

"You owe me my merchandise." Tarik's statement was loud, hot-headed.

"When did my delivery instructions ever tell you to go to my house?" Rubin held his question tightly to cold business. First Janssen and now Tarik. The cabin was supposed to be untraceable, something in the line of shell companies that purported to own it must have broken. Maybe that was how Goran had stumbled on the payments being filtered through Balancia, why he'd been talking to Patricia Dryant about it.

He called up the live feed watching his lynxes, turning

the camera's field of view from one side to the other, a full pan. He'd never suspected he needed to record it but he'd apparently been wrong there.

A man lay by the remains of the first outbuilding, now collapsed in on itself. He'd been eviscerated and bled out, judging by the surrounding snow. How had the lynxes got out?

Rubin swung the camera around, same thing on the house, the stone walls carved and gouged, the wood looked as though a novice lumberman had used it for axe practice. Debris from the explosion had been travelling at some force to do that. He needed to reconfigure the boobytraps, clearly his new explosive was more destructive than he'd appreciated. A slow smile, a confirming nod. It was a better product than he'd thought.

The other outbuildings appeared untouched, their access panels unbroken. Tarik hadn't got what Rubin had left there. His grip relaxed around the sat phone.

"Your men triggered my failsafe, is that what you're calling to tell me?" He took a sip of his drink. The curse of dealing with these people who shot first and asked questions later was that they never listened to instructions. He'd thought Tarik's time at Oxford had changed that in him, a lesson to him to never assume.

"Failsafe?" Tarik spoke English better than Rubin, but his vocabulary left a bit to be desired.

"My instructions have always been clear. I actively dissuade people from going to my home. That's why any drop-off or pick-up of merchandise is done at carefully selected locations to avoid just this situation. I don't keep my weaponry unprotected. Your men set off one of the traps protecting my equipment. I can't be responsible if you don't keep the rules. They're in place to protect both of us."

Rubin sipped the hot toddy again, let Tarik rant. Too much of a hot-head. If he wasn't such a good customer, Rubin would have kicked him free a long time ago.

At the point where most of Tarik's shouting had reverted to Urdu, Rubin stepped in.

"I can't understand you if you don't speak English. Remind me again where you're from."

Rubin's admission he didn't pay attention to his customers prompted another volley of Urdu.

"Tarik," Rubin cut over him, "is this helping? Where are you from?"

"Pakistan, you should—"

Rubin had no time for his childish tantrums. "How about I upgrade your shipment?"

"What do you mean, upgrade?"

"I have something very special, just out of prototype, you can be the first to use it. And I know exactly the way for you to get what do they call it, the most bang for your buck?"

Tarik was cagey, not quite done with his anger yet. "Tell me more."

"Something on a bigger scale?"

"I'm listening."

"An explosion no one can trace to you? Bullets are all very well but they're too piecemeal. Explosions get the job done faster. This new product produces little collateral damage which will be better for your cause."

"I might accept that, yes." Tarik's switch around was extraordinary, as Rubin had expected, especially when he realised the potential.

"There are conditions," Rubin warned, "if you are to receive these weapons free. They are proprietary, not to be reverse engineered, sold to competitors. For this reason, one of my men will stay with them until they're used. He will direct you and observe because the data will be valuable for refining it. This will be the first time this weapon will be deployed on live targets."

Rubin's gaze strafed the wall on his right, in big letters in the midst of the framed certificates of seaworthiness, his yacht master qualifications, the sporadic splattering of photographs, hung a canvas on which beautiful calligraphy proclaimed his guiding principle, 'There is no planet B'.

"Yes, I accept. Your usual caveats apply?"

To only use his weapons on centres of population, to only destroy man-made structures, the new target almost ticked both boxes.

"My man will advise you. I will, of course, cover the funeral costs for the men you lost today and for those you might lose in this test."

"Always a pleasure to do business with you." Rubin could hear Tarik smiling. He disconnected the call, sent the instructions. That would be an extraordinary test.

His desk clock, a marvel of precision engineering that Balancia could showcase, showed him it was 9:45. He needed to hurry. 11:15 where he tried next. Unsurprisingly, his call wasn't answered. He typed that he wanted to speak into the chat they'd set up. She must have been waiting for his contact, because his phone rang almost immediately.

"You have good news." She never asked questions, assumed always her will was done. He liked that about her.

"I thought you might like to know the next test is going ahead in a couple of hours. The news channels will broadcast it but I will send you footage."

"Very well." She disconnected, a woman of few words.

He just had time before leaving for some of the delicious soup the chef kept for him. He knew it would be cold in St Petersburg.

30

When the jet levelled out, Eva called Lily and got her voicemail. Anya's mum picked up first ring.

"Hey, Tricia, how's Lily, is she behaving herself? She's not picking up her phone."

Tricia laughed. Normally it was infectious, but Eva was too tight, tensed against Lily not calling her, not texting, not missing her. Which had to be the best thing, but she'd yet to persuade herself of that.

"The girls are watching a movie. How you doing, nearly home?"

"The plane was delayed, you can probably hear I'm still on it. We've been diverted. So now I have to wait for a connecting flight. I'm sorry, I might not be back until really late."

"It's no problem, Lily can stay tonight if you're too late back."

Eva breathed out a strangled breath. One less worry. "You're a lifesaver, Tricia."

"We got this, girl, didn't you tell me that?"

"But I don't want it to all be on you."

"You're on your first trip, how's it all on me? I've been doing this long enough and you've helped me out all that time, don't you worry. Listen, go, don't want to eat up all your allowance with that expensive plane wifi. We can talk when you get back. If I haven't heard from you before it's bedtime, Lily will stay here."

Eva prepared dinner for her and Luke. Whoever stocked the plane did an amazing job of catering to appetites. Luke looked at his, two sliced steak burgers on salad, at hers, salad, hummus and omelette.

"You get mine," she explained, "I'm vegetarian."

"I like travelling with you." His grin turned to a grimace as he shifted in his seat.

"Do you need more painkillers?"

He nodded "In my go bag, blue box, the strong ones."

It didn't take the painkillers long to send him to sleep. Eva sat with a coffee at the laptop, scrolling through the news. The snatch of a word stopped her. She clicked the entry and rewound the clip, zhuzhzhaniye. She had heard it right, buzzing in Russian. She replayed the entire news report.

The camera showed a suitably serious reporter, a young brunette with an Eastern European accent. "Authorities are still unsure what caused the death of thirty-four cruise ship passengers. The group had disembarked from the ship Liberty Queen in St Petersburg for an organised tour this afternoon. It is believed several assailants fired at the group. Their guide and the cruise company employee checking them off the ship survived and are helping police with their enquiries. Police are appealing for eyewitnesses and anyone who has any information is urged to come forward. So far, no one has claimed responsibility for this attack."

The lights of the Liberty Queen behind her looked welcoming, unlike the harsh arc lights that lit up the cordoned off quayside. Several white tents had been erected over the area and CSI techs in white and blue body suits were busy in and out of them.

"Mikhail Stasov was on the quayside when the shootings occurred." The reporter turned to an older man, with a weathered face, wearing a wool coat with the collar turned up, a knitted scarf and a shaggy fur hat. "Mr Stasov, can you tell us what you saw?"

Eva listened to the man's words, reading the English subtitles at the same time in case she misheard. "I saw the cruise ship people coming onto the quayside. They come every day to see the cathedral, the churches. The group was there." He gestured at the area where a police officer guarded the integrity of the perimeter with a mean glower. "All so normal. Then the couple at this end of the queue, they dropped to the ground. I heard a buzzing of bees but there are no bees now, they are asleep for the winter. Then everybody fell."

She rewound the last few seconds and listened again. No doubt about it. She dialled into S, copying and sending the link to the news piece while she was put through.

"Stamford."

Thank you, Gordon, for being such a workaholic.

"It's Eva, en route to London. Do we know where Carl Rubin is at the moment?"

"Why?"

"I sent you a link. It's his weapon. I'm sure it's one of the tests he was bragging about."

"Hold on."

Gordon's screen went blank. Eva waited, she was right, she was as sure as she'd been that there was something to find at Rubin's cabin. When he reappeared, his face moved over in its box to accommodate Sadie in a box in the Provisions department and Iago in an office Eva hadn't seen yet.

"The buzzing the witness heard." Eva explained. "It has to be a drone, he didn't notice anyone running away."

"They might have been long distance shots," Gordon pointed out.

"Is there any intel on the time of the shooting window? Was it really fast?"

Sadie shrugged. "Not sure yet. The Russians will be trawling the cruise passengers for any footage they might have."

"It's Rubin's weapon, I'd bet anything. Sadie, you've read our report?" Sadie nodded. "I've got the bullets he fired at us for you."

"Anything like this weapon recovered from the house in Norway?"

Eva shrugged. "No drones, no weird bullets that I noticed. But when he targeted us, we didn't see the actual weapon, only what it fires. The drone didn't look anything special." But they were learning much about Carl Rubin wasn't what it seemed. "He mentioned other tests, a group of people could be next. Do you know where he is?"

"We'll get someone tracking him down." Gordon said.

"Does he have any other homes, assets where he could be? I don't see an arms dealer operating out of rural Norway, no matter how much he loves the landscape, it's too far from the world stage to make him viable."

"How much do you know about arms dealers?" Sadie asked.

Eva shrugged away that it was precisely nothing. "I know about people."

"We'll be in touch." Gordon disconnected.

She felt the jet banking even as Gordon called her back.

"Rubin's in the area. His jet flew into Tallinn airport in Estonia early this morning and his yacht's moored there currently."

"Short hop from there to St Petersburg." Eva said.

"Exactly. How do you feel about seeing if you can bug his comms? We need to get more evidence and you're the closest assets we have."

Eva had done the training on that plug and play. She could do that. "Sure."

"We don't believe he's on board but he's flying a Panamanian flag, so be careful."

"What difference does the flag make?"

"If Rubin commits a crime while based on his yacht, he can invoke the laws of the country where it's registered. Panama gives him the ambiguity he needs. It's not just him, lots of boat owners use it, more favourable tax laws, just for starters, more flexible about everything else."

"Okay, understood."

"You need to be as discreet as you can be, we're straying a little here but it's within parameters."

"Straying? What does that mean?"

"We're out of The Society territory, more into MI6's."

"Aren't we on the same side?"

"We are, but we're accountable in a different way. And because we're not in the general MI6 briefing cascade, we have to be careful we're not compromising any of their operations we don't know about. You'll get a packet."

Luke slept through the rest of the flight while Eva focused on the encrypted brief from Gordon: a schematic of the yacht, berthing plan for Tallinn harbour.

Could she do this by herself? Luke was exhausted, in pain, in a drugged sleep. She had to.

Her phone rang, Lily surprising her.

"Hey, sweetheart, is everything all right?"

"Yeah, I just wanted to say hello. Tricia said you might not get back tonight."

Eva sighed. "I'm sorry about that, delays in the flights. Are you okay staying with Anya again?"

"Course, I, you," Lily huffed out a breath. "You're being careful, aren't you?"

Eva forced a laugh. "Not much danger being in a meeting room, other than being bored to death."

"Okay, I just wanted to say that."

Lily's careful tone took Eva back to when she'd been a teenager, lying in bed, unable to sleep beneath the worry of what would happen to her if something happened to her mum now that her father was gone.

She blew out a breath, pressed her fingertips to her eyelids, rubbing away the prickling of tears. She didn't want that for Lily.

"Mum, you still there?"

"Yes, sweetheart. You mustn't worry about me, I'm fine. Enjoy your sleepover. I'll see you tomorrow. Love you."

"Love you too."

Eva placed her phone on the table. That was how they'd always been. Had Lily ceased hostilities over Eva's hedging explanation as to why she couldn't visit Charles in prison?

All while the plane landed, taxi-ed to the private area at the rear of the airport where a car waited for her, Luke slept.

Using the code S texted her, she opened the padlocked comms cupboard and took a lapel camera and earpiece.

"Yo, Eva, I'm your eye in the sky." Iago answered her call.

"Thanks for waiting."

"You're welcome."

"I know, big doughnut run when I get back."

He laughed. "I knew I liked you."

She spun the laptop round, showed him Luke. "He took the strong painkillers before we got tasked, so I'm leaving him here. I did this training, I can do this."

"Right, let me set up your comms." Iago tapped furiously on his keyboard in London while she put in the earpiece and twisted the lapel camera into the top buttonhole of the coat she'd picked up on the way to the airport.

"Acquired." Iago's voice came in her ear, the inside of the plane appeared on her laptop screen. "Voice and visual. You're good to go."

She placed the bugs in their tiny travel boxes into her inside coat pockets, checked her Glock, and knocked at the cockpit door.

A man opened it. A woman was still in the chair, checking gauges, noting readings.

"Hi, I need something from the hold." Eva said.

He grabbed a hi-vis vest from a hook at the back of the cockpit and followed her down the cabin. Stepping off the plane, the wind tore her breath away.

The hold lit up when he opened the door. Two coffins stark in the space jolted her. She gulped in the frozen air, rubbed at her eyes as if by taking away the image, she could undo the reality.

The first officer handed her what she'd asked for, no explanation needed. She closed her hand around it.

Yes, she could do this. She was only planting bugs.

31

Eva pulled the hi-vis vest borrowed from the plane's first officer around her coat. But it wouldn't stop her shivering when the cold wasn't the problem.

The harbour master unlocked the tall metal gates that led to the VIP members' area of the marina, the jetties where the wealth of a small country would be moored during the summer. "Last berth, biggest yacht, you can't miss it. I'll be in my office, if you need me." His English was flawless.

"Is it too windy for helicopters to fly right now?" Eva asked.

He shrugged. "Air is not my area, water and boats are."

She walked down the sloped gangplank to the hub of jetties that spoked off the central platform.

"What the hell are you doing?" Luke's voice, groggy in her ear.

"How are you feeling?"

"Where are you?"

"At the marina."

"Send the car back for me. You can't do this on your own."

"I can, it's planting a few bugs. I did the training."

Eva stepped to the side of the platform to let a couple pass her. They barely acknowledged her, the hi-vis working.

"There's a lot of value in the target thinking we're out of the picture." Luke said. "Showing our hand so quickly's not good, we could get better mileage another way. And he might just shoot you for real this time."

"He's not here. I'll be in and out before he gets back."

The water hit the hulls of the boats she passed, tiny flickers of light split into shimmering drops as the small waves dispersed the reflections.

"Are you onboard?" Luke asked.

"Not quite."

"Then you don't know that."

She'd reached the spoke at the end of the spread, there were a dozen boats moored nearest the central platform and one right at the end, lit up like a buy me sales shot.

"Wow."

It was ridiculous to call it a yacht, even a super yacht wasn't anywhere close. It was something the Royal family would be at home on. She couldn't guess at its price tag, it was so alien a thing to her normal life in a rented flat in London, the kind of things she saw in movies.

She was under-dressed, under-armed, under—

"You need to wait for me to get there." Luke sounded more awake now.

"I'll be done by then." Her slow footsteps were taking her down the jetty far too quickly.

"Eva, he knows who you are, you can't bluff your way out if he sees you."

"He saw you, too. Have some faith in me."

The locked gate in the middle of the span opened easily to the key the harbour master had given her. She just had to persuade her heart rate to calm down. And her mind to stop rerunning the conversation she'd had with Gordon last October when he asked her if she was prepared to pass her father's legacy on to Lily. Her father had tried to ease her mind by telling her that the bullets he ran towards were words and recorded conversations, but they'd killed him anyway. And here she was, walking voluntarily towards where the man who had actually tried to shoot her had last been seen. It was one thing wanting him to pay, but another to risk making her daughter pay the price, gambling her life on an assumption when he might be nothing like Charles.

She pulled her hood up.

"Going quiet on your end." She followed the protocol her training had taught her.

She heard Luke not appreciating it, if the language in her earpiece was anything to go by.

A strain of music reached across the black water. As the distance shrank to the yacht, Eva realised she was tensing, hunching in on herself, nothing to do with the dropping night temperature. She had to seem confident. She pulled her shoulders back, marched faster. Security lights blazed at her, turning the peaceful darkness to a dazzling fury.

The yacht towered four decks above her, an enormous span of height. She'd have trouble looking off the top deck for sure, the draw that drop would wield over her would be strong. If that was the only way out, there was no way she'd be able to dive off it. She shuddered. She'd try and stay on the entry deck.

"Identify yourself." The demand through the tannoy split the silence.

"Harbour master's office, requesting boarding clearance,

compliance check with new regulations." Eva shouted.

Her camera feed gave Luke and Iago eyes on. She wasn't alone. She unzipped her coat and undid her holster, pressed her fingertips against the handle of her weapon. She wasn't helpless.

"Who wishes to board?"

"Harbourmaster's deputy."

"Come back in the morning."

"Non-compliance means you forfeit your mooring. You have ten minutes to leave."

The lights blazed on her, the tannoy stayed silent. Were they really going to risk it? If Rubin was on board, it could be they were leaving anyway, and she might have forced their hand.

Should she give it more than ten minutes? She had to act as though their decision just meant paperwork to her.

"Hey," she shouted, moving closer. "I'm not standing here freezing my arse off while you decide. I'm writing it up that you're in breach of compliance. You need to be gone in eight minutes." She threw a couple of Russian swear words at the implacable shiny blackness of the super yacht and walked away.

"That went well." Iago said.

"Give it a minute." Luke was suddenly on her side?

"You may board." The tannoy overrode them both. A gangplank slid out from the black hull and whispered to a stop on the jetty.

Eva breathed, reminded herself as the harbour master's deputy she was overworked, underpaid and now pissed that she had to do this with all the boats when she just wanted to sit in the office and drink hot chocolate.

A slim woman in black trousers and a red fine knit jumper, whose long hair fell perfectly back into place when the wind ruffled it, was waiting for her at the top of the gangplank.

"I'm Mr Rubin's assistant. Welcome aboard the Overwatch." She said it as though Eva had been expected.

"Curious name."

"The Overwatch is a one-of-a-kind. What do you need to see?"

"If I tell you, it would ruin the point of a spot check, wouldn't it? I need to inspect the whole vessel, I'll be taking notes as I go."

"This way." The assistant gestured to the double doors leading to the inside space, one of which was open.

Eva could have done with sunglasses against the glare of gleaming brass and wood so highly polished she could practically see her face in it.

"This yacht is a test bed of green ingenuity," she went on as though Eva was an investor she was hoping to impress. "We have a unit that desalinates seawat—"

"That's all very laudable, but that's not why I'm here."

"Why are you here?"

"What's your name?"

"Marai Bukowski."

Eva tapped it into her phone but let Iago do the searching for the woman's history. "Where's the owner?" The million dollar question.

"He'll be coming aboard shortly."

Eva turned her panic into annoyance. Tapped harder on her phone. "As if it's not bad enough I have to do this," she launched into Russian, interrupted herself. "When is shortly?"

"I don't know exactly."

"Well, find out, I don't want to be here all night. I have a hundred others to do. Night shift is supposed to be easy."

Eva stared at the woman. "Get to it, I don't need a chaper-one, I know my way round one of these."

She walked around the perimeter of the room, some kind of reception area, comfortable easy chairs and a couple of sofas, low tables. The chess set ready to play in one corner tempted her but knocking the king over, her forecast of Rubin's future, would just get her noticed. She scowled instead up at where the wall met the ceiling and down at where it met the carpeted floor. "Hmmm," tapped some more at her phone.

She peered harder at the join between carpet and wall, then squatted, gazing sideways, looking for plugs, anything to suggest comms she could tap.

Nothing on that side.

"Are you still here?" She asked Marai as she crossed to the other side of the room.

The assistant hovered at the door to the interior of the yacht. Eva gave the ceiling more attention on that side, tutted. "I'll need to speak to the owner about that." She frowned. "This is going to take some time."

"What's wrong?" The assistant looked worried. "I'll go and check his eta."

Eva gave her a minute before placing two bugs in the room, then opening the interior door which led into a short corridor. Through the porthole in the first door, the room showed her it was a dining room, worth one bug at least.

The next was the one she'd most hoped to find. No port-hole in the door signposted that it was where Rubin valued his privacy. Blond wood clad walls, such a reminder of his home, Eva could have been transported straight back to Norway.

"Office, I'd say." she murmured to her audience.

"Any chance there's a laptop or anything, I can echo it."

Iago sounded hopeful.

Eva's look around the room let her camera pick up the easy chairs clustered together as though they were having a conversation, the drinks cabinet and the expected globe beside them. Around two TV screens one side wall was decorated like an art gallery in extraordinarily clear photos of nature: a fjord, a waterfall, forests from the air, the tops of the trees looking curiously different when viewed from high above them, a nicer use of one of his drones. And Rubin's huge desk almost in the middle of the space, the night beyond the glass wall in front of her reflecting her tense face.

On the other side wall there were no photos, but many framed certificates, and a huge canvas, richly lettered, in the middle, proclaiming Rubin's public persona upfront and central: 'there is no planet B'.

But to the right of it all—what was that doing there? Out of kilter already, the memory drew her to framed print that reached into her childhood.

"How can that be writing?" She'd demanded when her father had shown her what he'd brought home. She'd run her finger over the curling swirling pattern of the calligraphy. "How do you read it?"

He'd laughed. "Shall I tell you a secret? I don't know how but I know what it says. It's pretty, isn't it, so much more poetic than our letters."

She hadn't really understood what he was saying then, but now she could see it. Amongst the other utilitarian framed certificates of seamanship and black-and-white typeface, the Arabic was much more inviting.

"Eva, what're you looking at? Bug the desk." Luke's urgent hiss was drowned by the sounds of a helicopter, deafening as it landed two decks above her.

32

"Helicopter's landing." Eva told Iago and Luke in case they hadn't picked up the noise through her earpiece.

"You need to leave." Luke replied.

Her brain was right with him, screaming at her to get out of there. "On it, I have to put at least one in here."

She pressed a bug behind the Arabic calligraphed print. It was thin enough that it wouldn't make the frame protrude so far from the wall he'd notice. Another behind the desk leg near the top where Rubin might not find it. No handy bookcases as per her training, but that was okay. She'd improvise. Come on, quick. The drawers of his desk were locked. No space between the back of the drawers and the desk front. The lights were recessed spots, the whole setup in place to not provide spaces for listening devices.

"If I put one too close to the TVs, won't it interfere with its signal?"

"It's a risk, don't do that." Iago confirmed.

No trunking hid the wires, they were buried in the wall.

The globe, on the underside of its support? Too obvious.

Beneath one of the chair seats could be a last resort. She searched with her fingertips for anything not fabric. There, a wooden strut in the middle of the seat pan base. She pressed the tiny device onto it.

"Eva, get out of there." Luke's voice insistent in her ear.

The tremendous clatter above her was fading, the helicopter winding down. She should have enough time to get out the way she came in, providing the gangplank hadn't been retracted. She got to her feet and pulled the gun out of her coat pocket.

She was a few steps away from the door when it opened inwards.

Eva sprinted to the back wall behind it. Pulled her hood up.

The tension she could feel down her ear in the jet at Tallinn airport and at S in London was worse than what she felt in the room.

Steady.

Focus.

She aimed at whoever was coming in.

As the door swung out of the way, Eva fired.

Carl Rubin wasn't wearing a coat. He stumbled into the room, the tranquilliser dart she'd fired at him lodged in his back. He twisted round, his hand reaching for it.

Eva pushed herself against the wall, lowering her head in her coat hood. The lynx had dropped after just a couple of seconds, would it work as quickly on a human? Rubin took a step towards her.

She held the gun up and fired again at his legs this time. She hit him in the thigh. He bent down to pull it out. She dropped the tranquilliser gun and held her Glock on him. Go down, go down, she begged him silently.

He stumbled, keeled over, dropped right in front of her.

Eva let out her breath. Her hands were clammy, the Glock slipping in her grip.

"Rubin's down," Perfect karma with the same drug that knocked out his lynx. "He didn't see me, I'm pretty sure."

"Get out of there."

"No sign of a laptop?" Iàgo still sounded hopeful.

"Not on him, it must be locked away."

"You've fulfilled the brief, leave." Luke said.

Finch probably wasn't far behind and Eva was out of darts. She wiped her hands on her trousers, holstered her Glock, pocketed the tranquilliser gun.

"Iago," she whispered, "are you hearing me through the bugs?"

"Confirm, ears are active."

"Ears?" Luke asked.

"Yeah, bugs is a ridiculous name for them. What do they do? Listen, so, ears."

She closed the office door, her hand hovering over her holster she pushed open the door to the lounge. The clinking of a stirrer against glass surprised her, Rubin's assistant mixing a drink. No sign of Finch.

Eva strode to the exit, muttering. "I'll have to get a team mobilised, it's worse than I thought."

"What's worse?" Marai looked like Eva was holding the gun on her.

"Everything. Your boss is not a happy man, I'd let him cool down for a bit, if I were you."

"But—"

"I'd also drink that, in my bedroom, away from everyone else for a while, let emotions settle."

The assistant swirled the liquid around the side of the glass, definitely considering it.

"I'll note in my report how helpful you were." Eva threw

a farewell gesture at her as she strode out of the door and onto the foredeck. Thank God, the gangplank was still in place.

On the jetty, Eva power walked to the steel gate, locked it behind her and, away from the spotlight of the Overwatch's security lights, she ran.

33
***

Rubin opened his eyes. He was on his bed, looking up at the ceiling. He patted himself down, nothing hurt except his head. No bandages, so no injury. What had his assailant been after? He got up, putting a hand out to steady himself, but the wall was too far away. He lurched to the side, stumbled onto all fours, nothing to do with the barely noticeable movement of the yacht. But lying there wouldn't help him find what the intruder had taken. He dragged himself to the door, gripping the polished railings for use in rough weather like he was an old man.

Inside his office, the only thing different was the slim dart on his desk. He turned it over in his hand, nothing on it to say anything.

No attempts appeared to have been made to get into his desk, but he checked inside the fingerprint activated drawers anyway. Still there, his laptop, his sat phones, the notes he'd been working on earlier.

He pressed the intercom and called Sean Finch to his office. He gestured at the walls as Finch came in the door.

"Already done." Finch confirmed. "Nothing."

"Do it again."

He watched him wand everything with no response from the sweeping device.

"What happened, Sean? What if I hadn't disturbed the intruder before they'd done what they came for?"

"You want to fire the staff?"

Of course he did. He hated incompetence. How could he do what he did if they couldn't be counted on to be on their best game at all times?

"Get Marai in here."

His assistant walked in confidently enough.

"Harbourmaster's deputy, you say? Doing a compliance check?" He frowned at her. "Didn't that sound the slightest bit suspect to you, at this time of night?"

She shook her head. "No, Sir, she had the key to the gate, she seemed very official."

She? Interesting.

"Was she caught on the CCTV?"

"I'll check, Sir. Do you need me to call a doctor?"

"I need everyone to do their jobs, is what I need. Get me some painkillers for my headache. Where else did she go?"

"Only the salon." Rubin nodded at Finch but he was already halfway out of the room to go and wand it.

The sat phone he gave to clients interrupted. He dismissed Marai with a wave of his hand.

"What is this?" The caller's words were staccato, spoken beneath a fury barely contained within an icy right-eousness. "You are an amateur. This is no good to me, this weapon."

"What makes you say that?" Rubin asked.

She made a noise that could universally be translated as 'are you an idiot'? "Your test failed is what."

He held the bridge of his nose with his thumb and forefinger. "The Lynx Assassin is good, the humans using it are the problem."

"I do not want excuses. I must be 100% certain you can deliver what you promise, my life will be on the line."

"As was mine when I shot my partner, I was standing right beside him, proving that the technology works. The person delivering the RFID tags in St Petersburg didn't follow instructions. He was specifically tasked with picking out random members to equate to half the group, but it looks like he touched everyone. I will need to verify this but, from the data I have, the weapon functioned perfectly, the bullets followed the electronic signal, as they are designed to do. The speed of assassination will tax the authorities but there's no evidence for them to get even close to what happened."

"There are no authorities to concern me. What does is that I and my husband remain safe."

"I can assure—"

"How do I know your weapon will target all the different tagged individuals, and not just pick the first RFID cluster? It is also no good to me if it leaves others standing. I will be more at risk."

"Let me show you," Rubin soothed. "I can prove it with a large-scale test."

"When?"

"Tomorrow."

She paused, one beat, two. Rubin waited. "It will take much to convince me." She finally said. "I'm not in the habit of gambling with my life."

"I'm not a gambling man, either. I deal in actualities and reality. The Lynx Assassin is what you need."

He could hear the line was open between them, but he let her think. He may not have met her but to accomplish what she had, what she did every day, operating as she did, he could appreciate however she chose to work.

"If this additional test is not a success—"

"I have other weapons coming online, equally as revolutionary. You may have your choice of them but I believe the specific technology of the lynx is most suited to your requirements. I have, and I did, stake my life on it. The method of delivery is critical, if you're delivering it, there'll be no mistakes, will there?"

"I need to see the test in real time."

"Of course, my people will message you."

"How many casualties do you anticipate?"

"How about a thousand, amongst a crowd of ten thousand plus?"

It didn't sound nearly high enough, nearly fast enough. There is no planet B, it determined everything he did. He would rather take out the entire audience, but that wouldn't confirm the weapon's worth to his client. If he'd thought she'd respond to the money angle, he'd have pointed out that he wouldn't do anything to jeopardise her payment. He had a lifestyle to maintain, hefty research and development obligations. Her paying him the highest amount he'd ever received for one weapon was almost as attractive as the fact that she was unwittingly helping him pursue his wider, most personal agenda.

"The numbers are unimportant. What concerns me is the efficacy of the weapon."

"This new test will convince you beyond any doubt."

"If it does not, our business is concluded."

"Let's talk again afterwards." But she'd already hung up.

The tech stood up, the imbecile he'd paid to distribute the tags was to blame for the failure.

He went in search of Finch. The clanking of pans and

utensils beckoned him into the galley. The heat and sharp tang of citrus were a welcome balm.

"You want some?" Finch gestured at the wok to which he was adding soy sauce. "Wild salmon, I've made plenty."

Rubin nodded. Finch took out two trays to carry the dishes of food through into the dining room.

"Let's eat in here." Rubin preferred the more cosy feel of the small dining table behind him. Another area of the Overwatch he'd upgraded. More like a kitchen in a mansion now than a clinical ship's galley, the extortionate price tag had been an easy sell for the rep.

"You want a sake?" Finch asked.

Rubin was about to say no, he had no idea what had been in the tranquilliser dart. But thwarting an enemy, that was worthy of a celebration. And his work today in soothing two problematic clients more so. Particularly as Tarik would be doing more than testing a new weapon when he followed Rubin's pointed suggestions, another furthering of his agenda.

"Cognac for me."

When Finch returned with the drinks, they toasted the day.

"Next stage."

Rubin forked the food into his mouth. The satisfaction of the sharp flavours, the warming bonhomie of the cognac eased his worries, untensing his shoulders and neck.

"I should sack the chef," Rubin laid his fork down on his empty plate, "have you make the food every day."

"You could but I can't make his tiramisu." Finch offered Rubin a second helping.

He shook his head. "Dessert for me. Change in plans. Do you have anyone around here you can entrust with a delicate task?"

Finch scooped the remainder of the food onto his plate. "Depends what it is."

"The cruise ship employee who was supposed to select the targets is helping police with their enquiries. I forget his name but we need him disposed of, immediately."

Even the promise of the rest of his very generous fee, to be given to his family in case of his unfortunate demise, wouldn't be enough to keep his lips together once the state police took an interest in him. Rubin had to tie up that loose end.

"I'll get it done." Finch confirmed, bringing a large tiramisu from the fridge over to the table.

Rubin considered, Marai was last on his list to ask, his Executive Assistant in Norway too connected to him. He called one of the techs from Balancia.

"Patron, what do you need?"

"Get me a subtle way into London for myself and Sean Finch as soon as possible, with a loud trail leading somewhere else."

"Any preference where?"

Rubin considered for a moment. "No, as long as you can tie in the official travel plans for us to be in London in two days for the contract signing with the British government."

"Consider it done, I'll send it to you in the usual way."

Rubin disconnected, took the bowl, nodding approval at the portion size. "I've been waiting all day for this."

34

When the jet landed at Farnborough, a reception committee was waiting for Eva and Luke.

"Standard procedure when we're carrying fallen heroes." Luke told her. "We join the vanguard."

When she opened the door, the rain was falling in stair rods lit up by the airfield's arc lights but it felt noticeably warmer than in Tallinn.

The ranking officer saluted Luke and Eva as they disembarked. Should she do it back? She did as Luke did, though he had one arm in a sling, and kept her hands by her side.

She followed him past the saluting soldiers, four in a 'v' shape from the plane door, a whole gaggle of them by the hold.

When the coffins were lifted out, she bowed her head. I'm so sorry. We'll get him. I promise you, her prayer to Fisher and Jacob, Rubin will face justice.

The ranking officer was calling out movements to his troops and, far too practiced at it, they loaded the Union Jack-draped coffins into two hearses that pulled up almost silently. Another salute as the hearses left and the soldiers wheeled away and marched off, their boots sounding like one heavy set of footprints.

"That's us." Luke nodded at the sole car left airside. "We'll be taking the kit too."

Once the hearses had reached a respectable distance, their car, a big black thing that looked as if it normally transported dignitaries, pulled up close to the plane.

"You get in," Eva said. "You kind of need two hands for this."

"Not gonna argue."

"Everything from the hold?"

"Everything."

She and the driver loaded the boot of the car with the black grip bags that Eva knew contained the weaponry they'd collected from Rubin's outbuildings. Most of them needed both of them to lift them in. Guns weighed heavy.

The last two bags had to go in the front seat and passenger footwell.

Eva leant into the car.

"The flight crew?"

"They have their own arrangements." Luke said. "We're going back to base to sign this lot in."

Eva shook rain out of her hood before she took her coat off and got in.

"Okay?" Luke asked.

Not okay. She fussed with the seatbelt as a distraction, folding her coat in on itself, limiting the amount of rain that ran off its waterproofing, directing the stream onto the floor mats. The harsh reality of what this job meant had driven away in front of them. Two families, two partners, maybe two sets of children, parents, friends, two worlds turned upside down. Two sets of possibilities of life plans, of goals, of potential, turned to dust in the bloody snow of a criminal's lair.

Eva leant her head on the backrest. She could imagine a similar scenario being played out in a warmer climate, wherever the hostile men had come from as families there tried to deal with their losses. The wages of man's inhumanity to man.

"Talk to me." Luke said after a while.

She gestured at the driver.

"Official drivers have clearance for run-of-the-mill stuff, no specifics, but we can do this." Luke pressed a button on the console between them and a partition slid up from the back of the front seats. "What's on your mind?"

"Is it always hard?"

"No, it's usually impossible. What we do, it takes a certain type of person. You worried you're not that type?"

"I'm thinking of Lily." Luke didn't say anything, and into the silence poured Eva's real worry. "What if I'd been standing outside when the explosion was triggered? It would have been me in one of those coffins, and where would that leave her? She'd have no one." Eva's words whispered to nothing. She couldn't voice the rest of it, it was too painful, too raw, even now. Twenty-five years since her father had come home in a flag-draped coffin and she still struggled with it.

"It has to be your choice." Luke finally said. "I don't think you should ever be comfortable with what we have to do. But I think you should be able to make peace with it."

"How long have you been doing this?"

"I've been in Six my whole life, they recruited me at university."

"What did you study?"

"Engineering, until Six approached me, then it got

boring because they'd opened my eyes, so I dropped out and embraced this life."

"Why do you do it?"

"That's a good question." Luke tried for a laugh. "Be a lot easier to answer if there was a drinks cabinet in here."

"You don't have—"

"It started off as revenge for my partner's death, you know that, an impossible challenge to bring The Society down. And once we did that, it just seemed an opportunity we couldn't pass up to do some real good, where we've always worked in the shadows. None of us go into this looking for fame and glory, well, maybe the glory bit. I'm good at it, turns out I can be a bastard, if I have to. It serves me well. I like that I'm cleaning up the streets, to use a really corny Hollywood line."

On paper, it was noble. In reality it was risky, it was hard, it was dangerous. People acting in the best interests of humanity to keep us on a righteous path, that spoke to her. But Lily.

"I've seen a lot of people come and go," Luke added. "Some permanently, others because they couldn't make peace with it. There's no shame in that, it doesn't do for us all to be the same. If this isn't for you, it isn't."

The car sped towards London, the road noise swallowed by the heavy chassis, big tyres.

"Do you think I was hard on you?" Luke asked.

"I see why."

"Do you? Tell me."

He was really doing this?

"I failed, it's all a mess. And two people died."

"It's semantics but, yeah, on paper it doesn't look good. Problem is that the review panel can't be told specifics, so they'll see the report as objective one—to persuade Rubin to fake his death and go into hiding—fail. Objective two—to have Agnetha Rubin arrested for money laundering charges —fail."

"But she is in custody."

Luke nodded. "The only way the secrecy works is with the oversight of the ethics committee."

"I don't understand, an ethics committee's that's okay with us carving up dead bodies and taking the claim for these deaths?"

"No, because it's a band of assassins doing that, not MI6. I told you the government is an odd master, they trust the checks and balances the Ethics Committee give. Nothing about this mission was a fair trial, Rubin was never going to agree with our protocol and, if the panel insisted on a trial, it should have been a fair one where you could have succeeded."

"Don't suppose the arms seizure goes in my favour either?"

Luke shook his head. "The panel can't know Rubin was involved so they can't know you were responsible for that find. The appropriation of it will be eyes only, the PM probably won't see it. This is how our work goes, we get no recognition, apart from at S. We get to sleep easier at night knowing that we're making a difference, but it's also harder having that glimpse of how things really are.

All her reasons to try this were contradictions like that, weighing heavily on her now.

"Me being hard on you is nothing to do with you, just trying to make the best of a bad job. I thought if everything else was faultless, it might count for something. It wasn't a fair test."

Luke stopped talking to the darkness beyond his window and turned to her. "You deserved that." He held her gaze, the streetlights strobing over them through the glass sunroof.

"Probably blown my chance to be an analyst again too," Eva said, but her trying to make light of her failure made it hurt more.

"Gordon will fight for you."

"I know."

"We all will."

"Thanks," it was a half-whisper. Did she want them to?

Luke's ringtone stopped her saying anything more. "You're on speaker with Eva and me." He held his phone on the console between them, "Iago."

"Got some dynamite already, Eva, from the ears you planted. Rubin has another test, tomorrow, one thousand casualties, being randomly picked out of ten thousand plus."

"Do you know where?"

"Nah, didn't give a location. We're scrambling to figure out where his yacht's going."

"He'll want to be there." Eva said.

"We're en route to S, put the coffee on." Luke terminated the call. "You need to be dropped home?"

Eva shook her head, Lily was safe for tonight and so would she be, behind a desk. "I promised I'd get him for Fisher and Jacob."

Then she was done.

35

Gordon called Eva and Luke straight up to the briefing room as soon as they were through the airlock entrance at St George's Grove. "Good job, Eva, on the bugs. We've got solid intel to chase." He beckoned them to weave their way through the members of S standing almost out in the corridor to the seats he'd saved for them. "We need to figure out where he's doing this bigger test."

"Shame he didn't say where he was going." A middle-aged man Eva hadn't met said. "The world's a big place."

"Where are his yacht and jet? Does that give us anything?" Luke asked.

Iago consulted his tablet. "Not so much. Yacht is crossing the Baltic Sea, jet's still at Tallinn airport." He made a flicking motion and a map sprang up on the briefing table, making Eva start. The screens on the walls displayed the same thing. He'd inscribed a red oval on a map of the Baltic, looping eastwards out from Tallinn.

"This is everywhere he can reach overnight and into tomorrow afternoon." Iago explained. "Timeline's vague, but for him to hit a crowd of ten thousand, we have to assume it's an organised concert, football match, something along those lines. Cross-referencing his projected landing zones with venues of that size, we get precisely six events happening. We've alerted our contacts to have the venues searched."

Eva shook her head. "He doesn't need to prepare before-hand. His weapon just has to have line of sight to the drone."

"That makes it an impossible task." A woman standing at the back of the room pointed out the problem.

"Luke," Gordon said, "explain to us what this weapon does."

Luke looked at Eva. "You understand it better than me. Explain how you beat it. If it wasn't for her, I wouldn't be here now."

Eva felt the gaze of everyone in the room. She gave them a quick rundown of what Rubin had told them about the Lynx Assassin, and her best guess at how Rubin had targeted them.

"Once Rubin docks, it'll give us an idea of where he's heading." Iago said. "We're contacting marinas to see if he has any berths pre-paid, habitual places he uses."

"Does he own a helicopter?" Eva asked.

A woman with long black hair tapped at her tablet. "Publicly, no."

"He arrived back on the Overwatch on one. If he had to rent it, has he returned it? If not, the company should know where they're expecting it back, what its range is?" Eva's suggestion was a wild guess.

The woman nodded. "I'll look into it. Any idea of the charter company?"

Eva shook her head.

"Could be a friend's, acquaintance's." A man added.

Could it though? Something struck Eva as odd about that. If he still had it on board, he could reach anywhere inland, a short helicopter ride, a car waiting.

"Is he still signing the accord with the PM the day after tomorrow?" Eva asked.

Several people around the room consulted tablets.

"No changes announced in the public arena."

"Nothing on the government briefing channels."

"PM's diary still shows day after tomorrow."

The responses drilled down into the resources S could access.

"We can work his timetable backwards too," Eva said, "to account for known variables, when and how he's arriving in London. That might give us something. I can look at that."

Gordon nodded. "While he's on the move we have a chance to get out in front of this. Anyone have anything else?" He looked around the room, but everyone remained silent. "Let's get to it. All non-urgent missions wait, this is our priority. I'm meeting with the Director in the morning, give me something to take to him other than casualty figures. Luke, Eva, stay behind, Iago will play you the recording we got."

Rubin's one-sided conversation wasn't much until he said "When I shot my partner, I was standing right beside him."

"He shot his partner?" Luke asked.

Iago paused the recording, looked at Eva. "That's why you asked us last night to check the bullet that killed Goran Willander."

She nodded. "A hunch, he killed Patricia Dryant in Copenhagen, an accountant at Balancia in which he's an un-named executive, there all the time apparently overseeing special projects. I figured he might have done the same with his partner at Futura Energy, and we just assumed it was his wife's first choice of assassin being a bad shot."

"The bullet came back a match to the one used in Copenhagen." Iago confirmed.

"To the ones Rubin fired at us," Eva said. "but it doesn't make any sense why he killed Goran Willander, the nice guy of the business, the one who dealt with all the pesky employees? He could have picked anyone, why him?"

"We'll get on that, after we find the test site." Gordon nodded at Iago to continue the recording.

When it finished, he updated them. "We're looking at the fatalities in St Petersburg, and those who were close to what happened but survived."

"But everything in Russia takes longer," Eva said. "What're they saying, the Russians?"

"It's quiet through official sources but the back channels are very busy."

"I'd bet money that's why Rubin chose a Russian site. There're enough cruise ships in Norway that he's unhappy about, but the political fallout there would be small, not enough for him. He wants to stoke conflict."

"Evidence?" Gordon asked.

Eva shrugged. "More instinct, as to who he is."

"I can't work with that. Bring me something I can show to prove it and we can talk to the Russians, get them onside. Last thing we need is another spat over there, they're only just coming round from the US Ambassador being blown up in Moscow."

Eva managed not to wince at Gordon's casual reference to another fallout from Charles' actions.

"Do you need to work remotely tonight?" he added.

"Not tonight."

"Clock's ticking." Gordon dismissed them.

Eva went back to her office via the kitchen where most of the worktop was covered in snacks and fruit and just the smell of rich coffee was enough to wake her up.

She crunched on an apple, looking for a logical way to tie all the loose ends of information together. But nothing seemed to fit.

What about the things Rubin found important enough to show, to remind himself of every time he sat at his desk on board the Overwatch? She zoomed in on the footage she'd got from her lapel camera. The images of nature she understood, and the canvas proclaiming 'There is no planet B'. Clearly a message of some importance for him, given its placement and his green agenda.

What about the Arabic? She was sure it was the same as the one her father had, something about the pen and hurting, wasn't it? The sweeping strokes were what she remembered. Each word of the translation triggered the memory in her until she could recite it as much as read it. 'The wound of the sword or gun will heal, but not that of the tongue'.

Her father must have kept it to remind him he had to make sure his stories were true before going to print. His words so powerful, his influence such that lives could be upended if he wasn't careful with what he said.

Question was, how did that saying apply to Rubin?

36

Tricia opened her door to Eva's ring looking as together as she always did, even at silly o'clock in the morning. Despite having grabbed four hours sleep, a very welcome shower and change of clothes, Eva felt a mess beside her. "Sorry it's so early, I thought Lily might like a change of school uniform."

"No problem, come on in. You staying for coffee?"

"Taxi's waiting downstairs for me," Eva didn't need to check her watch to feel the increasing pressure that today was the day of Rubin's test and they still hadn't figured out where it would take place. "Thanks again for having her."

"Really not a problem."

"It's hard, isn't it, juggling it all?"

Tricia nodded, her long dark curls bouncing. "Oh, yes, it's a bundle of stress and angst. But I think we're doing okay, our girls are good people."

"Mum!" Lily nearly bowled Eva over with her welcome hug. "You're back, you took ages." And Eva had thought she hadn't noticed.

"I know, I'm sorry. International travel isn't so glamorous when it all goes wrong."

"Where did you go?"

"Only Europe, though you'd have believed it was Australia, with all the delays. I brought you a clean uniform."

Lily squeezed her tighter. Eva smoothed her hair like she used to when she was little.

"Gotta get ready." Lily released her.

"See you later, sweetheart, have a good day."

Lily nodded. "Environmental studies today, my favourite. We going to listen to the rest of Carl Rubin's interview tonight?"

Just the thought of hearing his voice made Eva want to shudder. "That sounds great," she lied, kissing the top of Lily's head and she was gone to get dressed.

"I've never seen her so keen to get ready for school." Eva said.

"I have a little incentive," Tricia said. "I stretch the advent calendar thing all year long."

Eva laughed. "I'm stealing that."

THE DAY TICKED by too quickly, the countdown clock that Eva had set on her laptop screen was running too fast. Clocks.

Where did Balancia fit? Clocks, a jump to time pieces, the company line, a jump to timing devices, integral parts of bombs.

What about his obsessions? Eva entered time and climate emergency, remembering Lily telling her off that she didn't use that term.

'The UN declares a climate emergency' the first entry, more of the same followed until Eva changed the search term to 'there is no planet B'. That returned entries about buying merchandise sporting that slogan, books, t-shirts, drink bottles. Then she saw it. She clicked enter on the podcast episode list of the same name until she found number 127, interview with Carl Rubin, CEO of Futura Energy. Eight minutes past the point she and Lily had got to she knew where he was going to do the next test of the Lynx Assassin.

37

"That makes no sense." Gordon said.

"It doesn't," Eva agreed, "but he's gone to a lot of trouble to hide his tracks. Why else would he do that if it wasn't to throw us off? Iago traced Rubin and Finch flying into London an hour ago on a commercial flight into Stansted."

"Quite the commute into London." Gordon said. "And no weapons allowed on commercial. But all that aside, why on earth would Rubin target the audience who believe the same as him?"

"Because we'd never suspect he would." Eva leant forward in the seat opposite his desk.

"How Many Heartbeats?" He read from her message.

"It fits everything, the SSE Arena, Wembley Arena, can take twelve and a half thousand—"

"He said ten."

"He said ten plus and the rally's sold out."

Gordon ran his hand through his thick, grey hair. "I follow your logic but it's an indoor venue. You said he has to have line of sight for the drone to lock onto the RFID signals."

"Maybe he'll have it inside, a show of his tech capabilities for his client."

"Futura Energy's one of the rally's biggest sponsors. He won't sabotage his company name, surely."

"No one's going to know it was him, it's like he's two different people."

"I don't buy it." Gordon said.

"How Many Heartbeats?" Eva said. "Isn't that an odd name for a rally about climate change unless it's through the prism of population control? Click the link at the bottom of the message."

The chilling video that had convinced her she was right began to play. Recorded over twenty years ago, in it Rubin looked like the young impressed student he was then, watching a speech given by an idealist which felt uncomfortably close to eugenics. Had he taken it a step further?

Gordon dialled a number, put his phone on speaker. "Iago, you're on with Eva and me."

"I'm not seeing anything out of the ordinary around the Arena." Iago said.

"Would you though?" Eva's phone vibrated in her pocket. "He doesn't need anything special to be set up. He just needs his weapon."

"Which he didn't bring in on the commercial flight."

"That you know of. I could go down there, be boots on the ground, speak to the organisers. It starts in less than an hour, this is his shot, I'm convinced of it."

She pushed down the sense of panic, the dread of the clock ticking down to zero and them sitting there unable to do anything than just watch.

"You could," Gordon agreed, "But he thinks he killed you and I don't want to waste that advantage."

"Why's that necessary now?" She was playing devil's advocate. "What can it hurt if he knows I'm alive? That just shows him his weapon isn't the all-powerful thing he thinks it is." Though it would take a lot more than that to shake his confidence.

Her phone quietened to stillness.

"I'm not convinced he'll do anything to jeopardise the deal tomorrow. He'll be under the media spotlight while he's here."

Eva remembered the look in his eyes when he talked about the population doubling in his lifetime. "I don't think he cares about that." Her phone vibrated again, once.

"But he'll care very much about the energy deal with our government going through without a hitch, it's worth a lot of money to his company."

"Money's not his motivator." She had the measure of him, she was sure.

"A man with two companies, a private jet, a super yacht which is quite something and a wife who can afford The Society rates? Once we have something concrete, we can take it to the police and Five. If he's planning anything on UK soil, it's down to them. I know you remember from your time here as an analyst we have no remit to operate here." Gordon reminded her.

Eva nodded.

And she meant it until she checked her voicemail.

38

"Hey, Mum, is it okay if I get a T-shirt? Can you give Tricia the money? It's twenty-five pounds the one I want. Thanks, Mum, you're the best." Lily, bright, gabbling, excited against a background noise of lots of people.

Too busy to pick up when Eva called her back. Tricia answered first time.

"Thanks so much for having had Lily for the extra night. I'm free now, I can come get her early, give you a break."

Tricia laughed. "They've been no trouble, Anya's a lot easier to manage when Lily's there. They're at the How Many Heartbeats rally. A friend of mine—"

"They're at the rally?"

"My friend had tickets, but he's poorly so gave them to me. It's perfect because the girls were desperate to go. I'm in a café nearby, I'll pick them up when it's over and drop Lily home."

How Eva wasn't screaming, she didn't know.

"Does Anya have her phone on?" Eva asked, every word clipped and tight while she tried to hold onto her sanity.

"No, I told them to turn them off until it's over, save their battery. They're fine, I'm only over the road."

Eva thanked Tricia without knowing what she was saying. She took the stairs two at a time, out of the airlock as fast as she could. The front door closed behind her with the finality that reinforced what she was about to do couldn't be undone. Goodbye career at S, MI6, the whole security services.

"You've got Lily." Lily's voicemail played in her ear the entire journey.

When Eva got off at Wembley Park tube station, she didn't need to check Google maps, she just followed the crowd.

How was she going to find Lily in amongst everyone?

She reached for the reassurance at her hip, but that was safely locked away back at S. Her temporary access pass would have to do.

She brandished it at the hi-vis vested security guard searching bags, stationed in front of the line of staff checking tickets with mobile scanners, let him read it before telling him in a low voice. "Security Services. I'm checking out a credible threat." The words were dynamite, blowing up her career, but she said them as though they didn't matter, as though her fear for her daughter wasn't threatening to choke her. "It's just me at the moment, we're keeping it low key, we don't want to cause panic." She looked at the streams of people behind her, in front of her. The guard followed her gaze.

"No one's alerted us to anything." His voice rumbled like a wannabe James Earl Jones.

"The information's only just been confirmed. Can I go in?"

He hesitated. Was he waiting for a codeword, something

to prove Eva was who she said she was? He beckoned one of the ticket scanners over.

"Security Services, checking out a threat. You let her in."

A dart of fright flitted over the girl's face. She looked as though she should be at home doing her homework, but she nodded.

"Do you need us to do anything?" the guard asked.

"Are you on the door all night?" He nodded. "I'll come and find you if we do."

Eva charged inside, stopped dead. Where did she start? The high-ceilinged oval auditorium was nearly full, excited anticipation thrummed through the air. Her gaze searched the tiered seating from the stage at the top. Where are you, Lily? That wouldn't find her, better if Eva could determine there was no threat. That she'd jumped to the wrong conclusion Gordon thought she had, and she was just embarrassing herself.

She headed for the cordoned-off area on the flat behind the seating, a mixer lineup that wouldn't have been out of place at a concert, manned by five crew members, dressed in black jeans, T-shirts and sweatshirts.

"You on time? Can I give the nod?" She gestured at the stage.

The guy didn't look up from his screen. "We're still rejigging the change. Could have done with more warning."

"There's been another change?" Eva asked.

Now she had his attention.

"Not that I know about, we're working the first one, the new keynote."

"We've had several backstage. Which one are you guys on?"

"The one that makes a difference to things. You know, Carl Rubin speaking."

39

He was there. Carl Rubin was there.

Eva was right.

"That change, yes, of course, that one." She gabbled at the sound mixing guy. "You're on it, good. Time check?"

"Ready in five."

She walked away. Looking up into the stands at twelve and a half thousand people surrounding her. Think like an agent, not a mum. The ceiling, far above her head, was high enough to get a drone up there, not an easy flight in between beams and light arrays, but probably too doable for a good pilot. Their salvation, the bullets couldn't come in through that, the roof would effectively cut off the signal from the RFID tags if he'd managed to deploy them.

How have you done it, Rubin? How have you deployed the tags this time?

A shower of the powder from the ceiling was too hit and miss. Everyone could end up tagged. He was looking for a thousand targets. How had he chosen them?

A couple passed her with huge drinks in paper cups.

And then the stadium lights dimmed, and the crowd cheered, clapped and stomped to a slow drumbeat. A teenager dashed past Eva, barging into her, throwing a sorry over her shoulder.

The drumbeat was winding up, whipping the crowd up with it.

Eva thumbed through her list of phone contacts, finger hovering over Gordon, Luke, Iago. She hit Luke's name, cut off his answer.

"I'm at the SSE Arena, Rubin's here. It's going down here, Luke, right now, his thousand targets." She swallowed, clamped hard on her emotions. Lily had a one in a twelve chance of surviving. It didn't feel like very long odds.

Eva pushed steel into her spine, stood straighter. "I don't know how he's marked them, how he's going to release the bullets. A good drone pilot could probably control it inside the auditorium. The panic if he shoots them in here though," she forced herself to finish her sentence, "will probably kill twice as many as the shots."

She walked around the back of the sound mixing area, searching the floor. Between the seats on the tiered sections was too tight for a drone to be sitting there waiting to be instructed. On the stage? She'd have no warning before it took off, the drone would lift up and the—she wasn't thinking.

Her panic was drowning her logic. The drone didn't shoot the victims; the rifle did. She needed to be looking for a rifle that had line of sight with the drone. So many more places he could have hidden that, anywhere up on the lighting arrays. She swallowed. If she had to go up there to save Lily, she would.

She could barely hear Luke above the now pulsing music. "Hold on."

She ran out of an exit, into the relative silence of the corridor. "Go ahead."

"I'm taking it to Gordon, getting you reinforcements." Luke said.

"He forbid me from doing this," Eva said. "I shouldn't involve you. I know we have no remit here, and you can't help because of your shoulder, but we need to stop Rubin. Can you call the emergency services and all that?"

"Keep your phone on. I'll call you back."

Eva went into the auditorium, walking along the flat area, scanning the tiered seating above her for Lily and Anya. Please see me, sweetheart.

An explosion of music drowned the drumbeat, and a voice filled the air. "Hello, SSE Arena, put your hands together for your keynote speaker, the man heading the charge to stop the climate emergency." The announcer wound up to fever pitch as though he was announcing a world heavyweight championship fight. "Founder and Chairman of Futura Energy, green warrior, Carl Rubin."

All the ego massaging Rubin could ever want was present in the frenzied applause, whistling and cheering as he walked across the stage.

"Hello, London. It's good to be here." It was strange to see his grinning face on the big screens looking like a normal person when Eva knew what he really was, what his real agenda was. That he didn't value one of the twelve and a half thousand people applauding him. "Are you ready to disrupt some things?"

Apparently they were, if the level of noise was anything to go by.

"I thank you all, from the bottom of my heart, each and every one of you, for responding to the climate emergency call. For being willing to do what's necessary to reclaim our planet from the harmful effects of the human race. I salute you."

He let the cheering run for a minute, two, until he held his hand up for quiet. Quieter at least.

"Now I know you all understand about Earth Overshoot Day, you're kindred warriors." He paced from one side of the stage to the other. "Earth Overshoot Day, the day when we consume so many of our planet's resources that she can't replenish them for the remainder of time left in the year. This year, it falls in August." He stopped pacing, accused the audience. "August. Mother Earth cannot replace everything you consume in September, October, November and December. Four months," he punctuated his message with silence and stony glares, and Eva could see the real Carl Rubin on the screens, "one hundred and twenty-two days in which you are the enemy, when you are killing the planet. Every bite of food, every sip of water that you take during those one hundred and twenty-two days every car, bus, train or plane journey, every time you charge your phone, put heating on in your homes, every time makes you a murderer."

The thunderous applause, cheering and whistling had dropped to virtually no noise at all. Eva would at least be able to tell where the drone was taking off from. She flicked her phone to silent, vibrate only.

"But I own an energy company, I hear you pointing the finger. Let me tell you I would rather be out of business if it would make Earth Overshoot Day a thing of the past. Year on year, it falls earlier. Next year, it'll be in July, if we're lucky. What happens when it's in June, May, April? What happens when the global population has doubled to fifteen billion, when Earth Overshoot Day falls in January?" He gestured at the banner over the stage where the double-edged message shouted in huge green letters 'Too Many Heartbeats'. "Alone, I can't stop that happening." his voice rose until he yelled. "I. Need. Your. Help."

He was quite the showman, mesmerising. He looked as sane as her.

The applause surged, the audience congratulating themselves on being the warriors he needed, just not in the way they could ever have dreamt. He paced up and down the stage. Was the fizz of his energy something Eva imagined because she knew what was coming?

"Apparently, I need your help right now. I'm asking you not to panic— well, obviously, about the climate emergency, you should be panicking," he waited for the laughter at his joke. "But right here, now, I'm asking for calm. The staff have just informed me that we need to evacuate and there's an issue with the alarm sounder. So, please, follow the signs to your nearest exit. Once we're outside, they can deal with whatever the problem is. Whoever left their backpack in a public area's going to feel pretty silly." He laughed, wooing his audience. "Then we can come back in and get on with the show." He raised his arm to his acolytes. "Muster points are out in the car park. Stay safe."

40

The house lights came up, normal conversation changed to worry.

No, no, no. But even as Eva thought it, even as what Rubin had said sunk in, she realised the ushers were already opening the fire exit doors, people standing up in their seats, making for them.

She charged up to a member of staff. "Can you get an announcement out over the tannoy, this isn't an evacuation. No one should go outside."

"It's not my decision, somebody mentioned a suspicious package, the protocol is we evacuate."

Eva flashed her access pass. "I'm Security Services, where's your supervisor? Who's in charge here?"

The usher shrugged. Eva was being pushed by the stream of people behind her, rushing for a safety outside that she knew didn't exist. She redialled Luke.

"Rubin's evacuating the Arena."

"I'm on it." He rang off.

The guy beside her, in a red and white baseball jacket, was wearing a sticker on his forehead.

"What's that?" she asked.

"We're VIPs," his accent hinted he could afford to be, "shame you don't have one."

The guy and his friend shuffled on to the end of the jam of people leaving the safety of the building.

"Who gave it to you?"

They ignored her. "Interpol." She shouted at them. "I asked you a question, how did you get that?" She gestured at his forehead.

"They gave them out, to the VIPs." His mate said.

Was that it?

"Take it off, it's a target."

The baseball-jacketed guy laughed, pulled his hands out of his pockets. "Yeah, you and whose Army?"

"I'm warning you, if you go outside, you're at risk."

"You're just jealous, babe." He adjusted his drooping jeans, waggling his on display boxers at her.

"You'll die if you go outside."

"Still not having my sticker." He turned his back on her.

Eva pushed against the current of people behind her, working her way back inside. "Security Officer, coming through."

She charged into the arena proper, running around the tide of people toward the sound mixing array. Only two men now doing something.

"Can you get a message out to the crowd through this?" she asked.

"You have to evacuate, love, along with everyone else."

"I'm an off-duty Interpol Officer, I need to use the tannoy. Does it log into the mic on the stage?"

"You got ID?" The guy had a bandanna tied around his neck, white polka dots on red, looking like it had lost its pirate ship.

"Off duty, I don't carry it around. I have to stop this evacuation. The danger's outside, not in here."

"Yeah, above my pay grade, lady. We've been told to evacuate, that's what we're doing."

"I can have you arrested for obstruction. And you." She pointed at the other guy.

"The speakers use lav mics clipped to their lapels." The other guy said. "We don't have mics on stage any more."

"Fit me up with one."

"Didn't you hear the announcement? I'm out of here."

"This is ridiculous." Eva pushed her way up on to the stage, looking for abandoned mics.

She had to settle for yelling from the stage. "Off duty Police, the danger's outside, don't evacuate, you're safe in here. There is no suspicious package." But of course no one would listen, even if they could hear her. She probably wouldn't if she were them, especially if she had Lily with her. Lily. Still no sign of her, no shocked face turning towards her, that's my mother up there embarrassing herself.

Think, if she couldn't stop the evacuation, what could she do?

Her phone rang.

"They're evacuating, I can't stop them." She answered Luke. "Are the Fire Brigade en route? Can you tell them to soak the crowd? Water will disrupt the RFID signals."

"I can try, sure, but I know the response will be a big no unless they're on fire, they'll be worried about being sued."

"We're trying to save their lives."

"You don't need to tell me that. Messaging them now." Damned if she did, damned if she didn't.

Too long, too long.

She dialled Tricia, talked all over her interrupting questions. "Keep trying the girls, either of them, both of them. When you get hold of them, tell them to stay inside. I'm there now, there is no suspicious package. The danger's outside. They mustn't go outside, even to meet you, they need to go back inside the Arena. It'll save their lives. You understand?"

"Yes, but—"

"It's vital, they mustn't leave the site to meet you, they have to stay inside the Arena. I'm in there waiting for them."

Eva hung up, going with the flow of people leaving but across, not out of, the open exit doors. Where were the fire wardens?

She chased the glimpse of a hi-vis vest weaving in and out of people, going sideways to their going forwards.

"Hey, you work here?" The guy turned round, nodded. "You know where the tannoy system is?"

"Nope. Need to evacuate, same as everybody else."

"That's what I need to tell people, the danger's out there, inside they're safe."

"But Carl Rubin said—"

"Just take me to the tannoy system."

"I don't know where that is."

"Where do they do the countdown to the event beginning? There'll do."

"It's a recording."

"But where's it played from?"

He shrugged.

"Take off the VIP stickers, they're dangerous." Her best shouting was drowned by the noise around her, she was too short to pop up above the crowd collective, too female to be taken seriously, and not uniformed enough. "VIP stickers, hands in the air." Even her loudest bellow fell short.

Being short had its advantages, Eva ducked around the

crowd, passing through it as if she were avoiding rocks in a rapid. Security lights all around the exterior of the arena turned night into day. She squinted, scanning the sky, no sign of the drone. Was it round the other side?

A scream. Another, another, a round robin of terror. The shooting must have started. And then people began pushing, shoving, flooding away from the building.

Eva had not a hope of getting them back inside.

She redialled Luke. "Where are the police? It's started. I need ambulances, paramedics. Can you get a major incident declared? Can a helicopter make an announcement?"

"Two minutes out." Luke's voice reassured in her ear. "Armed and regular police, Fire Brigade, ambulances, all en route to you."

"I think the ambulances might be too late already."

The two guys Eva had asked about the stickers were sprawled on the ground in front of her. She wouldn't have recognised them but for the red baseball jacket, now splashed in its owner's blood and probably brain matter.

Lily.

"Can Iago hack the tannoy system?" she asked. "I can't get anyone here who can use it. The RFID tags are in a clear oval sticker with black concentric circles on it, like a target. It's a bloody target."

She hung up and turned around and around; her gaze flitting from person to person searching the fleeing, screaming, running, in full panic mode crowd. But no sign of a young girl with long brown hair. Lily was a child. There was no way she or Anya had a sticker.

"Get back inside," she shouted. "The bullets can't hit you if you're inside. The evacuation is a hoax."

But no one was stopping long enough to listen to her. "Off duty police officer, this is what the terrorist wants. He wants you outside." She grabbed the nearest couple, a grey-haired man and an Indian lady, "get inside, you're safe in there."

More screaming behind them. Another person in a green coat dropped to the ground.

"Please, I'm trying to save your life. If you see anyone with a sticker on, like a black target, get them to take it off."

The man nodded and pulled the woman back inside the building.

She had to stop more coming outside. Shoving her way back into the arena, shouting her warning at everyone on her way, Eva jumped up on the box office counter, waving her arms and yelling.

"Mass shooter event outside, you're only safe in here. The backpack's been disposed of. Police Officer, you're safer in here. Check your phones. Go back inside the auditorium, people are being shot on exit. Stay inside."

The steady flow out through the exit doors halted as those at the front saw the bodies lying on the ground.

"You may have been tagged and be at risk. Turn around, go back inside." Eva encouraged them and the tide started turning, people side-stepping the exits, turning back towards the auditorium.

"She's right."

"They're shooting."

"They're dead, oh my God."

The balance between order and panic tipped, and the pushing and scrabbling became more violent as the people's momentum reversed. The screaming and crying chilled her, but they started moving in the right direction.

"Turn around, you at the back, go inside," Eva screamed over the general hubbub. "There's a mass shooter event outside. Tell everyone. Stay inside."

Eva jumped down from the counter and ran round the building to the next exit where a trickle of people was easier to turn back. She swiped up a fire extinguisher from beside the open doors, checked the label. Definitely water, she couldn't kill anyone with water.

Another person dropped ahead of her, altering the wave of people fleeing. Eva grabbed at the teenager who collided with her, a young boy with straggly facial hair that tried hard to be a beard. "Stop." She held on to his jacket. "You need to take that sticker off, it's how the weapon's targeting you. Take the sticker off, get inside, wash your face then you'll be safe."

Young enough he believed her, she helped him pull it off. Sadie would need it.

"Take your coat off, fold it in on itself, there'll be some residual tagging on it. Go back inside, don't come out until the police tell you it's safe. They'll need your coat as evidence—" Eva hesitated, was it right to give away her name? "Tell them it's for Eva Janssen, Security Services. Okay, you got that? It's really important."

He nodded, pulling his coat off as he ran indoors.

"You're only safe inside the building. The VIP stickers are dangerous." Eva spun around at a scream right beside her. A warm spray caught the side of her cheek. The lady beside her dropped to the ground. Her sticker on a lemon-coloured coat caved into her chest.

Eva felt the lady's neck, no pulse. Her companion, maybe her daughter, screamed, shrieked, threw herself onto the dead woman.

"You need to go inside." Eva said. "You're a target, go inside."

Sirens split the air, but the screams of the people around Eva were louder.

"The paramedics are here, they'll take care of her. Please, she wouldn't want you to die." Eva bit off the 'too'.

She watched the girl run, sobbing towards the exit, pushing her way into the building. Eva yelled at those around her, her message mostly being ignored.

Still crowds streamed away from the Arena, flooding the side streets, running for the safety of the tube. The drone could pick them off easily, even as they dodged around others in their headlong flight. So many targets. Sirens from beyond the chaos, salvation on its way.

She dashed towards the sound of sudden screaming, a Chinese teenager in a bobble hat that had once been white, was lying on the ground, her friend practically jumping up and down beside her in terror.

"Off duty Police Officer, do you have a sticker?" Eva grabbed the girl's arm. "Do you have a sticker?"

The girl's eyes were wide, vacant, she was probably going into shock. Eva looked her up and down, turned her round, holding on to her so she didn't panic more and run away. She lifted her long black hair up and there it was, on the back of her neck.

She faced the girl and spoke slowly and clearly. "You need to take the sticker off. Can I do it?"

She nodded. But it was stuck too well, fragmenting in Eva's hand rather than peeling off like the others had.

"Close your eyes, hands over them, trust me. This will be cold but it'll save your life." Eva directed the fire extinguisher spray at the ground beside the girl to get the measure of its force. She took a step back and sprayed the back of her head.

How much was enough?

"Put your hands over the sticker, back into the building quickly. The sticker is a target for a weapon. If if can't read it, it can't find you. You must stay inside. Do you understand?"

Eva wasn't entirely sure to believe her nodding of her head, but the girl clapped her hands over the back of her neck and ran inside.

"If you've got a VIP sticker on, get back inside." Eva screamed. The crowd was thinning as more ran into danger in the open space between the shelter of the Arena's side and the emergency vehicles.

Above the sirens, piercingly loud now as the whole area was strobed in blue, Eva could hear the angry bees sound of drones. And there, ahead of her, remarkable in his stillness, Carl Rubin, watching his show. Mesmerised.

41

Eva quashed her first reaction. Running over to Rubin to plead with him wouldn't make him stop. But he had to be controlling the weapon somehow. He didn't seem the type to delegate something like that. She needed to distract him.

Hefting the fire extinguisher, she got closer to him than she wanted to. "Carl Rubin, put your hands up, you're under arrest."

His look of surprise was something, he'd had no idea she'd survived his attack on her nor, apparently, that it was her who'd drugged him with on the Overwatch. He pushed the lens of the odd glasses he was wearing up as if he could see better without it and so understand. "Eva Janssen? How are you here?"

"What are you doing?"

"Isn't it obvious? Didn't you hear my speech? We have to cull the population."

"This is murder."

"What do you think culling is? Strange, isn't it, that we

don't give it a second thought when we go out to shoot deer, massacre seals, tear apart foxes, all in the service of keeping the numbers of species down to what we believe are acceptable levels because we don't want them interfering in our human lives. Why should we not apply that logic to ourselves? It's true, what I said in there, man's hubris will push our planet beyond the tipping point where we'll have to move to another world for our species to survive. We're on course for that to happen before we have the technological capability to decamp." He waved at the building behind them. "Didn't you wonder about the name of the rally. How many heartbeats? Too many is what it is. I'm just redressing the balance on behalf of Mother Nature because we're outpacing her best efforts to keep us in check."

"You can't do this."

"I think you'll find I have. So, tell me, how did you survive? How did you defeat the Lynx Assassin?"

"Hands up." Eva tightened her grip on the fire extinguisher trigger and fired a stream of water onto the concrete until it pooled between them.

"You're going to soak me into submission? Try to drown me in your puddle?" He laughed. "You almost deserve to live with tenacity like that. I'll let you, in exchange for knowing how you survived."

"So you can tweak the weapon to make sure no one else can? I don't think so. It's all over for you, get down on the ground."

Her arms were tiring, the extinguisher was heavy. Now would be a great time for an armed officer to find her. But in her peripheral vision all she was aware of were other people falling, screaming, sirens, the noisy cacophony of a major incident. She dragged her focus back to him.

He shook his head quickly as if he were shaking away a fly. "You won't hit me with that, you don't possess the strength, your arms are tired already, nor do I believe you're capable of brute force violence."

He read her too well.

"Maybe not, but my daughter was in there." She ground out, pulling on her fear. "If anything's happened to her, I will make you pay."

She took a step forward. He took one backwards, as she'd expected. Another step forward and she launched the fire extinguisher at him. He dodged it easily. It swung beyond her reach, too heavy to bring back in for another try. She let it fall, a metallic clunking on the concrete.

"See this?" He opened his hand, a small black object in his palm. "It's as easy for me to operate this weapon as it is to unlock my car."

It looked exactly like that, the fob you'd have instead of a car key.

"You can't stop this." The fire extinguisher's metallic ringing as it rolled to a stop underlined his truth. "I've been enjoying manual mode, watching them fall one at a time. Time to try full automatic where the entire magazine's fired in one go."

"It's what you used in Denmark." she said flatly.

"It is, but only with three bullets, genius, isn't it?"

"Not enough to fool us."

"But if I fire it now, you'll lose your hands, probably your arms. Are you prepared for that?"

His gaze dropped to her hands where she held the stickers she'd retrieved.

"It seems I have the upper hand again, if you'll forgive the pun. Once again you're on the end of my will."

She charged at him, even while he was spouting his rhetoric. But it was too much warning, he stepped out of her way. She rushed right back at him, but he grabbed her coat, pulled her against him. "You're about to appreciate the real genius of this weapon. I can order a strike and shoot you, it won't touch me, even standing so close to you."

She twisted against him, raked her heel down his calf. As he shifted away from the pain, his grip on her loosened enough she could get her arm up behind her. She tapped the stickers on his back, elbowed him over and over to distract.

He hit her in the face, making her eyes stream. She held onto his jacket as he spun away from her. His leg kicked out and she was falling, her feet swept out from underneath her. She grasped at his trousers as she went down, but still fell fast, heavy, colliding with the concrete, the air smacked out of her lungs.

He kicked her hard enough to make her double over, catch the breath she was trying to get. He squatted in front of her, the victor all powerful over his prey.

It was the hardest thing. But she unwound from her foetal position, looked at him right in the eye. "I've beaten you." she coughed out.

"What, the stickers you've planted on my back?" He laughed, bounced up to standing, putting the fob in his trouser pocket, took his jacket off. "Ah, that's how you beat it, isn't it? You muddled the RFID signals. Clever. You had several stickers in your hand, so you've done the same to me. Your threat is useless."

Eva dragged herself to the puddle from the fire extinguisher and shushed her hands in it, wiping them on the ground, palms, backs, fingertips.

"You think that's enough?" He threw his jacket at her.

She kicked it away as if it was on fire, pressed her hands into the too shallow puddle again.

"I'm sure it's not." He retrieved the fob from his pocket and pressed it again and again so she could see him do it. "We'll see, won't we? Another test."

42

The bullet arrived with no fuss, no noise, though it would have been difficult to separate any sound it made from the general cacophony of the major incident response as it tore into Carl Rubin's leg.

He dropped to the ground, his face registering shock and disbelief.

Eva kept her hands pressed into the pitiful puddle, looking upwards, even though she was hardly going to see them coming if any of the other presses on his fob had ordered another bullet to her.

In the midst of the emergency lights of the police vans and ambulances strobing through the glare of the security lights, she could see the white lights of something else. Red lights flashed at its outer extremities, it hovered there, watching, an evil eye in the sky. Movement above it, another drone peeling away, flying to cause more destruction some-where else.

The real evil lay moaning on the ground in front of her. Eva got to her feet, bending over to ease the pain in her side where he'd kicked her, and prised the fob out of his grasp.

Light in her hand, larger than the one she'd used to steal his SUV, the array of buttons on it looked daunting, but, if she hadn't known better, no more deadly than lock and unlock. She put it in her pocket as though it might explode.

"Not so lucky this time, standing next to the supposed victim. I'm no Goran Willander."

Even where his face was screwed up against shock and pain, she saw him register the surprise that she knew.

Where she'd wiped the RFID tags from the stickers down his trousers, his leg was a mangled mass of bloody tissue.

"I'm not a doctor but you need to get that looked at right away, you're bleeding, a lot."

She frisked him, took his phone, left his wallet, removed his glasses. Heavier than regular ones, probably relaying a recording to somewhere. The lens was engraved with some kind of measurement marks. Sadie would like those, too.

"I have a deal this time." Eva said. "Give me the location of the rifles, and I'll get medical attention for you."

"Don't know what you're talking about." His face was growing greyer by the second, sweat beaded his forehead.

Eva squatted beside him. "You've deployed more than one rifle, same as you have more than one targeting drone. Tell me where they are and I'll get help."

He closed his eyes.

"Or, don't, it's up to you. Decide quickly."

"Your government doesn't want me to die. There's too much on the table for them, the agreement tomorrow is just the tip of the iceberg."

"You think I care what our government wants out of this? You're going to pay for all those your weapons have killed since you first knew what a bullet could do."

"You've got protocols—"

"Do I? You were right about my Interpol credentials being fake, I don't work for any agency, so what I decide is okay, you're just like my ex-husband and I never loved you so whatever happens, whatever fate I cause for you, my conscience is clear."

"You're still subject to the law."

"I am. But the law doesn't know about you right here, bleeding out." She put on the same tone he had to tell her and Luke how he was going to respond to any interest in why they'd disappeared in Norway. "I'm so sorry, officer, I last saw Mr Rubin on the stage, I hope he's all right, he's doing such great work on climate change."

"You wouldn't dare."

"We're done here."

"I have rights." His words were punctuated by rapid, shallow breathing.

"More than those people you've murdered? Where are the rifles? Otherwise, I'm walking away and directing the paramedics to the opposite side of the building."

Eva pulled the stickers off the back of his jacket. "You had your chance." She took a burst of photos of him on her phone and uploaded them to the S server. Deleted them.

She was two steps away when he called after her.

"All right. I'll tell you."

Eva kept going.

"It's in York House, Empire Way."

One more step.

"You listening to me?" He sounded feebler. "York House."

"And the other?"

"You can see it down that one's scope."

She walked back to him. "How do I bring the drone down?"

His breathing was becoming more erratic. She shook her head. "You don't have time to be difficult."

"It's a sequence."

Eva stared at the fob. Could she trust what he was saying? She wouldn't like to bet on what mattered more to him, his agenda or his life.

43

———

"If you lie, I'll walk away." Eva told Rubin. "If the drones do anything other than land right in front of me, I'll walk away. Do you understand?"

He told her the sequence.

She pressed the first button. The second. Felt a sudden jab in her back.

"Hands up." The voice behind her ordered.

"You know what to do." Rubin breathed.

"This is a traditional handgun," Sean Finch, Rubin's bodyguard, pressed the gun barrel against her. "I press the trigger another hair's width and you're gone. Give me the fob."

Eva gripped it tighter. But even as she realised she couldn't feel the gun against her, so pain erupted across the back of her head and she was down again, lying on the concrete.

The ground was cold and gritty against her face, hard against her body, but she couldn't quite understand how she'd got down there. The noise and brightness of the world around her faded in and out.

A rough hand grasped her wrist, and it was nothing at all for Finch to take the fob. Her hand bounced on the ground when he let go of her. The sound of the emergency services, everything around her, was coming from down a distant tunnel.

"Boss." Sean Finch was leaning over Rubin. "What do you want me to do?"

Eva struggled to focus. She could tighten and flex her calf muscles, move her fingers. She couldn't take Finch on if she was 100% fit, but brawn didn't always win. She focused on the men just a couple of metres away from her. What could she learn?

"Get me to hospital." Rubin's breath shuddered in and out, he pushed his words out as though they were dead weights. "She's got the glasses… show the client… weapon's reliable… raise price… make sure shipment's on time… time for lynx to change camouflage."

Shouting, distinctly now, was getting closer, the words 'over here, two more'.

Finch stood up, came towards her. Eva's frantic instructions to her body to move were going somewhere other than her brain. She pushed herself up on one hand, tried to hold him back from her but he swatted her feeble effort away, ripping the things she'd taken from Rubin out of her coat pocket.

His gaze met hers, he grasped her coat collar, pulled her higher off the ground.

"How're you doing?" An overly cheerful voice reached through the disaster movie soundtrack.

"Carl Rubin," she heard him gasp. "Get me to hospital."

"Don't you worry, we'll take good care of you." The paramedic responded.

Finch dropped her back onto the concrete and walked

off. The paramedic being there had probably saved her life. Eva closed her eyes.

"Eva, are you hurt?"

The man squatting in front of her made her think she'd taken a harder knock to the head than she'd thought. Was she dreaming? Light brown skin, shaved head. As if he wasn't recognisable from that, she couldn't mistake his grey eyes for anyone else's. They were really arresting. She felt a bubble of hysteria, just as she had the first time she'd thought that when he'd interviewed her thinking she was a suspect in her former colleague's murder last year.

"DI Smith?" She pushed herself up onto one hand, held the back of her neck. "What're you doing here?"

He smiled, he should do that more often. "I am police, police have been called. Luke Fox asked me to come down, see if I could help you. Are you injured?"

"I've got to find my daughter. She's here, somewhere." Her voice caught. "The man responsible for all this is there." She jabbed at Rubin. "He needs to be arrested and his body-guard, Sean Finch, he was here, but he's gone, probably to retrieve the rifles. He'll be visiting Rubin later; you could set up a sting."

"One thing at a time."

Eva opened her mouth, closed it again. Should she tell DI Smith about the rifles? Someone needed to know.

"I need to call this in." She got to her feet, staggered a little.

DI Smith held onto her. "You need to be checked out. You might be concussed."

Eva dug around in her coat pockets. "I'm not shot. The paramedics have enough to deal with." They were empty. "He took my phone. Can I use yours? I need to let Luke know."

"Of course." He unlocked it and handed it to her with Luke's number displayed. She hit call and walked slowly away from the detective, each step a little less wobbly.

"Elliot, you got her?" Luke answered.

"It's me. I'm fine, thanks for looking out for me. I got Rubin. His weapon shot him in the leg, don't know if he'll make it."

"Remind me to not get on your bad side."

"Sean Finch has control of the rifles. The first is in York House, Empire Way, Rubin said we'd see the second down that one's scope. They filmed the whole thing to show this mystery client how the weapon works. He had two on this, two drones for the firing side, probably more for the filming. Don't know if Iago can backtrack them. Can you set up a sting to grab Finch when he goes to visit his boss in hospital? He took the fob off me that controls the firing."

"You're making the rest of us look bad." Luke said. "I'll get on it. You staying on the ground?"

"I have to look for Lily, she was in the Arena."

Luke's sudden silence said it all.

Fighting the maternal panic clawing at her, Eva remembered to tell Luke to track her phone. "Finch took it."

"Have Elliott stay with you, so I can reach you when I get there. I'm sure she's safe, Eva, she's your daughter."

That wasn't nearly enough reassurance.

44

———

Inside the Arena it was eerily quiet despite all the people sheltering in the tiered seating.

"Lily, Lily Janssen!"

But no head of long brown hair popped up at Eva's yell.

"Anya Fernandez!" No cautious peering around anything at that shout either. "Has anyone seen two young girls, one with brown hair, one with black?"

Eva didn't know what Lily had been wearing.

The couple of negative replies shouted in her and DI Smith's direction were enough to send Eva out of the arena, charging for the toilets.

"I'll take the mens, you do the ladies." he said.

No one answered in either of the sets Eva tried. If only Finch hadn't taken her phone, one call to Tricia could have put her mind at rest because Lily was fine. She had to be okay. Eva should have memorised Tricia's number.

"Her best friend's mum is in a café, I told her to tell them to come back in here if they called." Eva ran her hands through her hair. The panic was winning. Should she go searching through the bodies outside? She gulped in air.

"It's okay, we'll find them." DI Smith said. "You know which café?" Eva shook her head. "You know her number?"

"Not off by heart." She was failing at being a mother.

"What would Lily do? Where would she go?" DI Smith led her outside.

"To Tricia, her friend's mum."

"So we need to find her then. What does her mum look like?"

Eva looked up at him. "Beautiful, she's Brazilian, olive skin, long dark curly hair, dark eyes, slim, tall. Anya's a lot like her, Lily has golden brown eyes, long brown hair, she's almost as tall as me."

A crushing tiredness hit Eva and, out of all proportion to what she was feeling, she yawned.

"You need to be checked out. I think you're concussed."

"I'll be fine, I have to find Lily."

"Okay, let's start there." He pointed at an adjoining road where there were several cafés, restaurants and bars.

"If you saw anything that can help us with what happened here today, please make yourself known to a police officer. If you need medical attention, please come to the ambulance bay outside the main entrance. Otherwise, please leave the area." Someone repeated the instructions over and over through the loud speaker Eva had needed earlier.

The shooting must have stopped, Finch more concerned about securing the weapon now. Getting it before the authorities did. Eva trotted beside DI Smith's fast strides. He looked the question at her.

She shook her head. "I'm fine, keep going."

The first café was packed. Eva ran inside, DI Smith taking the neighbouring restaurant. She pushed past the queue to scour the tables. No one she recognised.

She almost bumped into him as she burst out of the café. She was sure they could discount the bars but the Italian restaurant halfway along the street might be a possibility. "I'll take that one," Eva told him, rushing inside, nearly ploughing into the last person in the queue waiting for a table.

"They're full, not taking anyone else after us." he told her.

"I don't want to eat. I'm just looking for my daughter." Eva nudged past them and did a quick recce of the tables and everyone sitting at them. People laughing, chatting, having a good time while just over the road outside, others were having the worst or last day of their lives. She raced down the stairs, grabbing at the bannister when she felt another wave of dizziness, hanging on until it passed.

Back outside, DI Smith beckoned her from the other side of the road. "Eva, in here. They're all safe."

Eva's legs almost went out from underneath her. She rushed inside. "Lily."

"Mum?" Lily threw herself at Eva.

"You're okay." Eva repeated again and again, fighting back tears of relief.

"I told them what you said," Tricia said, "but they were already on their way outside so I told them to run over here."

"We have bomb scare drills at school, we know to get away quickly." Lily's explanation was muffled against Eva. Hopefully she hadn't seen any of the murders. Eva held her tighter.

It took a few minutes before Eva got herself enough under control to thank DI Smith.

"When I'm not questioning you, you can call me Elliott." He smiled.

She managed one back, remembering how tough he'd been when he had questioned her last year.

"Elliott, thank you."

His smile deepened. "My pleasure."

45

___

The office door to which Eva was escorted at Vauxhall Cross wasn't one she'd ever been through when she'd worked there. It was just a door on the outside, but the secrets discussed on the other side of it could bring down regimes, topple governments, change the course of world events. Probably had. It was a heady power wielded in there.

Just hours ago, she wouldn't have turned up to the summons. But the people she'd saved at the SSE Arena by being there—and those she hadn't—tipped the balance for her into wanting to stay with the Security Services. Being behind a desk was just as valid as being in the field, she could make a difference from there too. But going home to Lily at night, that was everything.

She'd thought MI6 could have appointed her as an analyst through Gordon. Perhaps she had to sign the Official Secrets Act again or they were putting her back in Vauxhall Cross.

Eva's escort knocked at the door and at the 'enter', opened it to let her into the lion's den.

She'd never met the Director of MI6, never seen him on the news, nor even walking around the corridors of the building. He kept a low profile, a lot quieter than Anna Bailey, his opposite number at MI5. Rumours about him circulated in the media when they thought about it, which wasn't often. What happened on home soil was better click-bait for their consumers, a fact that served MI6 well.

"Good morning. Eva Janssen, you asked to see me."

Sir Hugo Welch looked up from the monitor on his desk. If she'd passed him in the street, she'd never have guessed at what he did. He had an unassuming air, his neatly trimmed ribbon of grey hair, rimless glasses, keen blue eyes and ruddy cheeks suggested he was an accountant, a solicitor, someone who'd never raise their voice. The perfect disguise for the agent she imagined he'd once been.

"You've caused some waves."

She frowned. "Why?"

"Do you need me to spell it out?"

His desk phone rang. "Yes?" He sighed. "I'll take it." He moved his mouse around and clicked a few times, gestured at the chair by the wall. "You'd better sit, he won't be able to see you there."

A screen on the opposite wall sprang to life, and Edward Markham's face filled it.

"Good morning, Prime Minister." Welch said. "I'm here with Eva Janssen." He clicked and the PM's face moved to the top of the screen. He, with Eva tiny behind him, appeared in a box at the bottom.

"You?" The PM's greeting wasn't friendly. "You're the cause of all this trouble?"

Eva didn't know what to say to that, so she hedged. "Congratulations on your appointment, Prime Minister."

He inclined his head slightly. "I'm obviously extremely unhappy that this event happened on my watch."

She ignored that he made it sound like she was responsible.

"How can I possibly sign the green directive with Futura Energy now that their CEO is lying in a coma in a London hospital, shot on British soil?" The PM sounded petulant.

"By his own weapon." Eva interrupted the Director's reply. "Which Carl Rubin used to kill his business partner and deputy. The government might be grateful to not be associated with him. I'm sure that Futura Energy won't want to lose the deal, they'll find someone to represent them."

"This weapon that can apparently fire bullets on its own just into the air and they find their way to shoot the intended targets no matter where they are? It all sounds too far-fetched to me."

"This is apparently weapons dealing in the twenty-first century."

"You're besmirching the reputation of a man unable to defend himself, a man who does stellar work on behalf of us all. Welch, I'll be instructing my staff to focus on MI6 in our audit of the security services."

"Prime Minister," Eva refused to say with all due respect, she didn't want to weaken her argument before it was even uttered. "I wasn't there yesterday as a representative of MI6. I did what I could to save lives, as I would hope any of us would do in that situation."

"Precisely why I haven't ordered your arrest."

For what? Eva held her tongue.

"You'd better hope Carl Rubin doesn't die, because murder is something else again."

"It was his weapon that shot him." Eva said evenly, "his press on the remote to make it fire."

The Director silenced her with a look.

"Prime Minister, if I may. We are, of course, co-operating with your officers to give you oversight of our activities. The Official Secrets Act forbids Ms Janssen from discussing the events that happened as part of her mission and any of the ensuing consequences yesterday. As you know, she was on a trial mission, that trial didn't work out. She's no longer part of SIS."

46

Didn't they say you never knew what you had until it was gone?

Eva walked back to St George's Grove for the last time.

'You've always chosen to stay small', her ex-husband's taunt when she'd tried to stop him poisoning a city for his personal revenge. Taking the position Gordon had offered her had been a way to answer that and carry on her father's legacy. And now it had been torn away from her.

These goodbyes were going to be painful.

Her access pass still worked, letting her in through the sturdy outer door, the inner airlock. The closed door policy of beyond top secret meant the corridors and stairs were always quiet, so she reached her office without meeting anyone. She needed to tell Gordon, Nora, Luke in case the Director's memo hadn't reached them yet.

She booted up her laptop to perform a system wipe, even though she knew Iago would do the equivalent of a steam sterilisation to delete any data traces from her tiny footprint there as though they'd never existed.

Her notes folder—a throwback to when she'd been an analyst, anything and everything that struck her as odd, out of place, bizarre, against perceived wisdom—only had one entry in it. It made her feel worse, the image of the quote in Arabic that Rubin had on his office wall on his yacht. Another reminder she was failing her father. She deleted it.

Nora swiped herself into Eva's office. "You're going to be late. Come on."

"Late?"

"You didn't see Iago's debrief message? If we can, we like to tie up the mission as a team. This one, it's easy. Come on."

Easy? Nothing about this had been easy.

Gordon, Luke and Iago were already in the debriefing room when Eva followed Nora in. She could tell them then altogether, at least she only had to say it once.

"How's your shoulder?" Eva asked Luke.

"Can't wait to get rid of this." He gestured at his sling with his good hand.

"Sorry I'm late." Sadie bounced into the room. "It's hard to pull myself away from all the goodies you guys got me. It's like he was getting tech to bend to what he wanted, instead of inventing something and then figuring out how to use it. Iago, there's definitely stuff you'll want to look at, reverse engineer. Happy days."

"The debrief, Eva," Gordon explained, "is how we look at what happened to see if we can do better. Your brief as The Society is very different to how MI6 operates, as a whole. It also forms the basis of what we report back to the Ethics Committee."

"It's also a way to remember the good." Luke said. "For us that's the most important part. So, do you want to list the good on this mission?"

Five gazes turned her way, fingers on tablets, pen against blank paper.

"Start at the beginning, that's usually easier." He prompted.

"I was tasked to get Carl Rubin to agree to pretend to have been assassinated, but I failed. I tried to talk to his wife, who contacted The Society, to understand why she ordered the hit, but I failed at that too. I got her arrested under a DUI charge. We discovered Rubin is an arms dealer."

"From that list of failures, you've given us a new protocol," Nora interjected. "If we can understand why a hit's ordered, it may shine a better light on how to deal with the case."

"What next?" Luke asked. "Looking for the good right now."

Eva hesitated. Nothing about Fisher and Jacob being killed was good. Probably shouldn't class the killing of other gun runners as good either.

"Can I just say, getting our hands on what you brought back is no way a failure, I'll be using that tech in all sorts of ways. He's overcome all the reasons it shouldn't work." Sadie said.

The Lynx Assassin. The other gunrunners.

"It's not that." Eva said. "It's not that. It's him, he's the Lynx Assassin, I heard him talking to his bodyguard. He said time to change camouflage, a lynx can do that." She looked at Gordon. "The men killed at his cabin, do you have their identities yet?"

Iago swiped at his tablet, and photos of the two hostiles popped up onto the screens. The man she'd shot and branded looked so much younger than she'd realised.

"From your photos, Eva, we've identified them as members of a Pakistani military group."

"What's the number one rule amongst arms dealers?" She didn't wait for any guesses. "They said it at Rubin's cabin, they don't use the merchandise on each other. Otherwise there's no trust to do business." A couple of nods around the table, following her logic. "And what happened at the cabin? These two were killed."

She drew breath, finished in a rush. "Rubin had the place booby trapped everywhere. What if he believed the Pakistanis set one of his traps off, that he killed them? He'd have to make amends, wouldn't he, otherwise how could anyone trust him to do business with again? Who are the other members of the group?"

Iago tapped and swiped some more. A man's face nudged the two dead men out of the way. "This is the leader, Tarik Shah."

"Can you find out where he's based?" Eva asked. "Has he taken any deliveries from Denmark? I'd bet a lot of money Rubin sent him something to appease him. He told us he has a lot of weapons coming on line. What if he's using Shah to do a test for him?"

"Heads up," Iago said. "Carl Rubin just died."

The PM wouldn't be happy.

"Now we go to battle stations," Gordon said, "straying or not."

47

"Ready?" Gordon asked Eva as they turned into Whitehall.

Not so much. She trotted beside him past the row of well-maintained Georgian buildings exactly the same as each other. The gold plaques on either side of the Cabinet Office doorway signposted where they were expected.

"They're not going to like that I'm here seeing as I just got fired." Eva pointed out.

"I only have your word for that. I haven't had anything official so I'm playing the see no evil, hear no evil card. You okay with that?"

"Of course, but—"

"You're the one who made the connection. You deserve to take that credit."

Even if she'd rather not.

"Anna," Outside their meeting room Gordon stopped to talk to a blonde woman in her fifties who made Eva feel underdressed and would make Nora look under-groomed.

"You stepping outside your lane?" She asked Gordon, then looked at Eva. "What are you doing here?"

"Eva Janssen, Anna Bailey, Director General of MI5." Gordon made a clumsy introduction. But she'd already dismissed Eva, splitting her attention between Gordon and anyone else approaching the COBR meeting room.

"Is it true," she asked, "about Carl Rubin?"

"We've only seen corroborating evidence so far, nothing to disprove that actuality."

"The PM's going to be so pissed."

"Has he been anything other since he took office?" Gordon asked.

Anna almost laughed. "The deal with Futura Energy was his crowning moment as Foreign Secretary, probably what pushed so many to vote him into the top job."

"More than the India/Pakistan accord?" Eva couldn't help herself.

"That's Six's area, not on my radar." Anna Bailey dismissed her again, asking Gordon. "So why is she here?"

"Eva discovered Rubin's side business, she saved hundreds of lives yesterday at the SSE Arena."

Anna studied her harder. "You're the one who's got number ten all riled up? If you have to poke at the hornets' nest, best you have a long stick and fast running shoes."

As they joined the line of attendees filtering into the room, Anna added. "I should probably thank you for turning the PM's eyes away from Five. And you being here means this promises to be the most interesting COBR ever. I'm glad I came."

Eva wished she hadn't heard that.

The meeting room was almost full when they entered. The screens that covered the end wall acted as one at that moment to show the date and time of the meeting, white text on a grey background. Most of the seats down each side of the polished wooden table that took up most of the room's floor space were taken, three of the five at the top remained empty. Eva guessed the ones at the foot of the table wouldn't be used as they were so close to the wall of screens.

"You'll have to stand, I'm afraid," Gordon said. "They're out in droves, love a good fight."

"Is that what this is?" she asked.

"Don't worry, the PM rarely shows, even when they're needed. Stand opposite me so I can direct you, behind me you won't see."

Eva did as he suggested as he sat down and shook hands with the man next to him, Sir Hugo Welch. Eva focused on the screens, hoping he wouldn't notice her, call out that she shouldn't be there.

"All right, everyone," Mo Banerjee, the new Foreign Secretary, called the meeting to order. "Thank you for coming at such short notice, this could be extremely time sensitive. I'll hand over to the Director of MI6 as it's his fault we're all here."

"Thank you, Mo," Sir Hugo Welch ignored the jibe. "I know you will have all read the briefing packet and so appreciate the urgency of this meeting and why it's priority one." He looked around the gathering of esteemed people, up at Eva— no negative reaction, Gordon's call to him had apparently worked—back at the screens. "An update, Gordon if you would, as this is very much a moveable feast."

"Thank you, Sir Hugo." Gordon consulted his laptop, where Eva knew Iago was uploading everything as it happened. "Gordon Stamford, MI6, Do we have eyes on?" He asked the man at the end of the row whose bearing gave away a military past, despite being dressed in a dark grey suit rather than a uniform.

"We're tasking a satellite now, eyes on in," he consulted his watch though the time in London, Moscow, Washington and Beijing was displayed at the opposite end of the room on red LED screens, "two minutes."

Enough time for Gordon to give a run down on Rubin's public persona. "He came to our attention during a different mission as his true self, namely as an arms dealer. A very successful and profitable one, as we're learning."

"The bird is tasked; we have picture lock." The military man said. "The Indian Pakistan border."

Grey backgrounds melted away and the screens showed what could have been a prison compound exterior wall, tall struts of concrete laden with barbed wire. The clarity of the resolution was astonishing. The shot moved over what looked like newly built bridges, dense vegetation.

"I'm not seeing much here in the way of infra-structure or people to worry about." A man on Eva's side of the table said.

Gordon nodded at Eva.

"Can we see the Wagah border post?" She asked. "It's where they hold a ceremonial taking down of both sides' flags every day. It's a huge tourist draw."

"Getting co-ordinates." The military man advised.

"You don't believe that's the target?" The Foreign Secretary asked.

"We don't know for certain but knowing tensions in the region—" Of course it was, the Afghani proverb, 'The wound of the sword or gun will heal, but not that of the tongue'. Eva nodded, underlining her certainty. "Yes, it is the target."

"What are you saying?" He asked.

Gordon gave Eva that small nod again.

"The arms dealers using the weapon are Pakistani." she said.

"What have we got on the Indian border?" Someone said.

"No," Eva interrupted, "no, it's the Pakistani side which is in danger."

"You're saying they'll target their own people, that's ridiculous." The man was well-spoken, sure of his opinion.

"Why? We have to think about what they're looking to gain here. Only China supports the Pakistanis in their bid to rewrite the border with India. If they can accuse India of attacking their side, it gives them a sympathy vote. If it happens again and again, the number of dead and injured rise enough that it starts a movement, especially on the back of the accord that the Prime Minister got them to sign. India will be seen on the international stage to be breaking their word. Any casualties in the area can be written off to the ongoing tensions, but the damage to the accord that they've signed, they'll never trust each other again. At the very least more conflict is more business for the gun runners."

"We can't do anything without the say so of the PM." Another man noted.

"We've tracked the likely courier to a small town within easy reach of the border on the Pakistani side." Gordon said. "He arrived this morning giving him plenty of time to travel to the border and ready the weapon."

"Which is?" Banerjee asked.

"We don't know."

"It's all a bit vague, isn't it?" Someone else noted. "I don't understand the urgency when we don't have a full picture."

"The urgency," Anna Bailey was a surprising ally, "is clear. A weapon's in situ, your proof there, Gordon, is incontrovertible?" He nodded. "The courier will want to be out of there as soon as possible. The strike will probably be today, the longer it's in play, the more likelihood there is of discovery. What time is the ceremony?" She asked.

"Four pm local time," Eva felt everyone turn with her to check the clocks on the wall. "in around twenty minutes."

48

"I can't believe you called a COBR for this." The hook-nosed man said. "There aren't any British interests here. We should just let them spat; they've been at it for years."

Eva stared at him. "But now they're both nuclear powers, this border is more of a tinderbox than it's ever been, especially after the Indian Government changed the law in Kashmir. It's in no nation's interests for them to wage war on each other." She felt the stares of everyone in the room on her. "A spark like that could cause World War III."

The hooked-nosed man harrumphed. "You're being melodramatic." Just like a woman, his tone implied.

The military man answered for her in his quiet manner. "She could be right. If Pakistan are seen to be wronged by India in any grave way, they'll call on their ally, China, who will call on theirs, North Korea, who would be delighted to have an excuse to take it out on their enemy, South Korea, who will, in turn, ask the West for assistance. It's all very well having accords in place, memoranda of understanding between one nation and another but, in a situation like this," he waved an arm at the screened wall, "it's like dominoes. No one will be untouched. Of course, it could be the usual targeting of each other but we don't want to be anywhere near the agenda of a Pakistani arms dealer."

Mo Banerjee crossed to one of the phones hard-wired on the wall under the clocks and requested Downing Street from the operator.

Edward Markham appeared on one of the screens, interrupting the Foreign Secretary's explanation as soon as he saw Eva. "You? What are you doing there?"

"If I may, Prime Minister," Sir Hugo beat Gordon to reply, "Ms Janssen is the person responsible for bringing this intelligence to our attention. She has an excellent case, we should listen."

"I had your assurance—"

"Prime Minister," the military man interrupted, "time is of the essence. We need to decide what to do regarding this credible threat."

"It's hardly credible, the say so of one agent." The hook-nosed man observed.

Eva wanted to bang their heads together, shout at them all to stop being idiots.

Gordon brought Markham up to speed using his favourite phrase 'we have intelligence that' more than once.

"What kind of weapon is it?" Markham asked.

Eva took a huge gamble, filling the expectant silence with her best guess. "Based on what else Carl Rubin has produced, it'll be something unknown, unseen so far and very destructive."

The PM stared at a spot at the bottom of his screen. The room waited. Eva felt the changing of every red digit on the clocks as the tiny dashes of which they were made up shifted position to change from 8 to 9 to 0, a dance to destruction.

She pressed her lips together, shuffled from foot to foot until she had to remind herself to stand still. She'd done what she could do, she had to trust they'd do the right thing.

So much for being in the room, behind the cameras, one step closer to what was happening than an analyst usually got. And yet she'd never felt so helpless, such pressure. How she wasn't exploding into tiny pieces, she didn't know.

"What's your background in this area?" A man who hadn't spoken yet asked her.

"General."

"Specifically?"

"I was on the Russian desk for—"

"Shouldn't you be more concerned about what happened in St Petersburg then? Shouldn't you be wanting to expel Russian diplomats or whatever censure twenty-two British lives are worth?"

"That was Carl Rubin's weapon." She said patiently. "It was his agenda to stoke tensions in the area. It's an easy shot to get the world to blame and sanction Russia."

"And we're here on your say so that a dead man's agenda—"

"As the only person in this room who's been on the end of this man's agenda, I think I'm more qualified than everyone else to know what he was thinking."

"Target acquired." The military man clicked, and the satellite feed changed and now they could see a huge crowd of people congregated in seating and standing on either side of a continuous white line painted on the ground. "The Wagah border."

"Prime Minister, in case you weren't aware," Mo Banerjee said, "if this is a target, the timing will be during the ceremony which will begin at around 10:30."

In five minutes Eva's mind screamed.

"What can we do?" Markham asked.

"It's a benign satellite." The military man commented to no one in particular.

Shine a light on the truth, Evie. Her father's voice came to her from beyond his grave. Except he'd have been there in the danger zone, drawing the world's media to it.

"Excuse me, Prime Minister." Eva adopted the obsequiousness he seemed to respond to better. "As we can't deploy troops and we don't know how to stop this weapon, all we can do is show the truth of what's about to happen. Can we record the satellite's telemetry and broadcast it to the media? Pakistan and the rest of the world have to know it isn't India who's targeting them."

The red numbers seemed to have sped up.

"Is that feasible?" Markham asked.

The military man nodded, entering something on his keyboard. "We can sell it as a remote pass, a coincidence of a lifetime if there's anything to see and report."

"So what now?" Someone asked. "We just wait?"

"Yellowstone," Eva breathed. Rubin's agenda, too many heartbeats, culling the population. That's what he was using there.

Gordon caught it. "Go on."

"The super-volcano. Get those people out of there." Eva shouted over the PM and Foreign Secretary's back and forth of options. "Rubin talked about a weapon called Yellowstone." She gabbled into the thorny silence. "If it's anything like what it's named after, we have to evacuate."

"There's no having to do anything, that's not our territory." Markham reminded her.

"There's no confirmation there's even going to be a strike." Someone added.

"We can't do anything on one person's guess."

The dissension around the table became a round robin.

Eva shouted over all of them. "Rubin said he wanted to call this weapon Mars, after the god, the bringer of war."

"Satellite passing overhead, we can hold the view using a reverse shot." The military man confirmed.

"Do it. You are recording?" Markham asked.

"Yes, Sir."

"There's still two minutes until the ceremony—" Mo Banerjee's reasoning turned into a gasp.

The image on the screens changed.

The bickering in the room dropped into silence. On the screens a flash, an explosion on the ground probably, bloomed outwards becoming one, two, three, a daisy-chain of destruction that filled the screens. Even seeing it remotely from thousands of miles away from hundreds of miles above it, it was sobering.

The military man broke the silence. "We have assets en route for assessment."

"We can have humanitarian aid in the area in a matter of hours." The Foreign Secretary added.

The dust didn't take long to settle. There were no complex structures at the border, mostly flimsy seating, wooden fences, a couple of concrete huts, everything staged for posturing rather than practicality.

"Humanitarian aid for what?" Someone asked.

It was a good question. The Wagah border crossing was gone. There was no sign of any movement, no wounded, wandering around shocked, looking for survivors, for help. Apart from the smallest scarring showed dark on the ground, the infamous white line that represented India and Pakistan's divisions was barely touched but everything else was obliterated as if it had never been there.

49

───────

"What's the latest?" Eva went into Gordon's office for their meeting.

"It's been a couple of very tense days on the ground. India and Pakistan are equally edgy, not necessarily a good thing, but it would obviously be worse if Tarik Shah had deployed a conventional weapon on just the Pakistanis. Evidence suggests he did exactly as you said, the first explosion was on that side. He perhaps didn't understand how the weapon would function. It seems that first explosion fired another and another."

"Like a super-volcano," Eva said.

Gordon nodded. "Quite."

"So many people dead, if only we'd stopped the weapon being used at all. Any news on that?"

Gordon's turn to shake his head. "It'll take time to get our hands on any of the wreckage for analysis. But having the recording from the satellite stopped the escalation we all feared. Plus, our having been able to show the weapon's track into Pakistan. And we have you to thank for that. The PM's rather enjoying playing the concerned best friend of both nations, that seems to be how the media are spinning it right now. So have you decided what you want to do? Whatever your decision there'll be a review."

Eva smiled. "Isn't there always?"

"So it would seem."

"I don't want to be an analyst again, though I thought I did."

"Why is that?"

"Being in that COBR meeting felt so helpless, so remote. There was nothing I could do there to help any of those people."

"Sometimes it goes like that."

Eva looked at her hands, back at Gordon. "I want to become a full agent, to operate here in the field through S."

He had the best poker face Eva had ever known, but she caught his surprise. "Why?"

"At the SSE Arena, in the midst of the madness, I could do something to make things better."

"You saved a lot of people; we recovered a lot of target stickers."

"But not the weapon again." It weighed on her. If she'd got away before Sean Finch arrived on the scene, the Lynx Assassin would be in MI6's hands, not whoever was taking over Rubin's business.

"Now we know what we're looking for, we have a start." The helplessness in the COBR meeting felt far worse to Eva than being on the ground trying to stop Rubin. If Lily had been in danger in either scenario, Eva could only have done something to save her in one.

"Have you considered that in the room you stopped an all-out war in that region?"

"For the moment."

He nodded. "That's all we can do."

They sat in the heavy silence of being two people united in a common goal surrounded by the others in Gordon's unit, those in MI6 in Vauxhall Cross a short walk away, those in MI5 at Thames House further along the river, a set up mirrored all over the world to hold back the darkness and destruction of the agendas of the coldly brutal.

"You know it's not up to me, whether you can come back." Gordon said.

Eva nodded. "So where do I go for my review?"

50

———

"Well?" Luke was waiting for Eva when she walked down St George's Grove on her way back to the unit. "As bad as you thought?"

"Worse. Markham does not like me, he wasn't even supposed to be there, it was supposed to be Mo Banerjee, the Foreign Secretary."

"You're in good company, Markham doesn't like anyone."

Despite herself, Eva smiled. "You know that doesn't make me feel much better."

"Don't sweat it, he's been busy quoting you in the media all week."

She couldn't help thinking that was precisely why he might want her out of the picture.

"How's the shoulder?"

"Getting there, I'm only wearing this for the sympathy." He went to gesture with his sling, changed his mind.

"I see that."

"Iago's got something for us. Mission end, it'll cheer you up."

The atmosphere in the meeting room felt like a party.

One of Gordon's bottles of whisky was on the table with an empty glass beside it, Nora, Iago, Sadie, and a woman Eva hadn't met yet—tiny, thin blonde hair, big glasses with ornate frames that drowned her face—all had one each.

"Perfect timing, Eva." Iago said. "Grab a shot, we're toasting any minute now."

"Eva, this is Jackie." Nora made the introductions.

"Watchya, Eva." Jackie's voice was loud and Cockney.

"Jackie's one of our forensic accountants, she's been doing her magic behind the scenes." Nora explained.

"Nice to meet you." Eva said, frowning at the whisky. "Why's there never gin?" She stage-whispered to Nora.

"If we get the result we want with your review," Gordon chipped in, "I'll get you a bottle of gin for my office."

"And tonic." Eva poured the smallest swallow into the empty glass.

"We're celebrating." Luke upended the bottom of the bottle so it glugged into her glass and she had half a tumbler full.

"We're up, people," Iago shushed the laughing.

The screens around them burst into life with a bald man peering at them. "It's his webcam I've activated. He can't see or hear us." Iago clarified.

"Where?" Eva mouthed at Luke.

"Watch." He grinned back.

The man's expression changed, flitting from boredom to all Eva could think of was a 'holy shit' moment. A phone appeared against his ear and he said something she didn't understand.

It took a few minutes of the man pacing in his bland office, sitting back at the screen, pacing again before a knock reached through his PC speakers into the room.

He stood up and his body blocked the webcam for a few

seconds, talking to the woman who'd come into the room. He barked instructions at her, then moved away from the monitor and Eva was surprised it was Agnetha Rubin who sat in front of the PC. Her hair was tied back from her make-up less face.

She moved her right hand, probably using the mouse, and looked up in front of her, above the screen, then down at it.

"She's reading our email." Iago said, depositing it on one of the screens.

'The job you assigned to us has been carried out as per your instructions.' Eva read. 'Click on the link for proof. The Society.'

Agnetha's eyes grew wider.

Her expression changed to complete astonishment. "She's looking at one of the photos you took of Rubin when he was shot. We got lucky, in one of them he had his eyes open just right. I doctored it a little and voilà. She doesn't look pleased, you'd think she'd be grateful, it's what she wanted."

Agnetha actually looked furious. She tapped at the keyboard, a rapid succession of keystrokes, until a man in a navy uniform shot around the desk and grabbed her hands. She head butted him and hit the keyboard again.

"Probably didn't envisage it happening like this. Hard to spend all that money when you're in prison." Nora pointed out.

Iago swiped at his tablet. "There we go, reply from her says 'Get me out. Sean Finch will pay.'"

Agnetha was hauled out of the room screaming "it's mine, it should be mine". The link went black.

"Email deleted." Iago confirmed.

"That's good news. Yer face." Jackie grinned at Eva.

"You'll learn. It's good news 'cos she ain't made the connection between 'er being locked up and The Society. Damn, I'm good. Fifteen years for 'er for fraud plus whatever the Norwegians throw at 'er for the bodies that made the lynxes' dinner table."

"And for killing Ralph?" Eva asked.

"Nuffink doing there, can't give the authorities squat without compromising you. But she's paying."

She held her glass up and everyone toasted her.

Eva shuddered as she sipped the whisky. "What happened to Sean Finch?"

"In the wind." Luke said. "He hasn't done anything illegal that we can prove."

"Apart from holding us at gunpoint against our will?" Eva said.

"Apart from that." He agreed.

"And Rubin's business?"

"His legal ones are being sorted out by the Norwegian and Danish authorities as per his will. The arms dealing, we'll see. Nature abhors a vacuum; someone will step into it. We're watching."

"That was her motive," Eva realised. "It's not an exciting life unless you're leading it, when she said that she wasn't talking about green energy. She wanted to take over the arms business, that's why she wanted Rubin killed."

"Having met her, I'd say that's bang on." Luke agreed.

"In the meantime, we did empty a store he had in Copenhagen, the weapons are on their way here, where they'll be kept in deep storage until it can be decided who is best placed to take them." Gordon said.

"Until someone has the bright idea to use them." Nora added.

"Until then." Gordon agreed. He raised his glass. "I'd say

this mission was an outstanding success. I've persuaded the PM to start elsewhere with his audits and I think his attention has diverted away from SIS completely."

"We live to fight another day." Luke joked.

"Just watch out for those dangerous pavements, mate." Iago said.

Everyone laughed, an easy camaraderie that Eva hoped she'd still be part of once the outcome of her review was decided.

She stopped Iago when the meeting broke up. "Question for you."

"Shoot," he grinned, "or maybe don't, I hear you've improved."

"What's the protocol for me asking you for something very specific and how we could keep something like that just between us?"

Iago grinned. "Now I'm intrigued, walk with me, tell me what you have in mind."

"What do you know about the Kobayashi Maru?"

51

Eva waved her S temporary access pass at the guard in the security booth.

"What's your business here?" he asked.

She couldn't imagine they kept regular hours, but she played the game. She needed to get in.

"SIS, here to oversee the installation of a delivery. It should be here within the next half hour." She tried to look bored, as if she did this all the time.

"You missed it."

"What?"

"Only one delivery tonight. Got in about twenty minutes ago."

"Seriously?" She ran her hand through her hair. "My boss is going to kill me, I'm supposed to watch it being checked in, sign to say it's all as it should be. I was having such a good day."

"Warehouse 17B, that side on the right."

"Thanks."

As part of refitting the former light industrial park into an

SIS facility, all the signposts had been removed. Eva had to hope the numbers on the end of the units were chronological, otherwise she'd miss her chance completely, thanks to the delay on the train. Now would be an excellent time to be able to drive.

She jogged towards where the guard had gestured. Only at 15A? She dug in and ran, holding her access card on its lanyard with one hand so it didn't fly up and hit her in the face. 15B, 16, 16A. The busyness of unloading a delivery reached her in shouts and calls, the whirring sound of a forklift.

The bright lights of an open roll-up door showed her the way. She rushed into the building.

"Hold up, love, this here's a restricted area." One of the men greeted her.

"I know," she panted, holding up the access card around her neck. "SIS, here to oversee."

"You're late."

She nodded. "Train trouble. Where's the delivery? Is it all in?"

"They didn't tell us to expect anyone."

"They're not going to warn you. It's not you that's being checked, it's the other side." Eva waffled.

"Last crate's going in now. Aisle twenty-three, far side. Do we have to wait for you to do your thing?"

Eva nodded. "I'll be quick. I want to get home too."

"Chop, chop then."

Power walking towards aisle twenty-three, Eva saw the two hi-vis vested, hard-hatted men, one driving a forklift, the other directing him backwards. The crate on the prongs was bigger than she'd expected it to be. Three, Iago had told her, had been offloaded at Farnborough airfield. Rubin's store in Copenhagen had held a lot of weaponry.

"SIS," Eva identified herself, "I have to monitor the locking away of these crates. That the last one?"

The forklift driver nodded. "You should have the safety gear on."

Eva smiled, "I won't tell if you won't. You have to wait for me to do this so I want to be quick, then we can all go home. It's been a long day."

While she watched him slide it into place in the gap alongside the other two, she pulled on gloves that she withdrew from inside a thick bag in her handbag. He reversed and drove towards the entrance.

"What do we have here then?" Eva laid a hand on the crate they'd just placed. "You can go help your colleague if you like. I won't be a minute. Just have to detail it."

He half-shrugged, began walking after the forklift.

Eva pressed her gloved hands over all the sides of the crate she could reach. She dipped her hands back into the bag filled with the shimmery powder Rubin had wiped on her face. Considerate of him to have left containers of it in the outbuildings at his cabin for them to find and bring back. She pressed her fingertips over the next crate and the third. Re-dipped her hands and paid special attention to the areas where the crate lids met the sides.

That ought to do it.

Eva peeled off the gloves carefully and put them back inside a separate bag hidden in her handbag.

She walked towards the entrance of the warehouse where the men were waiting.

"All good. Thanks for that. You can lock up now."

She watched them. It was a secure building, even if the twenty-four-hour security hadn't been as hard to pass as she'd thought it would be. No one was going to get past the laser sights inside the warehouse that Iago had told her would trigger a direct armed response if they were interrupted. But it wasn't an opportune burglar breaking into the warehouse that worried her.

"We're good to go, offer you a lift?" One man asked.

"I've got it covered, thanks."

She waited until they accelerated away.

From her handbag she withdrew the tiny devices Iago had given her and leaning against the pillar return that made up the entrance, checked her watch in a grandiose gesture for the benefit of the camera while the hand behind her pressed the device against the brick.

Walking across the door, she looked down at her boot and bent to fiddle with the zip, pressing the other device against the pillar on that side. It wasn't that she didn't trust this place, it's that she didn't trust whoever would ever find out and whoever already knew what was in there. Some things needed to stay buried.

"Thanks, Carl Rubin, for the idea." she whispered.

She called Iago on her way to the security booth. "In place."

"And operational. What a team." he said. "I'll add them to my running in the background things to keep an eye on."

"I put enough RFID tags on the crates that if anyone opens them to take just one thing out, the sensors will pick it up when they leave."

"Knew I liked you. See you tomorrow."

She hoped so.

Out through security, Eva walked back to the train station. Outside it a man leant on the side of a sleek dark car that gleamed in the streetlight. He pushed himself up to standing, nonchalant to something dangerous until she recognised him and her fight or flight dissipated.

"Luke? What're you doing here?"

"Might have come up in a chat with Iago where you were going but I've got no idea what you're doing out here, didn't ask. Sometimes it's better to not know."

"Should you be driving?" She gestured at his sling-less arm.

"Yeah, I'm good. Automatic, easy one-handed. Gordon's heard from the review panel."

"So what did they say?" She tried to make her question nonchalant, scrutinising his tone and body language for any clue about her future.

"I've got no idea."

"For an agent, you're suddenly remarkably clueless."

He laughed. "Want to go find out? Looks like I can give you another lift."

THE END

DID YOU ENJOY THIS BOOK?

Did you enjoy this book? You can make a big difference to my career.

Reviews are the most powerful tools in my arsenal when it comes to getting attention for my books. Much as I'd like to, I don't have the financial muscle of a London or New York publisher. I can't take out full page ads in the newspaper or put posters on the tube or subway.

But I do have something much more powerful and effective than that ...

...a committed and loyal group of readers.

Honest reviews of my books help bring them to the attention of other readers and that allows me to keep writing.

If you've enjoyed this book (and want more!) I would be very grateful if you could spend just a couple of minutes leaving a review on the book's amazon page. You can go straight there by clicking this link:

UK
    US

Thank you so much <3

Coffee and movie soundtracks fuel my writing so if you've really enjoyed it, you can buy me a coffee!

https://ko-fi.com/karenguyler

And I'll send you a short story as a thank you :-)

FREE STARTER LIBRARY

GET A FREE BOOK AND SHORT STORY SET IN THE
SOCIETY'S WORLD

Building a relationship with my readers is the very best
thing about writing. I occasionally send newsletters with
details on new releases, special offers and other news on my
books. When you sign up to the mailing list, I'll send you:

Dare You? an introductory novella and
    There Can Be Only One, a short story

both set in The Society's world

You can get the novella and short story for free from my
website www.karenguyler.com

Being part of my readers' club also gets you access to free
bonus epilogues and short stories and book offers, what's
not to love?!

ALSO BY KAREN GUYLER

Have you read them all?

In the 'The Society' Series

Dare You, book 0

You instructed the assassins, but you didn't obey the contract. Now they're after you.

Trevor Young's money is gone but he knows who took it.

Instructing *The Society* to take out his embezzling, cheating business partner is easy. But Trevor didn't realise they're not just a gun for hire, that you mustn't break their rules.

So he did.

Now, *The Society* are in control. And his life is on the line.

Can he get the target off his back?

Free to download: **https://books2read.com/u/baZzoP**

The Society, book 1

If they know your name, you're already dead.

How did it come to this? It started with a slice of chocolate cake yesterday when Eva Janssen's life was normal, and she and her family were as safe as you. But today they have invisible targets on their backs. Has something from Eva's past come back for revenge? Or is it the secrets her husband's been hiding that will get them killed?

The faceless, nameless assassins of *The Society* don't care. All that matters to them is completing their mission - taking out those targets.

But they don't know Eva.

Buy it **https://books2read.com/u/bpzp8l**

The Lynx Assassin, book 2

What chance do you have against a weapon that's smarter than you?

Eva Janssen wants to be accepted back at MI6 so of course she accepts the trial mission she's offered. A quick trip to Norway and home to London before her daughter Lily has even missed her.

Her first mistake is thinking it's an easy test; her second is assuming she knows who she's fighting.

But she hasn't understood what it means to be part of *The Society*.

And, when she finds herself on the wrong end of the Lynx Assassin, a next-gen weapon deadlier than the sharpest human, can she even survive?

Buy it here: **https://books2read.com/u/b6O2zx**

In the 'Dateline Zero' series:

The Only, book 1

The Government stepped up after a devastating flu pandemic to save what remained of the British people. And if they are told where they live, what to eat, what job to do, the Government can keep their promise they'll be safe. Maya Flint wouldn't dream of breaking the rules, until her brother's life is on the line.

Buy it here: **https://books2read.com/u/mBZPvO**

The Disappeareds, book 2

Moved to London to work at Science Academy just like she bargained, Maya Flint has everything she wanted. Except her best friend, except her family, except her safety. And now something big is coming, something that has a dictator running scared. And a man scared is capable of anything. Stop him, Maya must, but what if the price is her soul and what if he gets to her first?

Buy it here: **https://books2read.com/u/mYZo8p**

The Reckoning, book 3

Set adrift in a stranger's life, remembering nothing before this summer, can Maya Flint find her way back to those she cares about? Will she learn that some things, some people, are not to be trusted before it's too late? And what happens if she does?

Buy it here: **https://books2read.com/u/bQJ9jd**

Standalone

Celebrations, but not as we know them

Ten teeny tiny stories of things we celebrate, only sideways.

Buy it here: **https://books2read.com/u/3k5rYL**

ACKNOWLEDGMENTS

Well, here's a conundrum... in the Dateline Zero series, it took me years to produce a new book so I had a lot of people to thank for each one. Now I've embraced the craziness of the caffeine-fuelled deadline and have this cracking idea for a series, I'm on track for my wild 2021 goal. Which means this book is being published only 3 months on the heels of the first book, The Society, so I have fewer people to mention here. The thanks are heartfelt, nonetheless, and I'm more grateful than I can say to have you along for the journey.

Huge thanks to my family – you are my world: Dave Guyler, Connor Guyler, Makenna Guyler and Kade Guyler, and to Adam Wilson and Natalie Wickenden (you've been enfolded into the Guylers now!). And a special thank you, Connor, for another outstanding cover!

To my street team – thank you so much for your beta reading and your feedback when I forget what I haven't put on the page. I'm sure the readers thank you too when they're not as confused as you were! Beverley Bishop, Katie Cooper, Deb Day, Makenna Guyler, Helen Hanna, a huge thank you to each of you for spreading the word.

ABOUT THE AUTHOR

Always being the new girl at nine schools on two continents was no fun at all so books became the only constant in Karen Guyler's life, even if they didn't help her get out of sports days. Now settled in Milton Keynes, England, Britain's best kept secret, she juggles reading with writing, her children husband and dog – a much nicer mix! On mostly sunny days she'll be trying to cajole her gorgeous dog out for a walk though has had to abandon the idea of dictating while walking because all the 'sit', 'stay', 'don't do that', 'leave', 'come back' played havoc with the characters' lives.

She also teaches Creative Writing for Adult Education with lots of laughter in amongst the word wrangling and discovery.